SPEAK WITH THE SUN

To Pam
best wishes

SPEAK WITH THE SUN

Madeleine
Keeffe

July 2006

Madeleine Keeffe

The Book Guild Ltd
Sussex, England

First published in Great Britain in 2003 by
The Book Guild Ltd
25 High Street,
Lewes, East Sussex
BN7 2LU

Typesetting in Baskerville by
Keyboard Services, Luton, Bedfordshire

Printed in Great Britain by
Antony Rowe Ltd, Chippenham, Wiltshire

A catalogue record for this book is available from
The British Library

ISBN 1 85776 725 X

Who in that land of darkness and blinde
eyes
Thy long expected healing wings could see,
When thou didst rise,
And what can never more be done,
Did at midnight speak with the Sun!

Henry Vaughan (*The Night*)

1933

I had intended to write it all down because I could not trust my thoughts to memory. I had a fear that my shaky courage would fly away if I ever had the chance to present Owen with the words. It was not the trembling sadness of those years that disturbed me but the happiness that grew so imperceptibly that I could not name a time before I felt such delight in being alive. That terrible happiness gave us a vulnerability that would not be appeased by the power of our love. Terrible, because in its mischievous simplicity it fooled us into believing we were safe when all we had was an interdependence that withered from the beautiful to the pitiful. We learned to measure our responses to the world in terms of our responses to each other and made our love all the more terrifying.

If this story is about love I should be able to speak its name but the word catches in my throat and only Owen's name remains alongside the confused sentiments contained in his letters. Violet tried to tell me about love when I was fifteen, as though I had just been brought back from some dark place where stars could not shine. But I knew about stars, I had seen them in Owen's eyes long before he was old enough to recognise them himself.

After he left I read all his letters but it was not a mere perusal of dates and events, it was a stripping to the soul of every thought and idea that he had put to paper. It seemed more heartless than any pain I might have inflicted on him while he was with me; more terrible even than his personal anguish over our daughter's death. Each time I thought about that hurt I had to wonder if we would have been together still had it not happened. It was terrifying to comfort him during those long agonised nights. The appropriate words never came; I struggled for smooth phrases when all he needed was closeness and to feel that I would not desert him.

If only he could have remained so pliant and accepting

of my tenderness. But I soon realised the conflict which was tearing him apart; to be my lover, my husband and the father of my children; and his despair at watching the principles which had given him the courage to defect, simply shrink with each fresh day.

Owen was never a hero, perhaps that was his problem. If he'd been allowed to grow through some heroic grief for the anguish he had caused those he loved, he might have recovered. Instead, he had malingered in some fading spiritless anaesthesia from which only the birth of his children seemed to lift him. And when those healing relationships began to shudder there was nothing left for him.

In plucking out and reliving those finest thoughts and reactions I was seeking some of that security and hope which had been detached from me. Owen had been able to share his fears with his comrades, putting them briefly into those letters. I was mystified why those feelings could not be expanded and refreshed with me when it was all over.

His simplest responses, to the sun sliding below the horizon or a snatch of birdsong or the shifts in mood of his companions: they had all brought him closer than he had been since. He had even talked about God and hinted at a spiritual presence surrounding the scenes of horror that he witnessed. But on his return all that was dismissed. Any moment which held meaning for him, he had an impulse to protect. It was almost as though he needed to guard his experiences jealously and keep them even from me, the woman he claimed to love. I felt that I would never know him as I had known him then. He was a different person through those hundreds of words. They had poured out in place of the anger and frustration that so many men were feeling and were able to express openly.

It had seemed so smooth when we were apart; words

were all that joined us together. The motes and threads of thoughts expanded and sparkled with our desire to keep our love for each other radiant and fresh. Words were never to be so important to me again and I guessed it was similar for Owen as a man who needed to express his life through language.

But his spiritual control could only last for so long. When he returned home the certainty and smoothness of the future could not nourish him. He had almost languished in those experiences as a way of learning more about himself but when it was all over he could not bear to live with the person he had become. He wanted to be punished for ever but he had to accept that there was a life other than miserable grey reflection; he should consider the risk of losing his wife and son. Was he willing to sacrifice those for some impulsive notions about punishment and self-realisation?

I fastened the letters with a faded blue ribbon, a childhood relic that I'd become attached to. I closed my eyes and blinked back the tears, angry with my own sentimentality, but I knew deep inside that my feelings were not a trifling sentimental notion; Owen had been my life and my life belonged to him. So many times I had wanted to tear up his letters, to shred them onto the fire and watch the scarlet flames consume the memories. They were a part of Owen that I barely recognised, an indistinct shadow of him that I no longer wanted but which held a fascination for me. He had to be different from now on or there would be nothing for us...

Almost at sea

September 3rd 1915

Dearest Mother,

I'm writing this in haste before we embark. Please excuse the untidy scrawl but I knew you would want a word before I left. I'm glad it all came off so rapidly. None of us had any time to dwell on it did we? Before you know it I'll be home on leave and it'll seem as if I was never away.

Alice told me about the other day and I made her promise to stay close to you. She must not let herself be carried along by all this unhealthy fervour. She should do her bit, naturally – I think she will make an excellent nurse – but she must keep some hours in the day for you and father.

I know that you will help Ruth while I'm away. She might seem strong and self-reliant but underneath she is soft and sweet and needs to know that you are her friends and support. In a peculiar way, I'm the lucky one – I don't know what I'm going to and everyone is rather excited. You, poor things, can only imagine.

Don't count on hearing from me for a while. I hear the passages of communication are somewhat archaic. But you know I'll be thinking of you whatever happens.

Tell father the tobacco pouch is very handy and has been admired by several of the chaps. Sorry, we've had the signal to make ready. Better close so this letter can be collected.

Much love,

Owen

September 3rd 1915

Dearest Ruth,

Strange, I don't feel confused or sad, it's quite exciting. I suppose everything happened so quickly there
was no time for jittery thoughts or panic. Looking
back at the lights, it seems impossible that everything
will go on as usual behind those cosy doors.

I wonder how many are sitting down to their
evening meal at this moment, not knowing or caring
about us; a crowd of bewildered and faceless men
cramped on this ship heading out for sea. Perhaps
there's a sweetheart somewhere, pausing over her
soup, a tear on her cheek, or a mother hiding her distress in the bustle of duties that still have to be done.

I dropped mother a few lines before I left. I know
she was in a flap about my leaving so suddenly. But
it was for the best – don't you think? Listen to me
asking questions as if you can hear me. Maybe you
can sense us out here – the ship plashing through the
dark water away from the sun? Are you far away with
your dreams or lost in some book? That's likely if I
know you. Keep to that book. Give your affection to
the words, they come from within, and can't be
mocked or shaken by all this idle cynicism and false
bravado. Of course it is false – who can feel intrepid
about this adventure when it's such an unknown?

I've been sitting with a couple of lads from
Manchester. Pleasant enough but they seem ignorant
of the war. I wonder how they know so little – they
must have heard from friends home on leave that it's
no picnic. But I won't disturb them by letting on I

know a little more. The youngster, Alan, has a clean, incredulous face. Poor lad, it's his first time away from home. I couldn't help noticing his fearful look as the ship slid away from the quay. He tried to make a joke about the muddle of sprawling bodies and baggage on the boat deck but I knew he would have preferred to find a hiding place and be alone with his thoughts. He comes from that pretty village up near the reservoir where we walked last summer. Says he can see the water from his bedroom window. Can tell what sort of day it's going to be by the look of the water – grim and lifeless or gleaming and hopeful. Went into raptures he did about that dull water. I never liked the place myself – something sinister and rather threatening about the stillness up there, even on a bright day. Closer to the sky and nowhere for any wild thoughts to escape. No place to snatch the sun and too exposed up there.

The other chap, Josh, is very different. He's a natural joker with a loud, irreverent voice. To tell the truth, his manner might be a bit coarse for young Alan but his heart is sound and in the right place – what Edwin would call a 'good sort'. His family are 'in coal', so he's not afraid of getting his hands mucky, he delighted in telling us. I think he'll be good for both of us if we're together for a few weeks – he'll keep my feet firmly on the ground and remind young Alan that life is basically absurd and the only way to deal with it is to seek out the bright spots and enjoy them. Sorry, I do seem to be going on a bit.

I'm sorry I didn't see Edwin. Tell him not to worry. We're all in this together. The worst possibility would be to face it alone. Our shared hopes and fears will give us the strength and unity we need. Forgive me!

I shouldn't philosophise. It must be the ship and its precarious place on the ocean. There's a constant thrum from the engine and you can feel the shudder beneath your feet. Anyway, the sea is calm. Let's hope it stays that way, this journey is going to be a trial. There are too many bodies for me to settle with my book. I'll sit and study faces instead. I can see your frown of irritation now, how it embarrassed you, my curiosity about my fellow man. There must be some sense and meaning in all this idle chatter. Look and listen! That's my motto.

What a handful! Most seem bewildered, pretending a nonchalance they can't possibly feel. The heaviness can't be hidden; the eyes give it away, bright and quick-moving or too pale and watery, and their features share the same flat resignation. I can't be inspired or offended by them. They're a peculiar bunch all right. A few are easy with a disjointed conversation or happy to flick the pages of a book, as though relaxing on a pleasure cruise – but they are few. There's an endless murmuring about trivialities, gallant attempts at jokes and bouts of uneasy laughter. The space all around, with sky and starlight, seems incongruous. The dark space beyond the ship is so immeasurable and the open sea with no moon to break up the shadowy power of it all – all that and my weariness – I seem to be part of a puzzling new world. I think I'll put my head down for a while.

Good morning! Well, we've landed. Secret though. We disembarked in the early hours and were loaded onto a train. The journey took hours. The train seemed reluctant to move without a stop every mile or so. Still, we saw some of the countryside. It's quite splendidly green and fresh in parts but dotted with sad reminders of the war: derelict villages, elderly farm workers coping with the harvest alone and the children, so many children... I must keep those faces in my thoughts – they are the reason we are here, after all. They are the future.

Do you remember that gypsy child we met, with the jar of sticklebacks? He had a look of terror in his dark eyes when I spoke to him. They all have that look here, wanting desperately for something to happen but afraid of what it might be; needing to ask what will happen next, in this unbelievable and terrible drama that has transformed their country, but struggling to find appropriate words.

There's too much to think about but at least it passes the time. Alan has been flat out for the past few hours. Poor lad, he was terribly seasick on the crossing, and didn't settle to sleep on the train. This billet may not be a home from home but it's warm and dry and it stays in one place!

Josh has gone a-wandering, to discover the town and all its treasures, he says. He's hopeful – but from the little we saw on the way through, there are only half a dozen streets, all of them unexciting. I think he's going to find the hours of sitting about a bit wearing, he needs to be up and doing. No one seems to know how long we will be here so we have to make the best of it and 'build up our strength', as the Sergeant says.

From the doorway I can see the hills in the distance, not unlike our quiet English slopes. They're changing from green to gold and then mauve as the sun slips behind the trees. There's an eerie silence to this place; an uneasy hum in the air that doesn't wish to be broken. But ... the new day will come, whatever, nothing will stop that.

I wonder whether you're watching the same sun melt into the horizon. Close your eyes dearest and say a gentle prayer for us.

Your Owen

September 13th 1915

My dear Owen,

At last I've received your first letter. It's quite exciting to think it came all the way from France. I had a
strange feeling as I looked at the words. I imagined
your quiet voice speaking them to me. So we're closer
than we think, my darling.

I hope you weren't terribly ill on the ship – I would
have been. The only time I went out in a boat, with
Uncle Edmund at Llandudno, I wasn't ill but I
remember the terror when I suddenly thought of all
that swirling water underneath the boat. I made poor
Edmund row us back to the shore in no time.

I like the sound of Alan. He'll appreciate someone
thoughtful and kind like you to look out for him.
Perhaps your medical studies will be useful after all;
you might help someone without feeling that it's
simply an exercise to help your father.

It would be good to know where you are. Edwin has
a huge map on the wall of his bedroom where he
marks all the offensives as they appear in the newspaper. Mother says he's gruesome and Lily refuses to
look at it. It's as well, I suppose, that I don't know
much – at least I can't worry as the news comes in –
but I should like to have a picture of you in my head,
some comforting image that will give you protection.
It's a talisman of sorts. If I can watch you doing
ordinary safe things and give you my blessing then
everything will be all right.

Of course I do worry. I never stop thinking about you and wondering how you are feeling. I imagine you shaving and drinking tea from a tin mug and stroking your chin as you try to concentrate on your book. You always did that. And the way you clicked your fingers as we walked along, impatient to be where we were going. The things that annoyed me are mere gestures now, a part of you, and I need to cling onto their comforting predictability.

How unbearable to live outside all time and never to be alone. How will you bear it? I know how precious those still moments can be. You might easily forget who you are as you become tangled in the lives of others. Imagine all those fears and frustrations all clamouring to get out – it's too dangerous. Quiet selfishness is preferable for survival – you told me that. But I suppose your survival is about something different now – something beyond enjoyment and satisfaction.

Edwin sends his love. He's been at the training camp near Liverpool for ten days. Every day he expects a call but I think he'll be there for a few more weeks yet. They can't possibly expect such green recruits to be thrown into battle straight away. Of course, mother can't understand why he's so excited and breaks into silent tears every time the war is mentioned. At mealtimes the topic is strictly taboo and it's a struggle to find fresh subjects to occupy our minds. It's rather absurd, when we're all preoccupied with it. It would be smoother to discuss it and bring our worries out into the open.

Edwin's birthday is on the 30th. Lily has been making him a muffler. He never wears one but I dare say out there he'll have a use for it. I found him a leather notebook which he can use as a diary or for notes.

He's not like you though, words don't matter to him too much – words on paper or in his head – between people, it's different.

It's strange isn't it, all these words on paper when we talked so much. I do miss our discussions. You made me aware of so many things I hadn't noticed before … wild birds, clouds above the hills, flowers and the shapes of trees in winter … and poetry, of course. I'm never without a tiny volume in my pocket now. I'm going to read *Autumn* to the children tomorrow but I don't expect them to find Keats's 'mellow fruitfulness' to their taste.

You've given me such confidence. That's how I like to think of you out there, with those confused young men, giving them an explanation when no one who matters has any answers to offer. I no longer feel a ninny when I'm with a group of strangers. I'm bursting to tell everyone it's because of you but I suppose they would laugh. Your directness and impatience with nonsense have made it easier to cope without you. I no longer see things in emotional terms only, the truth of things seems so obvious now.

Aunt Vi and Uncle Edmund are still here. Violet is such splendid company for mother. She won't allow her to hold anything in and asks searching questions about you and Edwin to slice through mother's protective layer. 'No secrets!' she exclaims, in that clipped whisper of hers. 'This is not the time for hiding in the shadows!' and she gets so cross if mother won't answer. At one point, she was silent when Edmund asked about your family and Violet went scarlet and asked her what would happen if you were killed – would she forget because she couldn't bear to talk about it?

Mother apologised afterwards. She thought I was

upset by her sister's bluntness but I was glad. I need to think about you and talk about you, it's the only way I can bear being separated from you. Violet knew all that. She's so sharp and sensitive to the way young people think. It's a shame they couldn't have any children of their own.

Apart from these minor irritations she had a notion to cheer up the house – said it was morbid. So, on Saturday evening we all gathered round the piano and she entertained us with a medley of music-hall songs and some war songs that they're selling on sheets. I was sad but I wouldn't have missed it.

Father almost had hysterics at her performance but Uncle Edmund was quite distressed. She should show more self-control at her age, he thought. Well, I think she's wonderful. She has an instinct about you and me and Lily and Edwin. She can talk of you without growing serious. Not like mother, who can't even breathe Edwin's name without floods of tears.

And poor Becca is in the middle of all this lunacy. She feels totally neglected while everyone thinks about you and Edwin. It's difficult for her to understand what all this is about. She hears only the sensational news or the snippets that friends boast about at school. She wants to write to you, to be a small part of it, I suppose. You won't mind, will you, dearest?

It's past five but it's still warm enough to have the windows open. The lace curtains have blown against my dressing table while I was writing and my bottles of perfume have fallen. There is a heavenly concoction of smells in here – I expect you'll catch it on the paper.

I can see the sun – see how you've made me consider such fine things. It's indescribable but I'll try.

It's like a large exotic fruit, the edges tipped with a bloom of pink as though they've been stroked with a brush. It seems so enormous that I could almost reach out and touch it with the tip of my finger. Then I remember you – the same sun reflected in your watching brown eyes and I could cry with the wretched stupidity of all this.

Yours for always,

Ruth

My dear Owen,

Edwin has gone to France. The letter arrived yesterday and he left last night. There seemed some terrible hurry and he was very mysterious about where he was going. I hope you run into each other, though with the thousands out there, I suppose it's a rather silly expectation. I think I'm allowed to be a little brainless at the moment, don't you?

I keep thinking about that last day when you wouldn't let me walk you to the station. I suppose it was best; you didn't want to be upset any more than I did. But I behaved very badly, shutting myself upstairs and ignoring everyone's enquiries when they meant to be kind. Poor Becca, she had some drawings to show me and your father came round with an invitation to tea. I must have upset them dreadfully. I hope they forgive me. Can you forgive me?

I wanted only to sit by the window and watch the sky darkening over the hills and imagine you on the train – reading or drawing or talking softly to some nervous young man who offered you a cigarette. I had to imagine all of it, even your walking up the Avenue alone, away from the house, because I couldn't watch you. Somehow the imagining was less painful for me – it lent the whole process a dream-like quality which helped me believe that as you had so easily left, so you would easily return.

After a while I ran into the kitchen, where Hannah was making marmalade, and I sat gazing into the fire as I'd done as a child. Hannah was quiet. We didn't need any words. She made me a cup of tea and put her arms round me while I sipped it. There's so much about Hannah that we don't know. That disturbs me. I never think she has a life of her own, an inner existence that is quite separate from what she does for us, but she never reminds us of it. Sitting under her arms I felt very humbled all of a sudden. All the incidents when I had been thoughtless and cruel came back and I wondered why she stayed with us but I didn't have the courage to ask her.

You must be prepared for a deal of this melancholy musing, I'm afraid. It's a part of my growing up which I haven't managed to escape, an unfortunate legacy of my mother.

I went round to sit with Lily. She's very upset. She and Edwin have grown so close over the past months and I don't know how she'll cope without him. She has little else in her life but her work at the shop, and with everyone's thoughts in Europe, they're not very busy. Her mother is kind but she's a widow and spends her time thinking of her two youngest children. Lily isn't allowed to be a daughter, she's expected to be a woman, full of good sense and self-restraint. I sympathise, it's not easy to be thoughtful all the time and I'm sure I couldn't be sensible every second, it would be so boring. I bet you're laughing at me with all this talk of good sense and responsibility when I was such a wild individual. It's lucky that I met you and you were able to divert all those high spirits and misplaced enthusiasm into something more useful.

Guess who I bumped into on the way back from Lily's. Albert Judd was in the park, shuffling along and stopping now and then to peer into a tree or pick up a conker or a sprig of hazelnuts. He's such a tragic young man with his secret sorrow that no one knows anything about. He doesn't appear to have many

18

friends and all the young men of his age are at the Front.

I wonder what passes through his mind during all those hours alone. I often wished that you and he could be friends. I'm certain you might have helped him. It's cruel how that generous spirit of his is being wasted. But what could he do? I dare say there will be many more like him before this awful war is over. He told me Henry has been in France since January. Having a rare old time, he says, but Albert wasn't taken in by his brother's yarns; he knows and understands about war. I wonder if he regrets not being able to play a part in this one.

It's fortunate that Lily wasn't with me. She would have been angry about Henry's glorying in the fighting. For such a timid soul she can still show some fury. That's good, don't you think? It shows she's not completely hopeless without Edwin. She's such a brave creature. Funny isn't it, how people will comment on her strength. I'm sure no one says that about me; Ruth is expected to be brave.

We parcelled up Edwin's socks and muffler and a few little treats for his birthday. Becca had made him a lovely book with poems and a story that she'd written, all coloured in the most beautiful colours. I do hope he receives it undamaged. We'll have a quiet celebration to keep him in our thoughts and to cheer poor Lily.

Let me know what you need. I don't know the first thing about army life. I suppose it's in their interests to keep you all as comfortable as possible, so you won't be short of much. Lily wanted to send Edwin things like tea and biscuits but I was worried how long they would take to find him and what might happen to them in the rain. Can't escape the practical woman in me! But it's just as well – I need to be organised for mother now or she would go to pieces. I have to sit with her more and more and she asked me yesterday if I would stay with her for the next few days. She's convinced herself that Edwin will be killed within the week and I dare not let her speak to Lily.

Enough! You'll be glad to reach the end of this letter. I'm such a dim-witted soul. Why don't I cheer you up instead of thinking only of myself? I remember when I was a little girl and had been sent to my room for some sin – I would hide under the bedcovers and imagine what it would be like if father forgot to tell me that I could go downstairs for supper. How would it feel to be alone for the rest of my life? I suppose half an hour was a lifetime to a small child. And of course we're not talking about years, are we – you'll be home in a few months and I'll be able to restock my store of memories to see me through the next barren months?

Take care as best you can. Heaps of love and kisses.

Ruth

P.S. The next letter will be longer and more interesting, I promise.

Dearest Ruth,

This place is almost a 'home from home' now that we are settled. That's Josh's expression, not mine, when Alan starts complaining. Josh is one of those individuals who refuses to be miserable. I think he works on his gleaming smile and his quips in the dark hours to prepare himself to keep us all from madness during the day.

The terrible thing is the boredom – the lack of any purpose. There was so much pressure the other end; the haste with which we were herded onto ships and then ... nothing at all. A heavy, miserable anti-climax. There is intermittent shelling in the far distance, about four miles away they tell us, but it doesn't seem to have anything to do with why we're here. It disturbs me to listen to it and to remain unmoved. Why can't I think what might be happening a few miles over the hill? It's not good enough to say I shouldn't imagine it or it would be too terrifying. I won't accept that – it's escape when none of us should be allowed to escape. If we've agreed to come we must accept everything.

I'm quite content, soaking up the countryside, taking in the queer folk, reading and scribbling when I can. But there is a fearful sense that those who are not so useful or self-sufficient will tire and grow tetchy and restless. That could be dangerous.

Do you know what haunts me most? Faces. So many faces, all with that same haggard, haunted look, a weariness as though they can't believe what their poor bruised senses tell them. Faces that I will probably see only once but whose person will stay with me for ever.

It's unkind to worry about them, they're too bewildered to respond on an emotional level. They
can only cough or shrug or nod, believing, but not
caring, that I understand their apathy and lack of
distraction.

But it's unfair to dwell on them. I've been attached
to 'C' Company, under Captain Drummond. He's a
sound chap, a regular soldier, though he can't be long
out of college, he's so fresh-faced and youthful. What
he lacks in experience is made up in understanding.
His sole concern is to make our existence as smooth
and comfortable as possible. He holds daily informal
meetings with the NCOs and tries to see all his
men at some time during each day. He has that rare
gift of sizing people up pretty swiftly – like you, my
darling, though you do it more prettily. But this
efficiency doesn't stop him being sympathetic to each
individual, lout or exemplar alike. Somewhat like a
mother, Josh says, though I don't think Alan would
agree.

It happens the poor lad was concerned about his
mother at home alone. She's a widow and strictly he
shouldn't have come out yet as he's the only son. But
they don't turn away eager and healthy volunteers.
Captain Drummond has put his mind at rest about
leave and so on. He'll feel easier now.

It's a shame about the teaching. It was good for you,
that intimacy with the young, and the days will
be long if you can't get out. I hope you can escape
for a walk. Those tiny snatches of freedom are so
important if you are to keep faith with yourself.
Independence is the key, my darling. Life is so
precious, you must make every little item a gem, no
matter how trivial it appears. And if your mother
were to adopt that philosophy it would be her

22

salvation. She wouldn't have time to worry about Edwin's safety. He'd be in her head, of course, but only as part of the other detail that would make every action valuable and worthwhile. She'd be happy to think about him, as you think about me, doing everyday things.

I'm preaching at you, what must you think? Defiant little spirit with a mind of your own. Talking of which, you would adore our chaplain. He's a complete and utter fool. Harmless and totally ineffective. He thinks he's deeply pious but he's still a fool for all that. I have to say, it's sad. So many men rely on their simple faith to keep them going. I don't blaspheme when I call him a fool, believe me, he's insensitive but gloriously innocent and is convinced in some mindless way that he is successful in his sacred calling.

He understands his role as a minister of cigarettes. Those tiny sticks of comfort he hands out are some form of divine panacea for every worry and ill. Poor Alan, he came back yesterday with a pocketful and he doesn't smoke. The dear Padre advised him to adopt the habit as a sedative for his nerves. I was furious but helpless and in the end we laughed ourselves silly. And Josh came off rather well – he swapped some soap and a tin of toffees for the lot. Toffees – that reminds me, you might send me some sweets. I never cared before but sucking a sweet seems a comfort through the long hours of sitting.

The men had drill today while the NCOs had a talk on explosives. I didn't take much in and I certainly can't imagine myself preparing to go out and kill somcone. It's like the guns in the distance, somehow I can't relate them to death but that's what they're all about.

Heavy rain. This is punishing rain. The men came

back sodden. Alan was slumped in his bunk with chattering teeth until the rum ration came to warm him. He woke later with a violent fever and was delirious. He rambled about a day on the moors with his dog. 'Come away 'ome, ye daft bitch!' he kept repeating. It was sad to hear his simple affection in this place but it's only thoughts of home that keep us cheerful.

Do you recall that little dog of the Judds' which you followed from the park? My father took you home, 'a little charmer' he said you were. That was the first time I'd heard about you. You ran into his arms outside the Judds' door. You'd followed Martha and the dog home and settled on her step, bright as a button, until she took you into her kitchen and found you a cushion by the range and a bowl of bread and milk. Mother was horrified at such adventures. I never told, did I, she had serious doubts about your suitability as a companion for Alice.

How comic and insignificant this seems, all these years on. Both of you grown up, sensible and caring young women. What nonsense some mothers conjure for themselves. I suspect they secretly enjoy it. When all the trials of dealing with babies and naughty children are at an end, they look round for something else to worry about and if it's not there they create it.

I can see the rain again. A thick grey sheet, like a shroud, hugging the hills. What misery there is there; no colour, no laughter, not even a song; the sameness of everything; the ugliness of everything. Faces, uniforms, the countryside through its shimmer of relentless rain. It's as though someone had tried to obliterate any lightness of spirit with a crude layer of paint in a fit of temper. Some entity out there doesn't favour us. But what else could we expect from war – soulless, not a glimmer of grace and all joy buried along with the sad corpses.

Are you enjoying the Lawrence poems? I'm glad I found them for you before I left. The lines I copied out have a strange compelling comfort. Josh is amused by my little collection of volumes, especially my notebook, which seems to be surrounded with some deep mystical significance for him. I don't think his reading has gone much further than passages from the Bible at Sunday school but I found him reading my Thomas Hardy the other day and he was quite put out and apologetic as though I'd stumbled on an unwholesome secret.

All is quieter at last. Only the snuffles and grunts of sleepers and the shell fire across the hills muffled by the damp air. Alan has stopped shivering but I can see his forehead glistening in the lamp light as I write.

Sleep safe, my darling.

Owen

My Darling,

I'm holding your letter and I can't read it. I sat for an hour, staring at my name until my tears dripped onto the paper and the ink ran. You've a very stupid girl, I'm afraid. I think perhaps it's not having Edwin here. I can't feel very courageous. Mother is so irritable. She cries at the smallest upset and is uncomfortable when Lily is around her because she reminds her of Edwin. Poor Lily, she has no one to talk to about him but me.

On Friday mother exploded at Hannah. She's never done such a thing before. She accused her of neglecting Edwin's room. Why hadn't she put a duster over his books and fresh sheets on his bed? Hannah was speechless. When he left, mother had forbidden her to touch a thing. Of course father was furious and made her apologise.

With such unpleasantness I feel a numbing panic. I want to run from them all and hide somewhere secret and alone until you come home. I often think of our little cottage hidden away in the woods but I've not been back. I could be so content there, waiting for you, with my books and my sewing and the garden. Am I very selfish, thinking only of my own wishes when mother is suffering much more than I can imagine? Why is it so terrible, the sons seem so precious? Would daughters be missed, I wonder?

Your Captain Drummond sounds pleasant. I expect you need more officers like him. I fear Edwin is not so fortunate. His CO sounds a regular tyrant; checks their kit at least twice a day and puts them on report if their buttons aren't polished and their uniforms spotless. He even checks their mess tins, can you believe it? There must be a reason behind all this conformity and cleanliness, but I can't imagine what it is.

Has your Captain a lady friend? I bet you compare notes. Tell me what she's like so I can visualise her sitting at home writing to him. Doubtless, she's some beauty of a country girl with an enormous house and tennis courts and a croquet lawn with fountains and swans in the grounds. I don't yearn for a life like that. All those house parties and trips to London and Ascot, pretty boring and pointless. I never understood the rules of croquet anyway.

I still love my books. Nothing pleases me more than to snuggle up in bed with your letters under my pillow and a book resting on my knee. I've been trying some Galsworthy but didn't take to it, there were too many intrusive chattering relatives. Hardy drew me back and I'm on *The Woodlanders* for the third time! All that rural philosophy is so gentle and reassuring, it keeps my mind from the war and what you must be going through.

There were two jays in the garden this morning. Such exquisite creatures, it's a shame they're related to magpies. Rowdy birds, chattering and strutting about, full of hateful self-importance. I can see they are reincarnations of politicians and people who think they know how to organise anything. They swooped down from the apple tree and smashed the coconut shells that Hannah had put out for the tits. I suppose you don't see many birds with all the people and the noise. You'll miss that.

After the service on Sunday I spoke to the Reverend Green. He's a most peculiar chap. He never mentions any family but he must have some, everyone does. He never smiles, not even at the tots who sit through his laborious sermons. I'm sure I was never so well-behaved. He didn't ask after you or Edwin. I don't care for him any more. I came home quite put out and couldn't eat anything for the rest of the day and Hannah had made a plum pie; she was very disappointed.

Mother says I expect too much. He's a busy man and can't remember everyone's husband or son. She's too generous to such an offensive man. What makes him so busy? He hasn't a proper job. His sermons are almost identical every week, he visits the sick and the old and talks about their gardens. The rest of the time is his own. Insufferable person! Father suggested that he begin some worthwhile war work – but not in front of mother, naturally.

I bought some peppermints from Frank in the shop today and when he knew they were for you he wouldn't take any money. Everyone is so kind. Troubles seem to bring out the best in people, don't you think? Have you ever wondered why some individuals are naturally good and others downright evil? Why was Henry Judd such a tyke and Albert so kind-hearted and gentle? I can't imagine him raising his voice to anyone. His mother is the same. Whenever I see her she's so cheerful and always asks after Lily and Edwin and you. I'm sure she doesn't know how to be angry.

There's been a dramatic change in my own mother. Is it the war or old age approaching that makes her so sour? She almost revels in the gloom and heartache. And poor father, he has such trials but he remains tirelessly patient. At school, the children think of nothing but the war and won't settle to any serious work. One of the pupil teachers is very lax and lets the older boys get up to all sorts of mischief. I'm glad I'm not there any more.

Naturally, Edwin is never far from father's thoughts and you, of course, but I suspect his feelings are pretty confused. He reads everything in the papers but is forever tutting as he scans the pages. He's unhappy because he feels so helpless. He can't see his role as a vital part of the war effort. I've tried to reassure him that it is important. Those children will be the next generation, what they inherit from us will have to make sense. He and the people like him are the only ones who can show them.

I'm sorry I sound like a prim dried-up schoolmarm. I'm so serious about so many things, I know, but it's my way of dealing with them. And here's some more dour stuff for you. I went with Lily to church this evening. It was so moving, I have to tell you. The atmosphere of the place; its perfume, the spluttering candles, the roughness of the stone seemed to hide secrets that might offer consolation; it was all so full of meaning. Of course, it was the people who made it what it was. They wanted to be there, not just to be seen there.

The mass was a total mystery. I couldn't understand the Latin and many things the priest did were puzzling but it didn't matter. The whole occasion was charged with some unfamiliar but fascinating potency. Do you see, I call it an occasion? It was special. By the end I felt changed. I felt a peace inside as though every little worry about you and Edwin and mother were in a safe warm place that couldn't disturb me. All my fears were softened, the images in my head were made gentle and blurred so I could choose whether I noticed them. I know part of it is the state I'm in, uneasy and tearful and oversensitive, but I don't care. Afterwards, I felt kinder towards everyone – even poor mother!

Father Fortune shook my hand and seemed pleased to see me. He told me I was welcome any time. When I mentioned you he held onto my hands more firmly and said that he would offer a prayer for your safe keeping. Wasn't that kind? Lily said that was what her religion was all about, real people and love, not superficial airy things like new hats or who had been invited to the vicarage for tea.

You won't understand all these ramblings. And even if you do you may not want to waste your precious time on such words. But you've taught me how important it is to talk about our feelings so I had to share it with you. Mother would have apoplexy if she knew. I don't understand why but she seems afraid of offending that insulting cleric. I might go with Lily again soon. It was such a comfort and the experience brought you and Edwin closer. Then Lily says we have only to think of you and you will be with us. I don't have to try very hard to keep you in my mind. You're there always.

With dearest thoughts,

Ruth

1921

1

Stillness

I imagined father downstairs waiting, listening for the gentle creaks and thuds that meant I was on my way down. On the table his books were spread open and untouched. He would not be able to concentrate, his memory clamouring with images too fragile to distract him from his wife, who lay dying upstairs.

It was strange how my relationship with mother had drifted in and out of shade and sunshine; partly from her struggles with the notion of family duty and her need for self-containment, partly from my own impatience and over-enthusiasm to please. The differences between us had become more apparent over the last few months; she was too old and ill to worry about them and I was too stubborn to admit a little flexibility might make her final weeks more comfortable. I was like father.

'Tell me about Lily again.' Mother's voice had become a muffled whisper but the insistence was still there.

'You're tired, mother.'

'Go on, please.'

It was puzzling why she wanted to hear about Lily now, when she had been so reticent about accepting her into the family. Maybe she was putting every little failure into a form which would ease her conscience. But it was easy for me to talk about Lily. She, more than anyone I knew, had earned happiness. Every part of her brief life held meaning; no experience, no matter how trivial or upsetting, had been wasted. And she lived with all that joy and response glowing from her bright face, never glancing over her shoulder or squinting into shadows. I loved Lily; we all loved Lily. Not for what she had become but for what she was. She, more than any of us, had remained true to herself, in spite of all her sufferings.

I smiled when I thought of her. 'They have the dearest little house, close to the river. She's planted flowers along the path – pansies and lily-of-the-valley and she fills the house with them. They are so happy.' I swallowed my sadness but mother heard it.

'What is it, what's wrong?'

'Nothing.'

Lily's happiness with Billie was always tinged with some regret. Their existence seemed too idyllic, too precarious, like a perfect sky before it is stained by angry clouds or the full-throated song of the evening thrush pushing back the darkness.

'No babies yet?'

'They're too much in love for babies.' I wondered where such words came from. I doubted mother would understand such sentiments. I smoothed my hands over my own swollen shape.

'What about our baby, how is she?'

'She's fine.' I wanted to clasp her hand, to compare her wrinkled skin with mine, but her insistence that our baby would be a girl was becoming an irritation. I seemed to have grown so easily into a woman who was not certain of anything. I found it safer and less disappointing and relished the unexpected as a thrill.

'And Owen, is he more used to the idea of becoming a father?'

'I hope so.' It was almost time to leave. She had closed her eyes and slid down the bed, her interest in me dissolved in her wish for rest. But each time I prepared to leave her it brought the moment of her death closer.

Death was unfamiliar to me and I was uncertain how to face it. I had listened to Owen's talk of his dead friends; I had been close to his shuddering body and measured the cries as he relived those moments of horror night after night. That part of marriage had been an unpleasant shock but I soon saw it as a distasteful experience that we would have to grow through together. Owen's helplessness drew my sympathy but there had been something cruelly unattractive about a man with his physique, quaking and tear-stained and unaware of his nightmare sufferings. There was an ugliness which I needed to colour when I discovered that I was carrying his child. I developed a senseless fear of being close to such disturbing outbursts. It seemed unnatural, his preoccupation with suffering and loss, when I wanted to thrill to the flutter of a life inside me.

I leaned away from mother's bed as though the sick woman might infect me with a similar sourness. I would keep my body safe and my baby untouched by such thoughts. My one fear was my presence at the end, when the breath finally left her lips, and how I would deal with it. This new fear was like a bitterness left after eating tainted fruit.

She gave a shudder and tried to turn on her side. I bent over her but the sweet sickly smell of her ailing body filled my nose and throat and I almost choked. I fled to the window to gulp at more delicate air and stared down into the garden. There, where I had dragged my feet across the damp grass and crushed windfall apples under my boot until Edwin had left his hammering and noticed me. The bird table he had worked on with such patience was still there under the lilac tree but the wood was cracked. No one put bread out any more.

With the approach of dusk the bed was almost in shadow. I was saddened and angry with my own selfish weakness; I was so infatuated with my own body and my future with Owen that I could feel nothing for this woman who was my mother. A flush of irritation tingled my cheeks. Had it been father it would have been different. He would have expected nothing less than strength and brave sympathy from his favourite daughter. But this fading woman under the sheets who had rarely credited her daughter with moral resolve, this was more than I could bear.

'Are you still there?' Across the dim room her voice was weak and I felt tempted to ignore it.

'Yes, mother, I'm here.' I moved to the foot of the bed and made myself look on those feeble features.

'Fetch your father. I need to see him.' She struggled onto her elbows and stared through the gloom. 'I'm all right, just fetch your father.' Her eyes seemed larger, glistening and more terrified in her puckered face.

'Mother wants to speak to you.' I avoided his eyes, convinced that he would see my lack of tenderness and my distaste for the sick woman upstairs. But when he looked at me I knew that he was remembering some gentle images of me as a child to soften the pain of the reality. He would never admit it but I knew that he understood my confused feelings about mother.

'I'll go up. Will you be staying?' He tidied the heap of books and rose slowly with an uncertainty and subtle appeal that was a test of my emotional resolve. His obstinacy in maintaining his independence was unassuming but it was none the less distressing to me.

'I must get back, Owen is expecting me.'

He held me in his arms, ill at ease with so much

tenderness now that his little girl was a woman and daunted by the growing fear of being alone.

'You'll be all right?' I brushed his cheek with the back of my hand, surprised by the warmth of his skin. I wanted to hold him longer, to feel his comfort again. All those years when I had displayed such precocious defiance and impetuous behaviour; not once had he shown impatience or disapproval; not once had he scolded me. In fact, I had never heard him lose his temper. He was a good man. Edwin, had he lived, would have been exactly like him.

'I'll be here tomorrow,' I offered with a firmness that I did not feel, not wishing to focus on his vulnerability.

'You shouldn't be dashing about.' He looked at my swollen body with guarded sensitivity and regret. In this state I had been drawn away from him. I was his daughter still but I was also Owen's wife.

'I'm not ill. It's perfectly natural. Don't worry, Owen is looking after me.'

'You're sure?' He clung to my hands until we had almost reached the door.

'Go to mother, she needs you.'

'It's almost dark.' He squinted at the thickening blackness that hugged the window.

'The bus drops me at the end of the lane. Owen will be there to meet me. Come on, she'll be getting upset.'

'I'm sorry for all this fuss. You're all I have left ... with your mother...'

'Have you forgotten Becca?'

'She has no time for us up at that college.'

'You have told her about mother?'

He followed me into the hall, where I struggled into my coat. Only the top buttons would fasten now and I smiled at my untidy shape.

'Yes, yes, weeks ago. She's written.'

I frowned. 'It's too bad. She could get home at the week-end, there are plenty of trains from Manchester.'

'I don't want her here. It would tire your mother.' He hovered in the doorway, feeling clumsy, still conscious of the distances between Becca and me in his affection.

'You know best.' I pulled on a woollen hat and wrinkled my nose. It was too big but Owen insisted as the buses were draughty in the evening. 'See you tomorrow.' I slid away, oppressed by the desperate sadness that was clouding his face.

The bus rattled down the hill away from the town. I liked the journey in the dark. The miserable houses were invisible and I could forget the untidy jigsaw of brick chimneys and concentrate on the trees and hedges that slid past the window and the reflections in the shivering pools of light on the road whenever the bus stopped. Night suited my mood. I could watch the images of people in the bus on the dark windows. There was only one other tonight, a young man in a cap with a scruffy tweed jacket and a shirt without a collar. He'd given me a quaint uneven smile when I climbed on the bus and I regretted the greeting I'd returned and tried to shut out his face beside me in the glass. Dark hairs from his neck and chest curled over the top of his shirt. I thought about Owen's smooth firm chest and the idea of resting my head on that other made me shudder.

I tried to relax, thrusting out my belly as a warning to the young man. The baby began to kick furiously, almost as if he knew that he was required to display his presence for my protection. The miracle of it all enthralled me still; so much activity from such a tiny creature; the magic of growth inside after those brief moments of bliss with the man I loved.

I doubted that mother had experienced such joy at the changes in her body. To her, motherhood had begun as a necessary part of marriage with no threads of love to unite it to her husband. Later she had used it as a device to justify her frustrations with her own weakness in certain relationships. And she was still using it, even so close to the end of her life. I could believe that mother's illness was an extension of her disapproval of my behaviour. After a great effort to heal the rift between us she had chosen this time deliberately so I would be left to struggle alone with a new baby and a husband still uncomfortable with himself. It was the final betrayal when she had loved her children so much – perhaps too much.

The lights of the Old Hall blinked through the shadows of trees in the distance. I wondered how long I would feel this excitement of coming home, the joy of seeing my man and feeling the closeness of his warm body beside me in bed. The dangerous fragility of Lily's happiness concerned me but I had no fears for myself. Perhaps it was all part of my new role as a mother. I had to feel exhilarated and favoured with the image of a tiny life to come. Lily had nothing but her love for Billie; a tenuous thread of emotion that could so easily be snapped.

Even after the desperate hours with mother I felt strangely comforted. My struggles tended to fortify and quench some inexplicable need inside, leaving me vigorous and resolute. Unlike poor mother I had learned to take each golden day for its own sake, my only rewards, satisfaction and a precious peace of mind.

Owen was waiting under his usual tree. The moment I left the bus he stepped forward and held me in his arms. We shared a kiss, a long closeness that hinted at the desire he had felt for me throughout the day; an echo of the yearning he had never repressed during our months of separation.

'You look tired, I wish you wouldn't go each day.' He guided me to the edge of the lane and offered his muffler against the cool air. I welcomed the comfort, the spiced smell of his tobacco and the mustiness of the books that he handled at the Hall. Our steps sounded flat on the damp road. A light shower had given the air a sweetness that stung my nose. I sneezed and clutched at my belly as I felt the baby lurch.

'I'm all right, we're both all right.' I smiled and guided Owen's hand to feel the tiny feet pressing against my dress.

'After next week you must stay at home, I insist.'

'Owen, don't lecture me, I know how I feel.'

He slid his hand down my body and found the warm place above my thigh and I sighed with the memory of him. 'I'm sorry. I want you and our baby to be safe.'

'I know.' I kissed his chin and we quickened our steps.

I could see the shape of the lodge ahead, like a doll's house growing out of the trees. I could not have wished for a more perfect home for my baby. When Major Burgon had offered it to Owen I had accepted without even seeing it. I felt from its name that I would love every part of it; the Major's wife had called it Lavender Hill before she died, because of the rich, aromatic heads that grew round the little house.

Owen pushed open the gate and I paused, holding his arm. The scent of lavender after rain made me dizzy and pleasantly muddled.

'Are you all right?' He fumbled for his key.

'I've never felt better.' I found his constant concern touching, as though he were making reparation for disturbing my life earlier. But I had forgotten all that and now that mother was drifting away I would have even less reason to recall it.

When we were settled in the tiny sitting room with our

40

tea in front of the fire he asked after her. I was hesitant and he leaned close, expecting to offer comfort, but I shook my head.

'I'm not sad. Does that sound heartless?'

He was not surprised.

'It's a relief,' I began, 'I won't have to worry about being strong and resourceful. Every moment I had the feeling that her eyes were trying to pick out some little hesitation in my behaviour, any signal that things weren't smooth between us.' I tried to identify his expression but he had grown accustomed to guarding his emotions. 'Don't you feel on trial? She's been waiting for the last two years for some disaster so she could gloat on what she'd thought but never had the courage to say – "I told you so!"'

'Aren't you overreacting a little?' He was still amiable towards everyone, seeing good in all, even those who had upset him or undermined his shaky resolve.

'No.' I slid from the chair and sat at his feet with my head on his legs. The lamps were not lit and the firelight sent shivers of orange across the ceiling and onto the mirror on the far wall. I closed my eyes and put my hands up to my flushed cheeks. 'There's a terrible cruelty inside us.'

'Hush, my love, don't think of such things.' He bent over and brushed my hair with his lips.

'It has to be said,' I insisted. 'Why can't we repay our parents' generosity with love – an unconditional love? Sometimes I'm afraid that I'm losing all the gentle qualities they tried to teach me.'

'Perhaps those gentler qualities are meant for your lovers and your children.'

'Is that all?' I was impatient for an explanation that would salve my conscience.

'Why should there be anything more? They are the future.' He paused and I recognised the pain of memory

41

behind his words. He had witnessed the future ripped away from a generation. His whole life would be clouded by those images. 'They will be, no matter what has gone on between us and our parents.'

'Then, I'm not so cruel?'

'You're like any other mother. If your mother hadn't been ill it wouldn't have occurred to you to feel guilty. She might have been a friend to you.' There was regret in his tone, an understanding of his part in mother's distance and incautious approach.

'I wish I could simply be myself.' I held my head in my hands and felt the throb of my pulse as the blood and that of my baby thrilled through my body.

'From now on you must think for two.' His tone was more hopeful and encouraging.

'It frightens me.'

'You should be excited. Think of the thrill when you see your baby and learn what you have to do to make him happy.'

'He'll need your love and attention too.' I pressed my hands to his face. 'You're his father.'

'I don't suppose I'll have much part in it.'

'What nonsense. Owen Webb, you're as frightened as I am. Tell me the truth.'

'I can't lie to you – this is a terrifying experience for me.'

'Owen?' His face seemed changed over the past two years; familiarity had lent it a comfortable more unconcerned aspect. To hear such thoughts was out of character. 'You mean that?'

He nodded. 'The responsibility of caring for another individual, one so dependent, is daunting.'

'Now who's overreacting?'

'We'll manage together, it'll be our challenge.'

I tightened my arms around him and drew him close.

'Owen, we will be happy, won't we?' The sweet scent of his pipe was on his lips; a comfort and a reassurance, like the nearness of my father. If I closed my eyes I might be a small child again with nothing to worry about except how pretty I looked.

2

Promises

I had been listening to the rain for hours. I imagined it splashing onto the glistening liquorice roof and gurgling down the pipes into the barrel behind the back door. By now the barrel would be overflowing, the water gushing across the path to drown my poor flowers. I tried to see through the window but the pattern of raindrops made a shimmering curtain and a sudden sharp pain burned the lower part of my back. I would ask Lily to look. Those little plants were so tender they needed protection. I called out but remembered that Lily was preparing breakfast for Owen, who had been sitting all night by my side, distracting me with idle talk of the past.

He still recalled vividly our first meeting during a visit to Edwin to borrow a book. He had been left alone while Edwin searched upstairs and I burst in. I was shamelessly inquisitive to see my brother's new friend; a friend who was smart enough to break up a fight between Edwin and Henry Judd with a few sharp words.

'Are you Owen?' I had accused and he smiled, that same slightly defensive smile that I knew now so well. I stepped forward and pointed at his boots where one of the laces was undone. He wriggled his feet, partly because the boots were stiff but mostly because of his fascination with my startling manners. I had been so unlike his sister Alice that he couldn't take his eyes from me. What he had seen, he told me later, was passion, an emotion that was disconcerting but exciting in one so young and unformed.

I was still intrigued by Owen's view of me and the way he constantly moved back to make comparisons with my childhood self. Father did the same but for different reasons. Father needed to keep the complete picture of his family near to his heart, especially when it was gently disintegrating. With Owen, each fragment that he pulled from the past was an affirmation of his acceptance by those who loved him. He did not need to be overwhelmed by the whole picture. His experiences had led him to be selective in what he cherished, which made each tiny tarnished shard specially valued.

But his seriousness over the baby was a concern. He was too reflective. I had to reassure him that we could be sure of each other so that his caution was no longer necessary. True, he was a different person from that fresh-faced youth who had stumbled over the scullery step and blushed at Hannah's chuckles. He had lost that startled look but I respected his wish to keep some parts of himself dim and untapped. Since the war and our closeness in marriage I was on my guard not to scrabble about too aggressively in the darker places of his mind. His caution was a warning at times, that I should suspend my eagerness to know all the answers.

I had been too insistent on change in those early days of our friendship. Father had warned me to measure my determination more carefully, but lightness and superficiality were inconsistent with the exciting philosophy of the time. I remember telling Edwin in 1910 that he could not expect women to be the plain diminutive souls that his grandmother had described in her journal. In my smug adolescence I had informed him that marriage, if women chose it, would never be the same again. The thought of my words made me blush. Of course, Edwin had been a sceptic of all these wild ideas. An intelligent young woman like me should beware of taking such sentiments to heart for when they collapsed around me I would have only myself to blame for the devastation.

A flurry of raindrops spattered the glass near my head and I shivered. There were so many hours of waiting and Owen had not left me until I insisted. He had wiped my brow with a damp cloth and smoothed my hair away from my face. He said little but I felt close to his thoughts and believed in some secret telepathy between us as lovers which preserved that constancy and quiet intimacy. How else was I to explain the feelings we shared through those fearful letters that had passed between us? At times during that dreadful war I had imagined the air between England and France throbbing with all those words of love and loss and comfort, pressing on the ocean and the sky.

And those feelings had been translated into an intimacy born, not from conventional desire, but from our relief at being allowed a closeness beyond words and sheaves of paper. I could hardly believe the first contact we experienced, uninterrupted except for our muffled apologies for ignorance or clumsiness. The resulting tenderness came as a measureless surprise to both of us. He had loved me for my hesitancy and lack of knowledge; he could not believe that I was not being artfully provocative. I had loved him for his gentleness and diffidence when I had expected more urgency from this man who had known such disastrous uncertainty. I had thought at the time that the only passion was our relief at being blessed in our love, but I know now that there was passion of sorts in the trembling of emotions held in check and released in our mingled tears of happiness.

As the first threads of dawn streaked across the sky Owen had crept away. I was relieved. The pains were more regular but alone I could settle to work through them, sensing that the baby could not be far away. Owen's father was expected even though I had it in my head that I was young and healthy and should be able to cope with such a natural process. The muscles across the arch of my belly stiffened and I tried to relax to meet the next wave of pain. I wished that Alice could have been here. She had her own baby and another on the way and she might have been more support than the timid Lily.

She seemed a frail girl, especially as she had joined with the strapping Billie Judd. For several years she had refused to consider any man but Edwin; then mother had finally persuaded her and the old woman's approval was like a blessed sanction from Edwin for this new attachment in Lily's heart.

The pain subsided and I took a deep breath and tried to focus on something definite and useful. It might be heartless but I was glad that mother had not lived to see the baby. It would not be the daughter that she'd expected; the power and determination of the vigorous limbs inside and my feelings of confidence whenever I thought about him made me certain that it would be a son.

As the pains grew stronger I struggled to call Owen but the words wouldn't leave my throat. I felt for the walking stick beside the bed and banged the floor, counting in time with the taps, to carry me up and over the pain ... seven, eight, nine, ten ... I closed my eyes. I couldn't remember what followed ten so began again at one...

'You're too late, we've managed without you.' Owen was sitting beside the bed with the baby in his arms while I lay quietly. He thought I was asleep.

John Webb looked on, a proud grin on his even-featured face, shaking his head at his son's achievement. 'Well done, mother will be tickled.'

47

'Ruth did all the hard work. She was so brave.' He glanced at me and I opened one eye and rubbed at my face. 'Hullo, my darling. How are you feeling?'

'I feel wonderfully tired. How does it feel to be a father?'

Before he could reply John had jumped in. 'More men should see what their wives suffer,' he scolded, 'they wouldn't be so eager to give them so many babies.'

'Even with all the pain and unpleasantness, it was still beautiful,' defended Owen. He squeezed the son, hidden under a blanket in the hollow of his arm, and the baby opened his eyes and thrust out a pink tongue, eager for food.

'He's hungry.' John felt for my pulse and gave me an encouraging smile but I wanted to get back to my cosy dreams. 'Would you like to have him?'

Owen slid the baby across the bed and helped me to settle him at the breast.

'Lily can sit with her.' John rubbed his hands.

Owen was laughing. 'Poor Lily, it was almost too much for her. I sent her out for a walk in the fresh air.'

'Sweet girl, exactly what Ruth needs, someone young and chirpy. Does George know?'

'We sent messages to everyone.'

'Good, good. Any thoughts on a name?'

'Joseph Edwin ... you don't mind there's no John?'

'Of course not. Joseph is a good firm name, I like it.'

Owen was staring out of the window onto the garden. The rain had stopped and everything glistened. The new grass shone and the tiny plants seemed brighter and more alert. 'I can't believe it's all over.'

'It's only the beginning.' John gave me a sly wink before patting him on the back. 'You'll know you're married now.'

'Oh dear, that sounds ominous.'

Lily tumbled into the room, her face shining, her sugar

48

curls tied up in a blue ribbon in honour of the new baby. 'Dr Webb, isn't it wonderful?' she planted a kiss on his cheek and sat on the bed and put her arms round me. 'I was totally useless, you know, all fingers and thumbs, and I couldn't hear what Owen was telling me to do. Totally useless.' She threw back her head and her hair bounced around her narrow shoulders. 'We deserve a cup of tea – well, you do.' She giggled and kissed Owen on the side of his chin. 'Aren't you happy? Oh, I wish Billie was here. He won't believe me when I tell him.'

John looked on, amused and gratified by Lily's simple affection, then turned his attention to me. The baby had sucked his fill and was nestling in my arms. There was a strange collected expression on his face as he turned towards the window.

He sat on the stool close to the glass and watched the tops of the trees shake the raindrops into the still air. It was going to be a beautiful day. The sun rose higher and warmed his head and he closed his eyes.

I woke with tears damp on my face to find John looking at me. There was a sadness about his expression which made me want to hold him and reassure him that my tears were not of regret but of thanks for all that I had. There was a far-away look in his eyes which told of daydreams that involved me.

'You look refreshed.' He patted my arm in his doctorly manner but I grasped his hand, trying to hold onto and share his sadness.

'Thank you for coming. I'm sorry it was all over.'

'I'm glad you managed without me.'

'How is Owen?' We hadn't spoken alone since the birth and I could not help worrying that it was all too much for him.

'Tired. He's very pleased with you – and himself, I suspect.'

I sighed. 'He's been able to do something right at last.'

He frowned. 'Now, now, none of that talk. He'll need your support a little bit longer, till he's used to the idea of being a father.'

'He's quite prepared for it, all these months of looking after me.'

'Good, good.'

'You needn't worry, he's quite strong now.'

'I never doubted it.'

I glanced at him sideways, a half-smile tempting my lips. 'You'll bring Maud to see her grandchild?'

'Of course, when you're up to it.' He shuffled to the edge of the seat, uneasy under my all-seeking gaze.

'Tell me, do you remember how you felt when Owen was born? I wish I'd known him as a boy, he seems to have an advantage over me.'

'He was quite unexceptional. We hardly knew he was in the house. It wasn't until Alice came along that he found his voice.'

'Was he jealous?'

'It wasn't easy for him. He spent so much time alone while I was out of the house. He felt his mother had an ally in this tiny girl, someone who might share the empty hours in ways that he couldn't.'

'He was sensitive even then?' I couldn't keep the regret from my voice. Peering over at the window I hoped that the sun would stay, hovering over the trees like a benevolent spirit. It kept my thoughts soft and manageable, and warded off the shadows of pain that I needed to forget.

'Oh yes. But he soon discovered that a sister could be quite interesting.'

My hand had strayed unconsciously towards the sleeping baby. He stretched his limbs against the soft blanket, still discovering what it felt like to be free. 'We'll give Joseph a little sister soon, so he won't be sad like Owen.'

'You get yourself strong first.' He stood up and stretched in front of the window. The sun was in my eyes and his figure could have been that of Owen. He bent down and put his cheek next to mine. In a husky voice, uncertain with emotion, he thanked me.

'What for?' I laughed.

'For being a good wife to Owen. There are many who would say that he didn't deserve it.'

'Nonsense.' I almost snapped at him then I thought of mother, grey-faced and disapproving, the tears coursing down her cheeks as she pleaded with me to think again before I tied myself to this man. 'The worst is behind us,' I said, taking control of my voice. 'Joseph will make all the difference.'

John looked at me with an odd smile. 'I hope you're right, my dear.'

I was sitting on the edge of the bed, trying to brush my hair, when Lily came in. She took the brush and began to stroke the long hair away from my face. There was a different look about her, not mere weariness, a flush to her skin, a shimmer in her eyes as though she had been running through a tingling wind, in a hurry of excitement to reach somewhere.

'Oh Lily, is it wicked to feel so happy?' I stroked her creamy cheek and she slapped the brush against her knee.

'Why would it be wicked?'

I was still moved by Lily's innocence but ashamed that she didn't possess the courage to talk to me as an equal, another grown woman. 'I feel uneasy. I don't deserve it. Later on I might have to pay a forfeit for all the good times.'

Lily put the brush down and moved closer. 'Didn't you pay enough during the war – with Edwin and all that Owen went through? This is your reward and your blessing.'

'Lily, you're too good. Do you ever think about yourself?'

She smiled. 'Most of the time I do, except when I'm thinking about Billie.'

'Will he mind you staying for a while?'

'He wouldn't dare.' She flashed her eyes as threateningly as her affability would allow. 'Truly, he's so pleased that you wanted me to be here; he's been worried about me.'

'Aren't you happy, Lily?'

'Oh we're happy, of course we are, but it's strange still. He works so hard and we're both tired.' She smiled again with some hint of a secret behind her soft eyes. 'So it's a relief to him that I'm distracted for a while.'

'He cares for you very much.'

Lily was quiet and her blue eyes filled with tears. 'Oh, he does.'

'Don't cry, Lily.'

'I'm sorry.' She sniffed. 'We're so fortunate, I can't believe ... and Mrs Cleery gone...'

'Don't upset yourself. Mother was ready to go.'

'I know. It's selfish to miss someone when illness made them unhappy.'

'Oh Lily, there's no one more generous than you.'

She shook her head. 'Owen is very happy.'

I leaned over the crib where the baby was sleeping, so still and peaceful, and whispered to her. 'I hope you'll have what we have, Lily. It's the best, the only thing.'

She nodded in silence. It seemed she was more in control of her excitement with me. There seemed no plain reason; perhaps she shared my uncertainty of too much bountiful happiness. We had grown up to accept every incident that life threw up with a mixture of gentle optimism and good sense. We had never let those tiny moments of delight lighten our heads. Even when the war ended we had kept a tearful control on our feelings. That dull November day in 1918 had the clarity and immediacy of a photograph that I was continually dusting.

'Lily?'

She looked up without answer, waiting for me to continue, almost sensing in her intuitive way the words that were forming in my head.

'Do you remember that day, the last day of the war?'

She nodded and stared towards the window as though she were imagining the raindrops beating against the glass. The garden below had been dripping after the hours of rain. I wanted to cry with the heaviness that rolled and stretched inside my chest and the desultory stuffiness that filled my head. Lily had been singing as her needle moved up and down through the material, a lullaby she'd learned from her married sister. It was a sad song but Lily was cheerful. She was content with her uncomplicated life, perhaps more at ease because she no longer had to worry about Edwin's safety. In a locket round her neck she carried his picture, his snub-nosed smile and unruly hair. At times she would stop what she was doing, snap open the silver and gaze at the face.

The tears came. I could hold them back no longer and as I rubbed them away so Lily could not see, Hannah came thundering up the stairs to say it was all over. Lily finished her song then laid down her sewing with such care, stood up, stretched and straightened her skirt and fell into my arms. Hannah had watched, her mouth gaping in a careless smile, before she was drawn into our intimate relief and gladness.

'I only think of the bright parts,' Lily said suddenly as though she had been identifying with my thoughts exactly.

'That day was so special, a blur of shining faces and laughter and handshakes and music... Do you remember the music of the band, thumping through the damp air from the town? When we walked in the streets everyone we met had a greeting to share. People we didn't know hugged us and thanked us for something that was not our doing. It was so peculiar. A young man I met on the way home put flowers in my hair. He carried a basket brimming with roses and chrysanthemums. Where would he have found such flowers in November? I've never been able to understand. It was another odd thing to add to all the others.'

Lily was breathless, with the same expression of thankfulness that we had shared on that grey afternoon. I reached in the drawer beside the bed and drew out a photograph. 'Do you remember this, Lily?'

She screwed up her eyes in the yellow light then a smile softened her mouth. 'Owen's picture. I was the first to see it in the tea shop. You were so kind to me and I thought you were only doing it to please Edwin.'

'Lily, how could you?'

'But you were sad. Why were you sad when you and Owen were beginning to fall in love?'

I stared at the photograph, recalling the intensity of his real smile as he tried to be cheerful when we made our farewell a few days after the photograph was taken. We both knew how miserable we would be apart but there was nothing we could do about what was happening. 'We were too young to be falling in love,' I said gently, leaning the picture against the lamp. 'We didn't know about life. We had nothing to distract us when we had to separate and survive alone.'

Lily's expression was one of shock. 'But you stayed together. You married and you have a son.'

'Yes, we have each other and we have Joseph.' I rose unsteadily and peered into the crib where the baby was making gentle snuffling noises. I spoke to Lily without turning round. 'Edwin wanted us to be friends, didn't he?'

'Yes, he did.' She was sitting on the stool by the window and held out her arms to the sun that was squeezing through the trees. She had the dainty figure of a girl; the open generous features of a person who has not experienced pain or misfortune. The ease with which she had hidden her pain was a puzzle.

There were many moments that Edwin had described to me, wishing me to love this fragile creature as much as he did. He had needed reassurance that Lily wasn't too insubstantial for him. He had confided in me when mother's reactions had been so unpredictable. We had never put it into words but we knew and understood her fear of Lily's position. She was a stranger in our family, a girl from a different social background, with different wishes and expectations. But in her love for Edwin, when her only hopes had been for his happiness, how could we not have welcomed her?

As with so many aspects of our ruffled existence, the war had made all that clear. Every strange unwelcome feeling, every bitter and intrusive thought, was juggled and rearranged until the whole collection, a farrago of unconnected dreams and fears, had to be accepted as an inseparable part of our lives. We couldn't live in spite of the war – the war was our life, we lived in the war.

1914

3

Uncertainties

I screwed up my eyes and frowned at the glare. The wicker chair pinched my back, making my shoulders ache, but I would not give in. I willed myself to sit motionless, my face turned to the sharp china-blue sky, until I could hear the sound of Owen's voice.

Something tickled my face. Tiny feet moved over my cheek towards my mouth and when I reached up a ladybird crawled onto my hand. The hurrying creature with its shiny coat moved across my fingers and flew onto my white dress... 'Ladybird, ladybird, fly away home...' The words danced in my head along with thoughts of Alice with her biscuit-coloured hair, sleek and straight, all those Christmases ago, sprawled on the rug in the living room, reading a story to Becca in the firelight. I tried once again to read my book but the sun was too bright on the page.

'You're clever,' chirped Lily from her spot on the grass under the apple tree.

'Me, clever?' I put up my hand to shade my eyes. As usual Lily was occupied with some sewing spread across her knees.

'To read those books. It takes me all my time to read the newspaper with Edwin leaning over my shoulder.'

'It takes me a long time to finish them sometimes, and I'll let you into a secret – I don't understand every word.'

'But you have Edwin or Owen to ask if you get stuck.

There's no one in our house who could talk of such things.'

'What about your brother?'

'He only thinks of his job and his young lady.'

'I can lend you some books, Lily, if you want to read. And I can talk about them if you need someone. It will be good for both of us.'

'Would you really? I should love that. I wouldn't feel so dizzy when Edwin starts talking about grand or important things.' She lowered her head to continue her sewing and smiled. 'You must think I'm a real pudding.'

'Who could think that?' Owen's voice came from the edge of the grass where he stood in his new grey suit.

I sprang up and held out my hand. 'Take no notice, it's Lily being silly. She wants to read to keep up with Edwin's conversation.'

'Very commendable.' He squeezed my hand and gave me wink. 'And will you help her?'

'If I can.' I led him across the grass and patted the pink cushion beside me.

'You're the perfect person.'

I bowed my head with mock modesty and peered up at his sunburnt face through squinting eyes.

'Where will you begin?' He sat down and looked suitably serious. 'The blood and tears of Florence Barclay or the sacred sensations of *The Sorrows of Satan?*'

'Don't mock. Florence Barclay and Marie Corelli have been most successful. If Lily is not familiar with them, it might be a wise place to begin.'

'I'm sorry. I wasn't teasing.' He touched the tips of my fingers with a kiss as an apology.

'I hope you're not becoming a literary snob, Owen Webb. I can't tolerate snobs.'

He ignored me and turned to Lily, who was observing us with amusement. 'And where is this terrifying

60

intellectual?' He curled my warm fingers inside his own. 'Is he on some secret educational mission?'

Lily spluttered then winced as she dug the needle into her thumb. She sucked at the crimson blood before it dripped on her dress. 'No, he's gone down to the vicarage with a book that he borrowed.' She folded her sewing neatly into her tapestry bag and stretched out on the grass and closed her eyes.

Owen plucked a blade of grass and began to stroke the hollow of my neck until I put down my book. 'Why are you distracting me?'

'That's my purpose here.' He laughed, sucking on the grass, and leaned closer. I flicked at a wisp of hair that curled near his eyes. It was smooth creamy hair like his sister's, hair which was made more startling with the sun behind it.

Lily sat up, rubbing her eyes, her fair curls tangled at the back of her head. Her face was glowing with that startled expression of unworldliness that made her so attractive. 'Where can Edwin be?' she asked of no one in particular. 'I should have gone with him. He promised to be only half an hour.'

Owen smiled. 'You know what he's like when he starts talking, he suffers from his sister's complaint.' He cringed slightly, waiting for my reaction, but I simply returned to my book. It was too hot to bother about childish insults.

'Perhaps I'll go inside.' Lily held her hands to her head. 'This sun is too strong, it's giving me a headache.'

'Shall I come with you and find you some sal volatile?' I asked anxiously.

'No, I'll be fine out of the sun. You sit with Owen.'

He watched as her dainty steps left the grass unmarked. She lifted the hem of her pink dress as though she were about to dance. I followed his look and felt a sudden elation in the warmth we shared for Lily. The girl's unsuspecting openness drew us closer together as though we were combined in some delicious inoffensive intrigue against the rest of humanity. I supposed that was the true meaning of friendship and felt honoured that I had been allowed to experience it.

Owen took out his watch. 'Edwin is late.'

'Too late.' I tossed my book on the grass and stretched up my arms. For what, I did not know. We seemed to have been lying around in this insufferable heat, waiting for something, for weeks. But it never happened.

'Phew! What a trek up that hill. I thought I would expire in this heat.' Edwin appeared round the side of the house, his damp hair clinging to his pink brow. He had loosened his collar and undone the buttons of his waistcoat.

'Have you run all the way?' I asked as he flopped where Lily had been sitting only minutes before.

'Almost. Then I met Albert. He wanted to talk.'

'Do I know Albert?' Owen was away from home so much that he felt a distance from the local people.

'You remember Albert.' Edwin lowered his voice. 'The South African war.'

'Why are you whispering?' I demanded. 'I know all about that war and what went on there. And I remember Albert Judd very well.' I leaned back and closed my eyes, recalling my first sight of him as a little girl, shortly after he'd returned, maimed after that infernal war. I'd run away from Hannah in the park and found him sitting alone, lost in his thoughts, but not so distracted that he didn't notice a mischievous child when she offered him a flower from her hat. 'He was kind to me. Not like his brother.' I rubbed my fingers hard along the arm of the chair. 'I hated Henry. He was so bad-tempered and dishonest. I wonder how two brothers can be so different?'

Owen looked serious. 'It's difficult for them. Father told

62

me about their father. I don't suppose Henry ever had a job?'

'Don't feel sorry for him,' I warned, recognising the sympathy in Owen's tone. 'He had a job at Adcock's; he was foolish enough to lose it.'

'And Mrs Judd, how does she manage?' continued Owen.

'Mother sees she's all right, gives her little jobs.'

'That's kind,' said Owen.

'She's like that. Would give her last crust to a beggar at the door,' said Edwin.

'Who's that?' Mother was approaching from the back of the house.

She was still an attractive women, with only a sprinkle of grey in her dark auburn hair, which was swept softly back to the nape of her neck. As she crossed the lawn the hem of her grey skirt brushed the grass with a soft rustle. Her appearance always made people talk in sober, controlled tones.

'Good afternoon, Mrs Cleery.' Owen rose and offered his place next to me.

As she sat, she smoothed the fine material of her skirt with graceful fingers and waited for the conversation to continue.

'Edwin was praising your virtues, Mrs Cleery, as an angel of mercy in the community.' Owen knelt on the grass beside me, his chin on the arm of the seat.

'Edwin, you're too generous.' She smiled. Owen said I shared the same expression, a faint mysterious curve of the lips which suggested something secret and amusing in one's head, but I think he was simply trying to intoxicate me with words. Nothing was ever simple with Owen, most things had to be decorated in some symbolic language, not to impress, but to give the ordinary a special quality. That was one of the aspects of Owen that I found easy to love.

'I was telling them about the Judds,' explained Edwin.

'Ah, the Judds,' she began to twist her fingers in her lap, 'it's very unfortunate.'

We all watched as her soft features were threatened with concern. 'We're so lucky to have escaped tragedy.' She gazed into the dazzling sky as if trying to convince herself that no evil could enter this place of quiet sunshine.

I grasped her twisting fingers. 'How's Lily?'

She brightened at the mention of someone who needed her help. 'She's not at all well, poor dear. I've sent her to lie down and Hannah has made her some tea.'

Edwin made a move to go in but mother held him back. 'Let her rest, Edwin. She's working too hard. I may have a quiet word with Mrs Wallace, she will push those girls so.'

'It's not Mrs Wallace, mother. Lily drives herself. She wants to do the job so well and learn so much.'

'That may be true,' said mother sharply, 'but Mrs Wallace should not take advantage of her good nature or she will find herself without a valuable assistant.'

'I'll have a gentle word with her,' I said.

'Thank you dear, I think it would be best coming from you. Well, I must get on, tea in half an hour.'

Owen lay down and closed his eyes and I returned to my book. Edwin was watching the gentle rise and fall of Owen's chest, the relaxed skin around his mouth and the fall of his hair around his neck. An insect crawled up his arm and flew onto his face, Edwin flicked it away and Owen opened his eyes. They had that startled expression that we had both grown to love over the years of our friendship.

'How's the family?' my brother asked.

'Well.'

64

'And Alice?'

'Oh, you know Alice, rushing here and there.'

'You should bring her up, Ruth would love to see her.'

'I've asked her but she prefers to sit at home with her books when she has some free time.'

'Sounds like me,' laughed Edwin. 'Give me a book or newspaper any day. I can survive without people.'

'Edwin!' I picked up a handful of grass and flung it in his direction. It landed in his hair and he shook his head.

'Not you, Miss Dizzy, or Owen or Lily. Just some people, they get me down.'

Owen slid onto his elbows and examined his friend's face with wide eyes. 'Not your family, surely. I've always found them so easy to get on with.'

'Yes, they are, most of the time. Father can be a bit straight. He wants reasons for everything. It's the schoolmaster in him, I suppose. Sometimes I don't want to think why I'm doing something. This must sound ridiculous.'

'Not at all. I understand. It was the same when I went to medical school. I had to stop thinking about it eventually or I would have gone mad. I simply had to accept it.'

I lowered my book and reached out to hold his arm. 'Was it very bad?'

'Seemed so at the time. Not when I look back on it.'

'Why didn't you tell me about it if it was so terrible?'

'There was no need to worry you. It was something I had to learn to handle myself.' He stroked my hand and looked away as though trying to forget something unpleasant.

'I've been lucky. I've never had to do anything I didn't want to do.' Edwin was apologetic, guilty at what he saw as his good fortune.

'There is something to be said for meeting a challenge head on,' continued Owen, 'character building and all that.'

I was amused to hear this conversation. These two were hardly men but they were talking so seriously about challenges as if their future happiness depended on their ability to cope with the unforeseen. Perhaps they would have been more content living in the Middle Ages when they could hop onto a charger and rescue some damsel in distress.

Edwin leaned closer and glanced behind at the house where all was quiet. 'This war business, it's a worry, don't you think?' He cleared his throat uncomfortably.

'Not really. There's more chance of war in Ireland than in Europe.' Owen's voice was so ingenuous I could hardly control myself.

'It's still war though, isn't it?' I almost shouted.

Edwin disregarded me. Owen's words were a challenge he could not allow. 'You can't believe that.' He made it his business to read every aspect of the current situation in any available publication. He knew that Owen did not wish to be so well-informed.

'But you only have to look at the papers, they're full of the Irish question. For years now Ulstermen have been arraigning themselves for some almighty open struggle. You only have to see their volunteer armies to guess at their plans.'

Edwin was on his feet and pacing the patch of grass between them. 'All wild ignorant threats, they won't come to anything. They're the ravings of bellicose Blarney men.'

Owen looked at him seriously, he was considering why Edwin should be so concerned. Owen and I had discussed the possibility of war in Europe and he was convinced that Britain would be drawn into it. It was because he found that thought so disturbing that he preferred to concentrate on other more palatable possibilities.

'Don't be so sure,' Owen continued. 'Asquith is making

66

an unholy mess of law and order over there and the country is all set to be swept along on some course of mindless violence. And Bonar Law has a lot to learn about shrewdness before he can claim any diplomatic victories over there. He openly supports their threatening behaviour, justifying their resistance at the expense of peace.' He glanced at me for reassurance, knowing how upset I became with all this talk of unrest.

'I wish I could believe you,' Edwin sighed. He looked up and the sun caught his face as it filtered through the web of leaves on the apple tree. The small immature fruits were beginning to swell and ripen, promising a rich harvest in the months ahead.

'You've been talking to old Green again, haven't you?' challenged Owen. 'That's why you were late.'

Edwin nodded and I shook my head. 'Edwin, you haven't? How could you when he's so insufferably smug and distant from everyone?'

He glared at me. 'Did you tell Owen about your jaunt with Lily?'

'No.'

'She went to mass with Lily the other day when you wouldn't take her to church.' He was being deliberately provocative. I knew very well that he found Lily's staunch faith almost touching. He had told me that although he could not identify with the religious ideas that guided her, he sympathised with their appeal. She lived within a consistent and ordered routine and her youth made her impressionable. Her bright fluttering vitality reminded him of a soft honey bee, beautiful but determined on its course for the good of the swarm. Her head was full of lively ideas for the others in her life but her lack of any sustained concentration might be disturbing to a character like Owen.

'She didn't tell me, no.' Owen's face was stiff and

Edwin, realising his thoughtless blunder, thought to make excuses for me.

'It was a frivolous prank, done out of pique because you refused your company.'

Owen put his hands on Edwin's shoulders. 'You don't know your sister very well, do you? She would never involve herself in anything frivolous, unless of course it heralded the start of an exciting adventure.' He was laughing by now.

'Then you don't mind?'

'Why should I mind? Ruth is perfectly free to do as she pleases.' The words were crisp and ungenerous and I was quick to answer.

'Excuse me, but I happen to be a part of this conversation and I will decide what I may or may not do.'

Edwin turned to Owen and their eyes met. Owen winked and they fell into uneasy laughter. After our dismal discussion it was good to see them so cheerful and I hoped they would not be drawn into such negative thoughts again in a hurry.

1915

4

Bliss

I worshipped the sun but the cool twilight and the
water nudging the edge of the grass were a great relief.
A breeze whispered across the lake and over the parched
grass in front of the house. Owen was watching as I
caressed the rough stone wall that separated the house
from the lawn. I loosened some amber lichen with my
fingernail and it fluttered onto the bodice of my white
dress.

He put his hands across my shoulders smoothing the
bodice. 'I like it.'

'I was worried we wouldn't finish it.' I pinched the
ruches of chiffon folded across my breasts. 'Lily was so
busy in the shop. Everyone wanted dresses for this party.
She spent hours and hours.'

'It was worth it.' His hands fell to my bare arms. 'You're
both very clever.' And he kissed the top of my head lightly
before drawing me close.

The sun slid lower in the sky, flushing warmth into the
grey water.

'I've been looking forward to this,' I whispered close to
his ear. 'I wanted everything to be perfect.'

'I hope it is.'

'But I feel sad now.' My eyes drifted across the water
and the gently stirring reeds.

'This beautiful evening?'

'The sun like that. I don't know why, I can't bear to look at it.'

'Don't say that. It's a part of this perfect evening and you'll want to remember it.' I felt his arms more firmly around my shoulders.

I found it difficult to explain the strange sensations that had haunted me since our unruly discussion in the garden about the war. 'Is it the end or the beginning of something? How will I know so that I can save the memory? I'm afraid, Owen. Memories have never seemed so important before.'

'Let's pretend it's a beginning,' he suggested.

I rubbed the tears from the corner of my eyes and tried to smile. 'Of course you're right. We shouldn't feel sad.' I straightened up and spoke in a brighter voice. 'Tell me, what have you been doing today?'

He took my hand and led me down the slope of trimmed grass. It was dotted with whispering couples and a loud group laughing at a young man's attempts to juggle with a handful of oranges.

'I helped father this morning and played tennis with Alice this afternoon.'

'Is she good?' I was interested now and the sight of the other young people, amused and relaxed, restored my good faith in the evening.

'Better than her brother,' he laughed. 'I need some practice.'

'Edwin is very keen. He wants to teach Lily.'

'Good idea. Are they here yet?'

'They're inside. Lily is so self-conscious of occasions. She's probably hiding in a dim corner.'

'Poor Lily. She has a lot to live up to, with you as Edwin's sister.'

'What do you mean?' I pulled him up.

'You're too modest to see it but it's obvious the way she follows you around that she worships you.'

I dipped the toe of my slipper into the edge of the water and watched the ripples move away. 'What rubbish. Edwin is very fond of her. I treat her like a sister.'

'She's lucky to have you.'

I closed my eyes and swayed back. I was listening, holding onto the precious moment, my doubts about remembering forgotten. My hair was held close to my head with a number of tortoiseshell pins lent by Aunt Violet. I longed to pull them out and let my hair fall free but feared it would be considered bad manners so early in the evening.

'What are you thinking?' Even through my trembling eyelids I could sense Owen's fascination.

'My hair. How terribly severe and unimaginative it is under all these pins. I hate it.'

'It's lovely,' he smiled. 'You have the look of a woman tonight.' He ran his fingers under my chin and followed the line of my hair.

'Don't you like me as a girl any more?'

'I like you as you are, and tonight you're a woman.' It seemed from his look and the way his hands grew more protective around me that he had wanted to say those words for a while.

'If you say so.' I looked down and noticed the mud on his boots. 'Owen, where have you been? Look at your feet.'

He looked down. 'Oh that, that was Edwin. He insisted on dragging me through the rhododendrons to see the new barn.'

'He's quite stupidly proud of that, I can't think why. It has nothing to do with him, not directly. He simply ordered the materials.'

'He's happy, don't mock his modest triumphs.'

I swung at him with a hurt frown. 'I'm not mocking. Please don't think that. I feel disappointed for him sometimes, that he couldn't do what he wanted.'

'He's enjoying his work with Carter's?'

'Yes, he is and Lily is so proud of him. I suppose working in an office appears very grand to Lily.'

'Is that her?' Owen nodded towards the terrace, where a slim figure in a blue dress was searching the grass for a familiar face.

'No,' I giggled, 'that's our birthday girl. Really, Owen!'

'Patience?' he screwed up his eyes to see through the dusk. 'So it is. She seems to have mislaid Arthur.'

'He's deliberately escaped. Large doses of Patience are too tiring.'

'I've always found her pleasant enough.' He sat down on the grass and drew me towards him.

'You're too charitable. She's a daddy's girl.'

'Councillor Morris is no softie.'

'She charms him. He accepts all her suggestions and dips into his bottomless pockets.'

'Hence this celebration?'

I nodded. 'She made it appear his idea but she planted the seed. Look at this – lights, music, all the food and drink we can manage – what more could a daughter ask for?'

'A bit grander than your humble do, remember?'

'Oh, don't remind me.' I cringed. 'What a horror I was. Poor Alice and poor you.'

'And you haven't changed one jot. I've still got my work cut out to keep you in hand.' He pinched the end of my nose and when I protested he put his fingers to my lips. I was seeing a new Owen tonight. There was something excited and impetuous about his manner and I wanted to show him that I knew.

'You know what you said to me a few minutes ago, about my being a woman? Well, I want to say the same to you, you seem more like a man tonight.' It was odd how I could not chart the progress of our relationship from friendship

74

to attachment. We had known each other for so long that the responses happened gradually and imperceptibly and it wasn't until we reached a turning point, a balance between our physical and emotional feelings, that we paused to grasp their true impact. In this way love had not come upon me suddenly, like the blinding realisation that I read about in those sensational novelettes, but with a subtlety and hesitancy that made it poignant.

I lay back. The coolness of the grass on my neck sent a delicious shiver down my spine. The figures on the terrace appeared comical upside down, with coloured lanterns waving under their bobbing heads. They added to my general feeling of dreamy happiness.

'What are you smiling at?' Owen lay down beside me and ran the back of his hand along my bare arm. 'You're not sad any more?'

I was trembling with suspended emotion. I didn't want this moment to end.

'No, I'm not sad. I'm blissfully happy.' I rolled so my face was close to his neck and whispered into it. 'There's so much to look forward to. Think, a whole two months together, with nothing to do but enjoy ourselves.'

'It'll pass soon enough.' There was a disturbing edge of unease in his reply.

'Owen?' I leaned up on my arms and searched his face for a hint of his change of mood.

'I'm sorry. I wish you hadn't mentioned time, that's all.'

I clutched at a head of clover near my feet and twirled the flower between my fingers. 'It's this war, isn't it?'

He put his head on my shoulder. 'I've tried to forget but it won't go away.'

'Edwin talks of nothing else.' I tossed the flower over my shoulder and rubbed the ends of my fingers where they were yellow with pollen.

'Lily told me. She's very upset.'

'Poor Lily.'

'Edwin should be kind to her.' He hesitated. 'There's something so pathetic about her delicacy. She needs protecting from all this.'

'Don't I need that too?'

He nuzzled my neck. 'I think you can take care of yourself. But Lily will need you.'

I made myself still and quiet, to take in his words and the sounds of the night; the gentle lap of the water, the muted voices of couples as they offered their secrets to the dark sky; the bright tinkle of laughter from beyond the lake and the strains of a popular song, squeezed through the brilliant yellow windows. I heard Owen chuckle beside me as he sat up, gripping his knees to his chest.

'That's not Arthur, is it, that singing?'

I tilted my head. 'I believe it is. He sang the same song on the church outing last Easter.'

'Not exactly religious, is it?'

'Reverend Green wasn't there. He cried off at the last moment; a visit from the bishop or something.'

'He has a good voice but I'm not sure about the sentiments of the song. I can't visualise Councillor Morris in the front row of the music hall.'

'Neither can I.' I kicked off my slippers. 'Come on, let's explore.' I tucked them under my arm and tripped across the grass. Owen called after me but I sniggered in the childlike way that irritated him and headed for the woodland at the far end of the garden.

A few yards under the arch of trees Owen paused to glance back at the house where the lanterns danced through a mosaic of leaves. They were part of a separate world, a world bright and trembling with chatter and the chink of glasses, remote from the quiet shadows where I had hidden from him.

He sensed my fumbling movements and crept towards me, close to the ground until he could see the edge of my dress flutter against the silvery bark of the tree.

'If you want to be inconspicuous you shouldn't wear white.' His hands were fastened over my eyes and I turned slowly so my face was only inches from his.

'Will you kiss me, Owen?' I whispered.

He held onto my face and kissed my cheek.

'No, kiss me properly. I've never been kissed by a man.' I waited for his mouth, my lips slightly apart, my eyes pressed tightly together. I felt him stroke my hair then he ran his cool lips down the skin of my face until he discovered my mouth in a long kiss where our lips hardly seemed to make contact. He had never kissed me like that before.

'Oh, Ruth.' He held my face close to his chest. 'Don't change, will you. Don't become like those belligerent suffragettes or a retiring dry intellectual. I want you to stay as you are now. You're so fresh and alive and I don't want to spoil that.'

'I must grow older, nothing can stop that.' I drew my face away from his warmth and licked the sweetness of his kiss from my mouth. 'Surely, if we change together it will be all right, we'll be safe?'

'I'm sorry, I shouldn't upset you. It's just...'

'What is it?' I leaned against the trunk of the tree and the curls of bark caught in my hair. He reached up and pulled out the hairpins one by one until my hair flopped across my shoulders and the bodice of my dress.

'When I look at my mother and the way she's grown tired and serious over the years, I can't imagine her youth and vigour any more. I expect it's being married to a doctor.'

'I won't mind being married to a doctor.' I traced the outline of his brow and nose, the fullness of his lips and the cleft of his chin. 'I'll never have to worry about being ill,' I laughed.

'A small consolation, I suppose.'

'I wonder what's for supper, I'm ravenous.'

He stared at my bright face, blinking back his disbelief. 'You're incredible, how you can change from one mood to another with almost a magical eagerness. You remind me of a dragonfly; one moment you're still and beautiful, the next, light and playful, flitting close to the surface of the water.' He ran after me across the grass, treading in the damp shadows where my bare feet had stepped.

'Who's that?' I pointed at the steps that led to a wooden jetty where a rowing boat was moored. A young man was sitting on the top step, his arms resting on his knees. He seemed lost in some desperate search for something unknown which had been swallowed by the dark water now that the sun had gone.

'That's Matthew Parker.'

'I've never seen him before.' I lowered my voice to whisper. 'He looks so sad.'

'Serious, that's all.'

'Should we try to cheer him up?' I moved towards the steps but he held me back.

'No, leave him. He's not sad, he enjoys being alone with his thoughts. We should respect that. Come on, I'll race you back to the house.'

5

Dreams

I had never walked so far from home. To leave the familiar streets behind; to turn at the top of the hill and look back at the jagged pattern of rooftops, the church tower and Adcock's Mill with its empty windows blinking at the cold sky and the neat rows of villas clinging to the side of the hillside like the broken parts of a child's train, was an adventure.

I was tempted to hide behind Owen's firm figure in his thick overcoat but as he stepped out with his enthusiasm for the open air and his warm hand clasping mine, I felt a thrill of freedom that prompted me to match his step.

As we squeezed between the trees it was like entering an immense and mystical building filled with hushed nervous figures leaning towards the light. The air changed; it became warmer and gentler with every muffled whisper that passed between us.

Owen unwound his muffler and looped it round my neck. I was so glad to see his face; the precise chin, the even-shaped nose, his mouth so generously set in a smile. I wished that I could believe that he was constantly happy as his face suggested. He reminded me of Lily, chattering and laughing like spring water while hidden inside were droplets of unease.

'You're like Lily.' I squeezed his hand.

'In what way?'

'You want me to feel that you're happy but underneath there's something else.'

'I'm sorry.' He rubbed my face with the back of his hand. 'It's not very easy to keep up the pretence of confidence hour after hour. Mother is so demanding.'

'You don't have to, not with me.' I caught his hand and traced the edges of his nails with my thumb.

'I'm fine as long as I have you in my head, your face, your smile, your voice. If I lose them I panic. The most ridiculous thoughts try to squeeze you out and I have to fight.'

'Poor Owen.' I smoothed the skin under his eyes and the roughness along his chin. 'You mustn't despair when I'm not there, I think of you all the time.'

The pines on either side seemed to be growing more powerful; their tops were out of sight in the dust-scented shadows above. He led me on and our feet were soundless on the soft spring of needles.

'A week.' His words were suddenly desperate and I felt sorry for having made him lose his smile. It was my fault that he was unhappy.

'I will write to you every day.'

'You will?'

'Of course. What else do I have to do?'

'Aren't you going back to the school?'

'Maybe. It'll pass the time but my heart isn't in it.' I was bored with the clamour of eager impudent children. I needed the soft security of my own secret thoughts and all my emotional energy to control my fears for Owen's safety.

'I forget how young you are.' He picked up a cone. The end was nibbled to a smooth point. 'Perhaps I don't want to. You have a certain power over me, you know.' He tossed the cone high into the branches and it landed yards away and a pair of wood pigeons clattered out of the tree tops and disappeared into the grey light at the wood's edge.

'What, little me?' I tried to pout but his startled expression made me laugh.

'What's funny?'

'You're doing your best to look miserable now I've told you about pretending happiness.'

'But I am miserable, desperately miserable. I don't want to contemplate life without you. For almost as long as I can remember you've been a part of it, a precious and irreplaceable part. It won't work without you.'

'We can still be together in our thoughts. Imagination is a powerful thing. We'll have letters and you will have leave, won't you?'

He did not answer. I tried to remember a time when I was not thinking about this man beside me, when my actions and thoughts were not driven by his needs and expectations, his impulses and his spirit. The unsettled months away at college seemed like a gift which we would gladly grasp now instead of this unknown that was almost upon us.

I embraced a nearby tree, running my hands over the stippled bark and breathing in the pungency of its essence. When I turned, his figure appeared suddenly hunched and pathetic inside his overcoat. He had lost that confidence that he'd set out with and seemed a dark shadow against the backdrop of the gentle tree. I held out my arms for him and he moved to me unsteadily.

'We'll have to make the best of it, won't we?'

'Everyone else will,' I agreed.

'But we're not everyone else,' he protested.

'That's part of being in love, we think that we're special, as if we're the only ones to have felt this way.'

'It's very selfish, isn't it?' He was frowning. 'Perhaps that's why mother looked so weary and forlorn when I mentioned that I was coming up here with you.'

'She feels excluded, it's not me personally?'

'Of course not.'

'We must try for these last few days to share you even though I want you for myself.' I held onto him, trying to shut out the image of his leaving on the train. I had not forgotten those dreadful occasions when he'd not wanted to go back to college and we'd sat in glum silence over cups of weak tea on the station until he had to run for the train as it was leaving. How lucky we had been. He was only going a hundred miles away and he would be safe with his books and his thoughts of home. This time where he was going was a terrifying mystery.

'Thank you for going to see her the other day.'

'She's afraid, Owen.'

'Did she tell you?'

'She didn't have to. The thought of her son with all those faceless figures plodding through France towards the unknown is agony for her. And Alice's enthusiasm for any activity associated with the war doesn't help. There was something interesting though.'

'Yes?'

'She thought the one consolation, if there is one, might be the opportunity of escape for you from your medical career. It's a diversion that will allow you to examine what you want. She knows how important creative things are to you and she hates the idea of your father's ambitions tainting your imagination.'

'I never knew she felt so strongly about it.'

'She thinks you're sensible enough to use your experience wisely, and develop more maturity through your contact with others.'

'Why didn't she tell me all this? She's not afraid of father, surely?'

'I don't know.'

'He does find it difficult to show his feelings. It's part

of his generation, which looked on susceptibility to pressure, especially from women, as a sign of weakness.'

'But he must have shown his feelings once. How did she fall in love with him?'

'He didn't have to be very forthright. Mother, with three older sisters all seeking eligible husbands, was delighted with such a charming and self-confident man. She felt so lucky that she accepted him without question.'

'She still loves him very much, I can tell.'

'Yes.'

'As she loves you. It's unfortunate about Alice. She came in while I was there and your mother was upset because she didn't have time to talk. She announced while I was there that she had an interview at the hospital for a nursing position. Your father had arranged it without telling your mother. She was most upset.'

Owen gave a sigh and heaved me up the final part of the slope. We paused to look back at the path twisting into the trees the way we had come.

'I don't think I was much help to her.'

'Nonsense. She would appreciate your sparing the time when you have things on your own mind. She's very fond of you. I've done nothing but talk about you. She understands how I love you.'

'Oh Owen, don't. I can't bear it, I'll make a fool of myself again.'

'Again?'

'I'm afraid I shed a few tears in front of her. I think it was being there, in your home. It was so easy to sit in your chair and touch your books. She was quite moved by it.'

'She considers you almost part of the family,' he said gently and kissed me. 'You are, aren't you?'

'What a question.' I buried my face in his overcoat and the gentle odour of it filled my head with its evocations of the past months; his father's pipe tobacco, his mother's heavy perfume; the fresh scent of his own soap. I could not remember a time without him and during the last two years our friendship had flourished and become my focus for living.

'We'll be strong together,' I said, turning up the collar of his overcoat.

'You're so sure, aren't you? In a way, you're more grown up than I am.'

'That's what I tell Edwin but he doesn't listen to me. He's too wrapped up in Lily to see anything serious in anyone else.'

'Lily's good for him.'

'Perhaps. She may have made him more human. His moods are softer, he's more gentle to mother and Becca.'

Owen knew what I meant. He nodded. 'Lily's power is as insidious as yours.'

'But it's a shame. I doubt that it can last. She's so different. Simple and hardworking, kind and attractive ... but she's a shop girl. Edwin is ... well, Edwin is Edwin, isn't he? His nose in a book, his mind on politics and what's going on around the world. She can't keep up with him, can she?'

'Sometimes differences can draw people together.'

I considered Violet and Edmund. They were different, their quirky behaviour complemented each other in a nagging and cosy way and they were happy. I could not imagine Violet with anyone else and Edmund would be lost without his battery of instructions each day.

'We're not too similar, are we?'

He drew me close. 'No, you're alert and bright, you chatter too much and ask idiotic questions and expect sensible and prompt answers. I am so boring I simply listen and wish I was more like you.' He gave me a wink.

'That's good.' I skipped away from him to the edge of the trees.

The woodland had a ragged appearance as though the edges of the fine building were crumbling away. Suddenly the ground came to nothing and Owen grasped my arms to stop me stepping over.

'This way, I have something to show you.'

I scrambled after him down a narrow rabbit track that only he had seen. I had to pick up my skirts to avoid the brambles and was soon out of breath with my efforts to keep up. 'What is it?'

At the base of the slope was a clearing.

'It's a secret, no one else knows.'

There in the hollow was a cottage. It was built of warm grey stone and the thick pink tiles on the roof were cracked and the chimney leaned at a crazy angle. I ran across the grass and pressed my face to the dirty glass. 'Who lived here?' I felt myself glow with childish excitement.

'It's been empty for a long time.'

'Can we go in?' I paused in the doorway, holding my breath until Owen was behind me. 'Ugh, it smells.' I wrinkled up my nose and gave a shiver.

'I think it's quite cosy, perfect for two lovebirds.' He folded his arms round my shoulders and pressed his face into my hair.

The stone walls were bare and the uneven floor was littered with leaves. Under the window was a battered armchair, spilling horsehair onto the floor. A kettle, thick with dust and cobwebs, sat on the hob but there were no cups or plates. In one corner was a low truckle bed with a straw mattress.

'Look, Owen, a garden.' I breathed on the grubby glass at the back window.

He leaned over me and peered out. Clumps of brown weeds had obliterated the tiny lawn and the twisted limbs of an old apple tree reached towards the house. The lowest branches brushed the overgrown tangle of grass like withered searching fingers.

When I looked back the room seemed darker and less friendly. 'There's something odd about this place.'

'What do you mean?' Owen blew dust from the kettle and lifted the lid as though he expected to find water.

'It's almost as if whoever was here has only just gone...' I plucked a cobweb from his hair and he trod ash into the floor.

'You're too sensitive to atmosphere.'

'It's created by people, they can't help leaving part of themselves behind.'

He gave me a gentle exasperated look and held out his arms. 'You're so special, my darling. There's almost a magic there inside you. It's been there since you were a little girl, but you've cherished and refined it over the years.'

His closeness almost filled me with despair; his skin glowing after the walk in the cool air, the firmness of his hold on me; his hair untidy around his face reminded me of a child who was looking for someone to care for him. 'It's your imagination, you love creating things with words, there is no magic, it's me.' I was trying to keep the heaviness from my voice but it was hopeless. I remembered he had said we would alter when we were apart and that worried me. 'Owen, what are you thinking about?'

'I was thinking of you as an unruly child, screaming at me across the park, waving down the church or pulling my hair when I refused to take you somewhere. And how pretty you've become and how attractive you will grow. Other men will want to be near you and to touch you and I can't bear it.'

'Owen, my love.'

'And – how much I will miss you.'

The silence between us was a sedative as we held each

86

other. It was enough to be close and listening to each other's thoughts even though we knew exactly what they were.

'We won't tell anyone about this place,' I whispered, 'let it be our secret, the little piece of magic which you think exists between us.'

'Yes. And will you do something for me?' He tried to cling onto me but I leaned away from him the better to see his expression.

'If I can.'

'Watch Alice for me. She's throwing herself into this nursing thing and I'm not sure she's up to it.'

I shrugged like a child who had been cajoled into doing something unpleasant. 'Of course.'

'You don't mind?'

'Why should I mind? She's your sister.'

Owen looked relieved. Perhaps the knowing was a reassurance of my constancy. I was close to part of his blood when he couldn't bear the thought of me close to another man. 'Good. It will be a relief to mother.'

'But will Alice mind? I think she considers me tedious, especially as I talk about you all the time.'

'She's the one who thinks herself dull.'

'Well,' I began, moving towards the trees, 'I can tolerate dull people – I'm attracted to you, after all!' I pushed out my tongue and started to run. By the time I reached the edge of the slope I was laughing. I felt gloriously free in the open air like a child. I was nowhere near the sophisticated young woman everyone assumed me to be.

6

Confusion

I closed my eyes and tried to keep the image of Owen's face clear in my head. The last weeks had passed so swiftly and I regretted how little time we had spent talking about us. We seemed to have solved all the difficulties of our respective families but we were left with the dreadful chasm of our separation. As the day of his departure grew nearer I was afraid of the familiar. How could we be the same when such tormented shadows brushed over us?

There was a creak as someone passed on the stairs but I kept my eyes closed, hoping they would think I was asleep. The door opened and a drift of mother's sweet perfume came into the room. I could visualise her wine-coloured dress, her hair pulled back from her thin face and her eyes, staring, almost distracted, as they had been since the announcement of the war.

It was impossible to remain silent with that picture in my mind. I rolled over and squinted up at the figure hovering in the doorway. 'What is it, mother?'

'I wondered if you were all right.' She rubbed her hands down her dress and the fabric rustled.

I leaned up on my arms. 'I was sleepy after lunch. Where's father?'

She crept into the room. She was uneasy about stepping into this place that was so special to her daughter and I felt sad for this woman who needed something that was her own and not part of her family. 'He's gone for a walk.'

I patted the bed beside me and she sat down and stared at her leather slippers. 'Why didn't you go with him?'

'He wanted to go alone. I think I disturb his thoughts.' Her voice was shaking.

I leaned close to console her. 'What nonsense. You're a comfort to him.'

'Not now. I'm rather a nuisance with my silly moods.'

'We all have moods. It's part of being an interesting person.' I tried to hold her hand but it was limp. I could tell she wanted to agree with my good sense but her mouth twitched rather than break into a smile.

'You always know the kindest things to say.'

'Do I?' I found that amusing when Owen often accused me amiably of not knowing when to hold my tongue.

'In a strange way you seem to have acquired more sense in your short life than I have.'

'Oh mother, what's started this off? Is it the war?'

She shrugged and one shoulder of her dress slipped off. She had become so thin lately, her clothes were beginning to hang on her. 'I suppose it must be.'

'It would help all of us to discuss it, especially Edwin.'

Her pale face stiffened and a terrified look flashed through her eyes as she fumbled for my hand. 'I don't need to talk about what might come. If the worst happens I don't have to be thinking about it for weeks before, do I?'

'No, but there are things that need to be said, to your son ... to me.'

She looked up, startled, perhaps realising for the first time my involvement in this imminent tragedy.

'I've never found it simple to talk about things, you know that. I prefer to do what's needed, quietly and without fuss. I can't be like Violet, chattering on about every little episode as though it had major significance.'

'It doesn't have to be chatter,' I defended. 'And a great deal of what your sister says holds truth.'

'I know. I'm not being unkind, it's just so purposeless.'

'You never see her withdrawn or in a sulk, so perhaps there's some medicine in her way of dealing with things.'

She was making neat folds of the skirt of her dress as a distraction from my suggestions. 'You must have talked a lot with Owen.' Her voice was reproachful. She sensed the end of her gentle hold over me as a daughter.

'So much, I can't remember. He's a good listener.'

'Your father isn't. He prefers to speak his mind and organise the conversation. He can't help it, it's the schoolmaster in him.'

'You're wrong. He listens to me.'

'You have valuable things to say.'

I ignored the implied plea for reassurance and tried to make light of it. 'Owen wouldn't agree with you. He considers a great deal of what I say to be rubbish. This war has stirred up too many wild and unexpected emotions. It's easy to lose control. I don't always think before I open my mouth, you must know that.' Remembered mischief made my voice dance and she was finding it hard to take my remarks seriously. She was uncertain how to continue on the subject that she had for so long avoided.

'I ... I suppose you're upset by all this?'

'Of course. I dread Owen going more than anything I can imagine. But I won't let him go without telling him all that's in my heart.'

'I wonder if we were so fortunate, not having to suffer all this uncertainty. Your love will be much richer, so much more precious, won't it? Ours was too easy.' These were strange, unexpected sentiments from my mother.

'Perhaps love should be worked for, real love shouldn't come smoothly or it's not worth having.' This brought a flicker of a smile to her face. 'Have I said something amusing?'

'I can't believe that we're talking like this. It's never happened before. I suppose I have Owen to thank for it?'

I was in front of the window but I hesitated to look out on the garden, which was so lifeless and insipid. But I was also afraid to look at the woman behind me. Owen had told me to talk, to make things smoother between us, but now that it had happened, I was wary of where it might end.

'Violet is very fond of him.' Her voice was suddenly firmer as though she'd made a decision to be positive. 'She said I should encourage you, but you know how I like to be free of my sister's influence.'

'You don't agree with her then?' I sat down before my dressing table, took up my brush and began to move it through my hair.

'Maybe you'll understand when you have children of your own. No one seems truly good enough, they have to prove their worth.'

'And Owen hasn't done that yet?'

'I don't know.'

I saw her expression change in the mirror. Her features seemed softer and the disconcerted look was lifted from her eyes, but I couldn't let her see things so plainly in her way. My relationship with Owen was not to be dictated by her feeble unconventional wishes. 'Perhaps this war will give him the chance.'

She jerked at the sharpness of my response and made fists of her hands on the bed. 'I'm sorry. It's unthinkable that I should expect such signals from someone I hardly know.'

'That's the difficulty, isn't it? You don't know him, not as I know him.'

'Has he told you why he's going?'

91

'We've talked of it – endlessly – but it seems to be a mystery. It's intangible. Nothing as simple as duty or heroism – what can they mean to a man who has no experience of conflict or disharmony and has no genuine responsibilities to protect?'

'He has you.'

'Is that enough for a young man to risk his life? It would be gratifying to believe it but it's rather a romantic notion, not of this century, is it? It's all very noble sacrificing one's life for love but if it's avoidable, I consider it rather a thoughtless thing to do.'

'Ruth, don't. I can't bear to think about all the dying.'

'We had to imagine the possibility, to prepare ourselves. It's still an unthinkable wickedness but once you've whispered its name, the horror can be pushed away, smothered in the rest of living. It's a charm. If we deny it, it's more likely to happen. Senseless things you have in your head when you've first tasted love.' I threw down the brush and swung round but she was staring at the bed-cover rubbing her fist over and over the pattern of pink flowers. Trying to obliterate their beauty. 'Mother, stop it.'

'Yes dear?'

I wondered if she had understood my words or had she refused to listen to them. 'You do believe that I love Owen, don't you? It's not some childish infatuation.'

'Of course.' Her voice was so hushed I could hardly hear. She unfolded her hands and looked at them flat on her knee.

'Are you pleased? We will marry when he comes back. We have to hold onto that thought or it will all be unbearable.'

'Yes dear.' Her head was on one side as though she were searching for something fresh in me. Perhaps for the first time she was seeing me as a woman. 'It's not easy to remember what it was like being young and in love.'

'Oh, mother, it's not so long ago.'

'I feel old all of a sudden.' She trembled and held her face as if she were about to cry then shook her head free and rose. 'I shouldn't talk like this, not now. We have enough depression to deal with.'

I reached out for her but her body would not relax in my arms. 'I don't mind. Please talk to me whenever you like. We should be friends now, two women together, isn't that right?'

Her pale face was near and the lines around her mouth and eyes were so distinct. 'Thank you, I'll try. We'll need each other, won't we?'

I nodded. I could not believe that she wanted to hold onto her wish for contact. We had shared so many false starts before and Owen represented the first serious challenge to her role as a mother.

Outside, I set myself some mindless task to keep my thoughts tidy. I loathed the feel of the wet leaves under my fingers but pushed myself to clear them from under the apple tree. It would be a help to father, who only set foot in the garden these days if the sun was shining. This unexpected turn of events had affected his life more than mother or I could imagine and he needed support as much as she. As I raked and scooped I began to feel calmer inside.

It had been a disappointment that Violet was so much more eager to discuss things than mother. And we frequently made mother the focus of such discussions. Violet spilled out such intriguing snippets about her sister. On one occasion I had been interested in some jet beads that sprinkled the bodice of her dress, almost to the waist, like droplets of black water.

'They are rather fine, aren't they?' Violet had slid her

fingers down the black crystals and her eyes had shone with a mischievous twinkle. 'They were mother's. Fay always wanted them.' She gave a wink. 'But I got them first.'

I leaned the rake up against the shed and crouched on the pile of logs ready for the winter fires. All those cold days ahead; dark spiritless months during which I would have to support this disappointed woman. I believed what Violet told me. She loved her sister and she loved me and she would not tell an untruth to either of us. But I wondered why mother was so weary and defeated now. We had Christmas to be lived through and that would be a serious challenge.

Last Christmas we had been so content; no one suspecting what unhappiness the new year would bring. When I was putting away the decorations Violet had exclaimed at a china angel I was wrapping in muslin. 'Good heavens, where did you find that?'

I told her it had always been in the basket and supposed it was mother's. Violet took it onto her lap, the folds of her dark skirt spread to receive it. She stroked the cracked wings and the halo where the gilt had flaked away. Their father had bought it for them for a halfpenny at the Christmas Eve market. It was the last one on the stall and mother had clutched it all the way home. No one was allowed to put it on the tree but mother. The pain of those memories was clear on Violet's face as she spoke.

'She doesn't tell you things, does she?'

I had to agree with her and my distress at such unconscious thoughtlessness could not be hidden from one as sensitive as my aunt. She had tried to cheer me with reminders of my mischievous childhood and how fortunate Owen was to have such a lively young woman for a friend. But there was no escape from the oppression of that afternoon. Those regrets so close to home, and the even closer moments with Owen, of which only whispers remained.

I felt the cool tears on my face as I bent to the last heap of leaves. A year ago and Violet had recognised the measure of our love, but only when Owen was being taken away from me did my own mother acknowledge it. I would encourage her to visit Mrs Webb; they were both anxious and had lonely hours to fill. They might give each other strength and relieve the nervous burden on their poor husbands.

'What are you doing out here?' Father stood on the edge of the grass, turning his hat in his hands.

'I was making myself useful.' I moved towards him and fell into his open arms. At the touch of his warm jacket, with its smell of chalk dust and musty books and grubby children, I let go. My tears came in great gulping sobs and father could say nothing to comfort me.

I celebrate the silent kiss that ends short life or long

W.B. Yeats (*A Man Young and Old*)

October 13th 1915

Dearest,

I walked into the village for the last time this morning. We're making preparations to leave tomorrow, to move further inland I think. Looking at those houses we'll never see again, I felt empty. As I strolled through the grey streets a small boy began trotting at my heel. Only about five but he pushed out his chest with such confidence, it might have been amusing had it happened in a happier place. His grubby face was bright with a huge smile but I was too moved to look into his blue eyes for long. Suddenly, he slid beside me and grasped my hand. His English was non-existent but with my moth-eaten French I discovered that he wanted me to go with him.

We scrambled through the empty streets but he was unaware of the miserable state of the abandoned buildings. It was odd, such a young child, alone – then most things about this situation are odd. We didn't talk but it didn't matter. He had a purpose and he wanted me to share a secret. I understood later how wonderful that must have been for him. Not many people here can have secrets, the hiding places – whether in your head or your few belongings – are not very secure.

We arrived at a tiny church and he pulled me towards the graves at the back. There, in the lee of the ancient wall and sheltered from the weather by a tumbled cross, he revealed his secret: a handful of

96

fluffy yellow ducklings. He was so proud and fondled their soft bodies with such tenderness, it brought me to tears. There was no sign of a mother and he didn't explain why they were in such an unlikely place.

His simple trust moved me. It was a peculiar honour, being allowed to share his sweet secret, and I felt it a suitably hopeful end to my stay in that place. I'll hold onto that careless smile for a long time. It was poignant because it wasn't a part of this dreadful war. It might have been a moment from anywhere or any time.

Before I left he insisted on taking me into the church. A little uneasily I followed – you know me and churches – and he was less sure of himself in there. His confidence seemed muted as he became part of that cool undefined interior. You'll be amused to hear what happened. That tiny church touched me. It possessed a tranquillity; it was set apart from what was going on outside and the tragedy all around could not touch it. I had a glimpse of truth, a hint of what holiness might be in that artless place. There was no demonstrative insistence, no overt challenge to my confused state of mind, so I could feel comfortable. It breathed in the centuries-old values of that forgotten village.

The boy crept on his toes, respectfully aware of the blessedness there. He knelt before a statue of the Virgin and lit a candle. Suddenly, I could see you in a similar attitude of patient supplicant, searching for answers to what you could not understand.

He lit two candles – one for his brother killed at Mons during the first devastating months of the war and the other for his sister, whom he hadn't seen since August. I left him there, alone with his prayers, his grubby fingers joined in front of his face, and I realised that I would have to start all over again. All my questions were obsolete in the face of such faith. I recalled what some insufferable Christian types used to spout at school about looking no further than yourself for solutions, and not to expect God to provide all the answers.

I'm relieved that I have you to listen to this. If I couldn't pour out my crazy thoughts I would go mad. You should read the letters I compose to my mother. I find plenty of practice in story telling! They have to be newsy and cheerful and full of answers to her snippets of trivial advice about keeping warm and eating sensibly. Little does she know how we live. I suspect sometimes she has a vision of me resting in some ancient chateau, surrounded by beautiful serving maids and giving orders to smart young men in spotless uniforms and shiny leather boots. She doesn't need to know the truth. This is a time for innocent lies.

I've warned Alice to restrain herself but I fear it will be near impossible. She is such a young lady of conviction all of a sudden, so determined and self-possessed. I hope she can keep her heart and her head separate. You've been so good for her. You've helped her to see more sharply and made her aware that she has choices and that she isn't merely a shadow of her mother. I hope I don't embarrass you with all this plain speaking, but it is the only way – to be wrapped up in others. It dampens all thoughts of one's own dreams and superficial needs which can only be destructive.

How is Lily? Often I think of her, so fresh and spirited, with her easy smile, and her teasing laughter as she nudged Edwin out of a mystical mood. Tell him to cling onto her – he'll need a creature of light like Lily when he's smothered in this godforsaken place. Our kit is packed and we're waiting for inspection before we move off. The day that started out so dull is now splendid. The air has a fine crisp quality, a sting of something mysterious and enticing that makes me excited about going on our way. It matches the exhilaration I felt before I set out to meet you, my darling. The sun is so high, the cool sky seems transparent, like fragile glass, at risk of being shattered by the slightest murmur of breath – the kiss of a butterfly, you called it. There could be snow. Let's pray it holds off for a few hours or our journey will turn into a miserable trek.

I've been separated from Alan. I'm to move to an RAMC group and the poor lad feels a bit forgotten. It's only weeks, our friendship, but there's something singular about relationships out here. So crammed together, we grow to know every wrinkle and weakness. It's almost as if we had never had any other life. Did we know any other place or other individual before this? I told him about you last night – you don't mind? It seemed a small kindness to share my happiness and good luck with him before I go off to start all over again. He has a strange old-fashioned respect for women, almost a deferential wariness. He was sheltered up there in the hills with only his dog for company. The local ladies hereabouts are a wee bit too much for him and he was relieved to return to his cards and his sketchbook after his one and only jaunt with Josh.

Did I tell you he was an artist? He has a rare gift. He can capture the mood of anyone. I had never realised how many different faces there were. Initially, they're all similar, under the same hats, inside identical khaki; pinched, worn expressions with a questioning weariness about the eyes. There's only a subtle fear, it's more an affronted confusion; 'the bewilderment of battle' Alan calls it. Rather dramatic but a perfect description. He sketched a group of faces: the Captain, the Quartermaster Sergeant, Josh and myself. You'd have loved his attempt at the Padre. He gave him a blatantly smug insincerity that captured every nuance of his character.

When I look back on the hours of preparation, it's been an odd mix of emotions, sights and sounds. On all sides there was an uneasy tension and bustle. One does not want to feel excitement but somehow one is drawn along with it. The roads are now all mud. The slow-moving troops make one continuous procession, their faces bleak and anonymous, like masks that someone has forgotten to paint with a smile. Their drooping bodies are weighed down with equipment. You'd hardly believe what we have to carry – ammunition, tools, emergency rations, wire cutters, blankets – although the last two are in very short supply, so may I put in my Christmas order now for a new pair of wire cutters? You won't be surprised to hear that it's not very easy to give an appearance of energy and determination under all that.

In all of us there is unease, not exactly fear, because tomorrow and the next bit of hillside or the next bridge are an unknown, but it's a persistent nausea that we cannot shake off. We know nothing of what we go to but for rumour and the shadows of the returning troops that we pass; drifts of shuffling bodies, their faces blank as skulls, smudged with the grime of despair. After seeing such figures I think I'm beginning to understand the meaning of battle fatigue. They were living ghosts.

Our first stop, so I have a chance to add a little more to this letter. We've moved into a different country. The pastoral of farms and quiet villages has given way to a harsh unkindness of coal fields, more dramatic and more suited to the painful groups who cross it that I mentioned earlier. As we entered, a party of New Army volunteers joined us. Their energy and keen curiosity won't stay for long in this ... I'm afraid to call it a land of shadow but I fear that's what it has become. There seems little chance of sunlight here.

I never thought I would welcome sleep so. Exhaustion brings some small relief – the possibility of dimness, a smudged-out picture with only a suggestion of real people and real landscape. My greatest fear is not being able to shut out the murmurs of those ghostly figures, yet I have never heard them complain, so the sound of their fear is a mystery.

I am sorry for this. The day began with some promise but has gradually darkened to a hopeless muddle of impressions that I don't wish to interpret. I need some of your sparkling thoughts to weave into my dreams. I'll send you all my love as payment.

Owen

We've arrived. I'm trying to scribble this on my knee but there are too many distractions and a wretched sense of menace about this place. Apart from the muddle of men and machines there is an alarming tension, a suspicion that others before us have felt the imminence of death. Maybe it's always this way so close to the front line. We are three miles away and move up the line after dark. I have to admit, now it's begun, I'm strangely elated and will be glad to get stuck in. I suppose those don't sound like my sentiments but we're drawn into this chill of expectation, almost amoral hysteria, without knowing what goes on. I expect it's the relief of knowing that for the first time we can legitimately show our emotions.

The last part of our journey was unforgettable. Miles and miles of muddy road throbbing with tired figures, all holding their suffering tight in a tense, uncanny silence. There were no words. Perhaps because there were none yet formed to describe their experiences or perhaps they feared that what they had to tell would be too horrific. French and British mingled together, indistinguishable in their stained uniforms, many with their heads concealed in bloody bandages. The sight of such suffering has knocked the zip out of our lot.

We halted at some desperate place, dark and chilly with echoes of suffering and despair. One hears of such places, redolent with fear and death, but never imagines the reality of their existence. There was nothing but crumbling buildings, burnt out and deserted, with a church clock stopped at a quarter to one – the beginning of the end. You used to chatter on about the power of such places and how their store of unpleasant memories could lower the brightest spirits, like an insidious ether that is inhaled unconsciously. That old workhouse at the top end of the town was one such place. I remember how distressed you were when we sheltered there from the rain and it started to grow dark. You could not explain to me then but now I understand.

Captain Drummond seemed to know of the place's tragic history. At the start of the war the patients from the lunatic asylum were trapped between two burning buildings and clawed their way out to run wild over the countryside outside the town. I felt the diabolic power of that place cloying at my skin like the heaviness before a storm, as though the demented spirits of those unfortunates wandered the ruins in an endless search for rest.

The trench line ran across some marshy land which couldn't support a complicated system, so it had been built higher with no communication trenches between. Very gruesome. Each unit was isolated in its own tiny command post, without the vitality that a full line of trenches must possess to sustain it. We were laid up there for a few hours and the spectacle of listless figures moving about their occult purpose among all those tumbled buildings was appalling. I thought of Alan and wondered how he'd settled after I left. How tragic that young men like him should have to be a part of this outrage. What right had any authority to submit youth to such unimagined torment when they knew so little of life?

You'll see from this how my mood is faring – it's not well. My poor character is becoming argumentative and obstructive and I don't much care for it. I've discarded my old unruffled ways for more confrontational ones. Everything is questioned and reordered into the context of MY life. I'm becoming more self-obsessed by the day but I dare say that's the nature of survival and sanity in this godforsaken land.

I managed a few minutes' rest in a run-down cottage on the edge of town. I drifted in and out of a hazy sleep, and the flaking walls and the dust, the sad shadows of earlier inhabitants leaving too rapidly, reminded me of our quiet place. We made a promise to go back, didn't we, to see the snowdrops and the daffodils in spring? There were no flowers outside this place, only the remains of an old cart that some-one had set on fire. It leaned against the wall like some charred skeleton, a gigantic insect that had crawled away into the shadows to die – another vic-tim of this joyless place. I tried to sleep but a group of sappers laughed and joked outside the window. It was a sad shock to find myself there and not in our secret place, with you close by, warm and fresh and smelling of violets.

All this crazed sentimentality may be quite in-appropriate but it holds me together and makes you seem nearer, my darling. Don't be unhappy with all the dreadful descriptions, my heart tells me that I will survive to see another summer in our valley. Nothing will take that from us.

I wasn't sorry to say goodbye to that soulless place. Physically we were revived by the break but spiritu-ally, we were drained. As consolation of sorts we had to suffer hymn singing on the rest of the journey. Not as unbearable as it sounds, they were cheerful ones, although the more irreverent insisted on substituting their own indelicate words. I suppose it was a mildly cynical tribute to their sentiment.

I don't know how the Padre felt, poor chap. He's fortunate to have a horse to carry him about. I expect in his ambling up and down the troop, the uncouth humour of the lyrics would be lost. When he returned to our section his features were flabby with smiles; he seemed quite innocent of the smirks and whispered blasphemies that followed him. One of these days I'll have a heart to heart with him about what is happening out here. He treats it like some Sunday school outing, with bland cheerfulness, as if he resents the German presence as an inconvenience, an upset to his divine order. They were no part of his plan when he came out here.

Naturally, if I misjudge the chap, I apologise, but from what I recall of the Reverend Green, the clergy cherish a bewildered sense of what being part of a community entails. They're wary of offering the hand of friendship for its own sake or answering a non-clerical question. Everything outside their experience has to be treated with suspicion or total denial. Perhaps you, my darling, with your finely-tuned insight into human thoughts and motives can give me a candid and objective opinion. There seems some doubt as to the non-religious aspect of their role. Sorry, I'm rambling again.

One more painful note. We crossed an area of unfriendly ground between two link roads, obviously the scene of some earlier skirmish. Someone had taken the time to bury what dead they could and had put up a hastily constructed cross of odd pieces of wood. On it were inscribed the names of the lost – Christian and nicknames only – and someone had laid a posy of wild flowers on the rough ground.

I hope you understand why I tell you these distressing things. I fear to keep things from you; the greyness of concealment would take you further from my memory. I seem to have increasing difficulty imagining you doing simple activities. There is little reality beyond this place. It has devoured my consciousness of anything light and frivolous and beautiful. I need you to describe what you're wearing next time you write and tell me how you amuse yourself. The hope of normal life elsewhere, in spite of all this greyness and misery, makes the pain more bearable and will keep me going.

I'm sharing a billet with two other NCOs. It's not too cramped but we expect more to join us any day. One of them, Maurice, is down from university like me, where he's reading classics. A subdued mellow chap, he's judiciously sentimental in his attitude to the war. After we had heard an argument between two sergeants next door he grew quite philosophical about the mess we humans have got ourselves into. I can't imagine him working up enough steam to go over the top and actually kill someone but we shall see.

The other, Sandy, is a lively Geordie. An amiable red-head who has his personal view on the enemy, which has nothing to do with Maurice's cautious one. He'll have no trouble when the whistle blows! He insists on trying to distract Maurice when he's contemplating but so far he's failed. When he gets too loud and offensive Maurice wanders off with a book in his pocket and squats somewhere under a tree. Sandy has nicknamed him 'weird bugger', but there is a peculiar affection between the two.

We began preparing our kit for stand-to this evening when a strange thing happened – the church bells in the village began to ring out. Everyone drifted outside to listen and as it continued, their faces became relaxed and quiet as though the chimes were a consoling sedative against the ordeal that lies ahead. I thought of that little boy with his ducklings. I can still see his fingers against my palm as he led me into the church. Then your face gradually appeared, flushed and bright-eyed, as you raced up the slope through the trees in the park to beat the insistent chimes from across the valley. I remember your annoyance when they wouldn't stop and the sun melting in a glorious blush of orange behind the trees. It was spoiled by that tuneless din, you said ... there is a past out there which I crave to brighten this joyless existence.

But I am too sad. Forgive me. I must read some Lawrence so the whisper of his words in my head will carry me through the long night. Tomorrow I go up to the support line to receive the wounded for the dressing station. Pray for them, my love.

Owen

'Greenways'
Carleton
Lancashire

October 11th 1915

My Dear Owen,

It was such a relief to receive your letter. It's only a month since you left us but it seems much longer. After the first excitement of young men leaving the town there is a terrible lull until there is news from France. I am glad you are comfortable, though I won't believe all that you tell me. You know your mother too well to tell her the truth if it's painful, and I thank you for it. We have some small idea about conditions out there, and I can picture you cold and hungry when the winter arrives, but I will try not to let the thought of you make me sad.

It is good that you have made friends; I was concerned that you might try to shut yourself off like you did as a small boy. You need companions more than anything else to see you through this terrible time. And try not to let yourself get wrapped up in books. They will keep until all this is over.

There isn't much news. Alice has been several weeks at the hospital and works all hours. I never know when I will see her as she seems constantly to be working extra shifts. At the moment there are no servicemen there but they are very busy with general patients from other hospitals in the area. From the little she has said she is enjoying it, if one can enjoy such an experience – I certainly could not. Strange, isn't it, a doctor's wife and I can't bear illness or injury? Anyway, your sister is a credit to you. She

108

insists that she is doing it all for your sake, so I'm sure that you will remember her in your prayers.

I know you never had much time for religion and though I might not have had the courage to say so, I did understand. When you are young, life seems so important, ideas of sin and forgiveness and death are very low on your list of things to be dealt with. But, believe me, if you can spare a moment or two to think on deeper things, it will be a comfort to you, especially if you are surrounded by wounded or dying friends. Pray God that you won't be, but who knows?

I haven't seen Ruth this week but she is very kind to me, popping in when she can and bringing me little gifts of flowers and sweets. I think her own mother is very depressed since Edwin came over and she needs her daughter's support as much as possible. I forget sometimes how young she is, she shows such good sense and a healthy determination. I can hear you laughing at my generous expression when I was so sceptical of her influence on you and Alice when she was so daring. But it was obviously the correct way for her to behave and has done her no harm – or you or Alice. In fact, they have become very close and they draw strength from each other. But what am I saying? They won't need all that strength because you'll be coming home to them soon, won't you?

You may wonder why I haven't mentioned your father. It's not deliberate, I assure you, but he is here less than Alice at present. He is thinking of you and sends his love. It's probably not the time to say this but I know that he feels sorry for the distance between you. He believed he was doing his best for you, sending you into medicine, and I'm sure when you're older you will be able to thank him for it. Even if you never use all your knowledge, you will be a better person, won't you?

I am sorry for being so serious. I should be trying to cheer you up. I have been thinking about what I would write for so many days that now the time has come my mind is a silly blank. I dare say Alice and Ruth do cheer you in their letters, so you'll have to put up with my dull predictability. Alice is developing quite a sense of humour working in that place, but that will be no surprise to you.

That seems to be all that I have to say at the moment except to urge you to take care of yourself, keep warm and make sure you eat enough – you always picked at your food. Hannah has mentioned baking you a cake and Ruth will send it with some knitting that I have for you when I have finished.

I know you won't have much spare time and you will be very weary with all your duties, so don't worry about writing to me. As long as you write to Ruth she will let me know that you are all right.

Much love from us both,

Mother

Although I am writing this as part of my diary, it is meant for you, Ruth, and I hope that when all this is over and we are allowed to tell the truth of what is going on, you will read it and in some small way understand.

I was roused from the strangest dream to find Sandy's freckled face smiling down at me. I was lost, far away from here, in some fresh green country with clean kind air shivering with birdsong and whispers of trees reaching for the sun. I had nothing to do but sit under a tree and stroke the soft head that rested across my lap.

Then, to open my eyes to this ... I can only describe it as horror. There are no whispers in this air, only the crackle of shells and mystified screams. I will never smudge the agony of those unashamed cries from my head. It was not simply the agony of pain but the protest of souls, held in some place that they could not imagine. Sandy has offered me some of his whisky but the sweet smell of it makes my empty stomach heave.

I have to return to the dressing station before night-fall but I must put down these images in case I am not able later. The thought of going out into that bleakness of cold and shadows is more than I can bear. The land around is so desolate; a true reflection of the atmosphere of death that colours everything. The only features are the colliers' cottages and the entrails of the pit machinery like some gigantic metal monsters striding across the cold earth. This is a place of forgotten people.

I promised to tell everything but for the first time

111

I hesitate. There are certain things it is better to push to the darkest parts of the mind in the hope that they will shrivel and die and become nothing – not even memory. Certain things are not worthy of memory.

As we waited in the casualty clearing station all sorts of confused messages filtered back, the most disturbing that our shell dump had been bombed by German air fire in the night and that our stocks of shells were painfully depleted. We stood around, limp and speechless and sick inside, waiting for the colourless dawn that was too close and knowing that the gas should have been released hours before. The light when it came was damp and cruel with rain. None of us could speak what was in our minds, except for one brave chap, more knowledgeable than the rest. He suggested that we were a bunch of fools if the gas had been used in these miserable conditions where there was not a breath of moving air, as it would not disperse.

Shortly after dawn, a familiar confusion of sounds trembled across the dripping air; the crack of rifles, the stutter of machine guns, the dull thud-thud of shells exploding as they buried themselves in the sodden unresisting ground, and above all, the screams of the men.

As the first casualties began to trickle back we learned the awful truth of what our courageous friend had said. The yellow faces gasping for painful breaths and the tarnished buttons confirmed our fears. The gas had hovered over No-Man's-Land in an evil haze that drifted back to our front line to squat in a monstrous layer over our unsuspecting young men. Our flimsy cotton masks were no protection against this devilish weapon. The horror that everyone had dreaded had happened.

112

As I was forced to witness the agony of those choking men, I tried to imagine the individuals who could devise such evil. What creatures could inflict this on their fellows? What has happened to the world that such wickedness is allowed in the name of a just war?

The initial fear became nightmare as more casualties from the gas party were helped back. German shell fire had shattered our unused canisters, creating havoc in the main part of the trench. I don't know where we found the strength to deal with what we found. It can't have come from God; how could God be a witness to such unspeakable horror between men? We could only make them as comfortable as possible before the stretcher cases arrived. The courage of those poor men has left me numb and disgusted. I am ashamed to call myself Christian. I find no dignity in being human any more.

One lad in particular seemed to have more than his share of guts. He was part of the Reserve Battalion that went over in the second wave, a party of Royal Welch Fusiliers. He escaped the gas but sadly sustained a serious wound in his thigh. He looked hardly old enough to carry a razor let alone a rifle. When they brought him in he refused my help, insisting that others more seriously hurt deserved my attention. He'd been wounded trying to help an injured comrade so this was no surprise. I knew that he was in a worse state than he realised; hit in the thigh, he'd suffered a great blood loss and was showing signs of shock. We patched him up as best we could and when I had done all that I could for the others I went back to his side.

He was delirious, rambling in some dreamy world of his own to a loved one. It might have been you as he described her dark hair and sweet face close to him. He needed no comfort from me but held my hand in his clammy fingers. Not once did he complain about his pain or about what he had suffered. Maybe we possess some secret sedative deep inside that shields us from reality at such moments. I am sure the images from his past that misted his eyes were a comfort, a blanket on the face of the unimaginable.

He is safe now, gone to the main dressing station at Morlancourt and then to hospital to wait for a ship to carry him home. It is tragic, but in less than three months he will probably be back. God help him. God help all of us to manage this nightmare so we don't all descend into madness.

I have not heard from you, Ruth. No doubt a bundle of letters is held up in some miserable French railway station. Strangely, it is a relief, because I don't have to think what I might write and I don't have to struggle with the hurt of lying and keeping things from you.

VICAR OF ST OSWALD'S CHURCH, CARLETON, LANCASHIRE
FIRST SUNDAY IN ADVENT 1915

'Prepare ye the way of the Lord, and do penance...' Strange words, you might think, but those words of John the Baptist are fitting for this Advent time. They point to the preparations that should be in our hearts as we approach this special time of the birth of Jesus Christ. And in this period of unrest and distress when you and your families are surrounded by fears and misunderstandings about the conflict, they have a unique significance.

Truly, this is a time of darkness and desolation, of pain and confusion, a time during which we anticipate the approach of peace and stability and an end to all suffering.

Many people have asked me the question, why? Why does God allow His people to suffer in this dramatic way?

Surely, they protest, in allowing these tragedies to happen he is neglecting us; He is turning away from our cries for help in this dark hour of need. This cannot be the God of love, they say.

I have thought on these disturbing issues deeply and long and after much soul-searching I can tell you that I know why God has countenanced this fearsome conflict.

Some of you do not remember Christ. Some of you have never known Christ. Why should you presume to question His neglect of your pain and your suffering? If you had not filled your hearts with thoughts of material things and self-gratification; if you had not let sinfulness creep into your lives; if you had not turned your back on Christ, then perhaps Christ would still be a comfort to you.

My words need careful attention. They demand it.

Try to recall the last time that you denied yourself some pleasure for Christ's sake. When did you last say a prayer for the relief of another and not simply to satisfy your own selfish need? If the answer does not come swiftly and sharply, it is because you are guilty of the very sins for which Christ died to save us.

Faith has lost its place in our lives. But it is not too late. This conflict, if you are ready to answer the call, will give you a chance for redemption from all your past laziness and self-obsession; your loss of attention to Christ's wishes and your failure to put others before yourself. Through our representatives in this conflict, the generals, the young soldiers and their selfless sacrifice, they will be offering up one meaningful prayer to our Saviour. There is no doubt that he will listen to such a united voice.

I am frequently asked, why should we respond to this call, what has it to do with us?

It is simple. Consider the tragic events of the last months; the German atrocities in Belgium, their horrific use of gas at Ypres when so many of our gallant young men were maimed and murdered; the callous sinking of the *Lusitania*, when innocent civilians lost their precious lives.

Do you need to search further for reasons?

Germany is guilty of the most heinous crimes against humanity. She represents our gravest enemy, Satan. If we take up the challenge to destroy Germany we are indeed answering the Lord's command; to shun the devil and all his works.

But beware of thinking this is a struggle for our honour. It is not for the honour of England that we fight, but for the honour of God. This is the most serious challenge we have been offered. If we are bold enough to meet it with open hearts, we have a chance of lasting salvation. It is for everyone to fight for the wrong our enemies have committed against God. They have lost respect for His name. Where there is no respect there is no love. Sinfulness and despair and loneliness are the only results of this failure. So it is our task, our duty, to restore the sacred power of that name.

Germany, that most wicked state, ruled by despots, represents the Antichrist, the evil one foretold in the Book of Revelation. There is no limit to the crimes she will commit in the name of this devil.

This, therefore, is a Holy War. We should feel proud that we have been offered the opportunity to fight in this holiest of battles. It is a spiritual duel with evil. And there can be only one possible outcome. Goodness must triumph. She will be our victor. Peace will be our prize and a life without suffering will be our reward.

Generations to come will be eternally grateful for this, our sacrifice. Our brave response will have saved them from future perils at the hands of the German people. In the end even Germany will be in our debt; she will thank us for saving her from the threat of hell and eternal damnation.

There will be deaths; innocents will perish. In a conflict of this scale these cannot be avoided. But take heart, we shall not have their blood on our hands. The citizens of Germany have approved the terrifying actions of their government. They have given their consent to the wickedness planned by their representatives. They do not deserve our pity. They do not deserve to live.

What of the babies and children, I hear you ask? Surely, they are innocent of such evil intentions?

Those same helpless babies may one day grow into killers of English babies. Can we allow sentiment to cloud our judgement? Could we let them live? Indeed, we could not.

Finally, what of our soldiers?

There is no other calling more worthy; there is no other calling more courageous and unselfish, than that of the soldier. Our soldiers are God's agents on earth. They have His divine approval for their actions. They are not guilty of murder when they slaughter German soldiers, for when we kill in the name of the Lord, it is a sign of our love for Him. He will thank us and in return He will grant us everlasting peace.

Our gallant soldiers are not fighting individuals with faces and names. They do not know the men they are going to kill. They are simply executing God's law in a just and meaningful war, so there is no murder. Soldiers are granted the highest privilege in their calling. There is almost a sacred quality to their activities when they are carried out in the name of the Lord.

Ladies, look to your husbands. Mothers, appeal to your sons. Persuade them – should they need persuasion – that theirs is the noblest calling. Their place on the battlefield will be one of glorious victory. Even in suffering and death, they will be transformed by God's splendour and guaranteed a place in Heaven. Be assured, ladies, that it is better if your husbands and sons fall in battle than that they live in the perpetual darkness and dishonour which follows cowardice and a duty unfulfilled.

To give you strength, hold close to your hearts the magnificent words of our hymns: 'Fight the Good Fight', 'Onward Christian Soldiers', 'Soldiers of Christ'. Listen, mark my words, they will lead us down the golden pathway to peace.

Peace. The only perfect state of harmony, not only between nation and nation and man and man, but a spiritual harmony between man and God.

Go now, prepare yourselves to be Soldiers of Christ!

Somewhere in the hospital

November 28th 1915

Dearest brother,

At last I've found a free minute to write. You know
what a hospital is like, if I sit for a moment, sister
finds me something else to do. But I've done extra
duty so I consider that I deserve a few seconds alone.
I've shut myself in the laundry cupboard and I'm
leaning against the door so she won't get me out
until I'm done. We are very full but there's no one
as interesting as soldiers. Boring gallstones and pneu-
monia – oh, I did help with a birth, a lovely little boy
but the mother heard last week that her husband is
missing.

You remember May? You always thought her name
unsuitable because she is so lean and pale. Well, she's
nursing in Harbury and they have started taking in
casualties. It sounds wonderful. You can really involve
yourself with those patients. Trust me to be stuck in
this dull old place.

Judging by the food you have, you'll be gross and
ugly before too long. Make sure you take a good long
walk every day or you'll regret it and poor Ruth won't
recognise you. I'm quite worried about her, by the
way. She's hardly eating enough to keep a mouse
alive. The school and her mother keep her busy and
she's involved in some charity thing with Lily. Perhaps
you'll have a word with her, you know how to be
gently diplomatic – but don't say I told you. She must
keep lovely for you, mustn't she?

I rarely see father unless I bump into him here.
Mother is very agitated about everything: you, my

work and father's refusal to talk about anything. I've told her to come out with it, force him to speak, but you know our mother, if it's going to be unpleasant and upset someone she keeps it quiet.

I've come to the conclusion (not very difficult) that medical people are some of the most selfish imaginable. They pretend to be hardworking because they are caring and compassionate but in truth it's an escape. They can do nothing else, least of all become involved with their families. I fear our mother is rather grey and tedious after the excitement of the hospital but father can't exclude her from his life, not on some silly whim that he calls professionalism.

You will understand from this that father is not my favourite person at present. I have never forgiven him for what he did to you and now he's not only making mother's life a misery but trying to organise mine as well.

As soon as there's one free I'll get a room in the hospital. I'll make time to see mother, and of course Ruth is very attentive to her. It's a pity mother can't be more sociable. Mrs Cleery would love to see her, there's such a lot she could become involved with if only she would push her position a little.

You are very like her in that. I wonder sometimes how you are coping with all those strangers and having to give orders to young men you've never met before. I expect it's like hospital – the layers of authority make it easy to identify your place and as long as you don't stray into someone else's territory, you survive. I must say you don't sound too despairing. You might have an interesting time with those new friends of yours. How dare you complain about sitting around for hours when I yearn to put my feet up for longer than two minutes.

121

You will have to get used to your sister's nonsensical ravings, I'm afraid. I'm sure you have enough to worry about. If I were in your position, I should be worried about practical things like washing my hair and how I was going to find the time to do my nails or shorten a dress that I needed for a party. My nails are a terrible fright after all the soapy carbolic water. You're lucky to be a man. You can get dirty and not worry about it.

Let me know how things are. We don't get much news of actual fighting. It's hard to imagine that it's happening across that short stretch of water. Write in code if you can't tell me, I was always good at puzzles.

Must go – sister is hammering on the door.

Heaps and heaps of love from your best sister.

Alice

December 9th 1915

Hello again! I'm adding some more to this as mother has just told me about your move. I am glad for you. You'll be safe there and although I know you hate it, you may be some small use in a hospital. Don't worry that you haven't written for ages, I understand that the hours simply slip away. I think that's why I find my work so rewarding. Even though we are falling over each other to get things done, I know that every little thing is useful. But naturally, I don't enjoy it.

For the past week it has been quite dreadful here. We took in some unfortunate men from Harbury because there was no room and it was distressing to see their poor damaged bodies. I never knew how hateful this war is. Why didn't you warn me? Does Ruth know what is going on? I've kept things from her but she's been so preoccupied lately that I'm certain she knows the truth.

They were so young. Surely they should not have been there? Most of them would not talk about what they had been through, it was too painful and they all needed to save their energy for dealing with the pain. But for some of them there is little we can do. Their bodies are so broken we would need miracles to rebuild them. These are the boys – yes, I think of them as boys – I have the greatest of sympathy for. I sit and listen and talk with them for hours. It is all I can do. But even when the pain has gone I will still be haunted by their experiences.

One in particular is especially brave; Stanley's his name. He's a local boy, from Manchester. He had been at Loos but he wouldn't talk about it. He only told me how brave everyone else was, how their strength had swept everyone along into the heart of the battle. He has to lose a leg above the knee. No one has told him yet, but I suspect he knows. We were discussing him today and sister asked me to tell him. She thinks I have a way with them because I am so young. I said I would have to think about it.

I wish you were here, Owen, to ask about such a brutal thing. How do you tell a man that he's going to be a cripple for the rest of his life? It's impossible to tell mother about this. It would be too upsetting for her, and father is still so wrapped up in himself he would be no support. At times like this I wish I had mother's faith. She would say, pray to God for help, but I'm afraid I can't see a place for God in all this. Perhaps you, in the middle of it, with a view of the whole situation and not simply the disturbing part, can see where He fits in. If you can, I'll be glad to hear your explanation.

I don't suppose you know about Green's devastating Advent sermon. It was unspeakable. I will not go into detail, enough to say that I will never go inside that church again. Ruth was so angry I had to drag her away before she set about him. She had only agreed to come with me as a favour because I was so upset about Stanley; normally she goes with Lily to St Theresa's. Anyway, I don't feel I can respond to a God who inspires such lies and bitterness. But Ruth and I may be alone on this one. There's been no positive denunciation from any of our parents.

I hope you are truly all right. Mother is very concerned about you. She has some notion that you may have reached a crisis and that you won't be able to cope. Nonsense, if you ask me. You were always strong. Nothing frightened you or made you give in. Look how you pushed yourself through the medicine when you hated it so.

I loathe these letters. It isn't me who's writing the words, but some silly young woman trying to amuse someone miles away who might be killed at any moment or already be dead. The things I long to tell you are too painful and precious, the things that I can, are trivial and pathetic.

Forgive me, dear brother, I fear I am changing into a woman at last. I can't fill the pages with inane jokes or trivialities any more. They're a burden, I know, my doubts, but it's a consolation to know that you will read and digest my words.

Bless you and keep safe.

Alice

7 Lilac Avenue
Carleton
Lancashire

December 14th 1915

Dearest Owen,

This is going to be a desolate Christmas – for all of us. I hate this time of the year. The garden has that bleakness of the in-between days when we still can remember the richness of autumn but the crisp silvery days have not come yet. The air is thin and sour, muffled with impatience. Something to do with the war, I suppose, and our not being allowed to experience emotional things, except for grief and sorrow.

Lily has been miserable at the thought of the celebrations while Edwin isn't here. You would notice how different she is, you who appreciated her irrepressible gaiety. There is a docile acceptance of unhappiness about her. I've been trying to persuade her to come and stay for a while but she refuses to leave her mother and younger sister. I'm expecting her later to help with a few things for Christmas. I hate using the word but how else can I talk to you? We won't be doing anything exciting, only preparing fruit for a cake and some marzipan sweets. It sounds pitiful, our dull life, but it is exactly like that of so many other young women. We live from day to day, never planning too far ahead and praying for a routine unbroken by the expected tragedy.

Do you remember that afternoon under the apple tree, Lily in her pink dress, her cheeks flushed with excitement and embarrassment at your good-natured teasing about Edwin? Life was so uncomplicated then. There were no secrets between us. We were balanced on the edge of young lives, intoxicated with the anticipation and freedom of all that was before us. It was simply good to be together, friends under the sun. And of course we knew nothing of the war – except for Edwin, who talked of nothing else. During those last weeks before Edwin left, it was the only time I saw Lily with a cool expression. She felt such contempt for the ideas that stuffed his head before they became reality and tore him away from her.

She believed that he couldn't wait to go. I tried to explain what pressure all young men faced. Would she have been happy if he'd moped about at home, reading about it all in the paper? He'd have become grumpy and unbearable. She didn't want to know. Naturally, a miserable frustrated Edwin was better than no Edwin.

Some of her sentiments seem cruel now when I think about them with you. She talks of the futility and despair of it all and her doubts ring in my head every time your face appears to me, because I know you will be thinking about why you are there and analysing the purpose behind every action you are called on to carry out. Perhaps this is a time for not too much thought – it simply drives one round in increasingly depressing circles. I have to recognise that your place is over there with all the other lovers and husbands and brothers and sons.

Lily's youth gives her the excuse of not seeing through her tears that this is all about freedom. The abstract seems too overwhelming and painful for her. She can only recognise the tangible, the pain, the loss, the desperate wives and mothers and the poor children left without fathers.

Even her dress has become sombre. She's taken to wearing severe, insipid fabrics. It may be a concession to Mrs Wallace's economies, of course, but I suspect that she is unable to enjoy a gay dress any more. She feels guilty at the explosion of colour and ornament that overpowered fashion before the war. She can't see the attraction of all this oriental nonsense when Edwin is out in France with not even a green field to rest his eyes on. I admit I agree with her but I was never one for delicious colours anyway. Give me my white muslin any day. Perhaps that is enough for one letter. Let's remember that last party together with you so relaxed and optimistic and me in my muslin and that first real kiss...

Ruth

December 16th 1915

Dear Miss Cleery,

I hope you will excuse the liberty, my writing to you like this. As Owen's commanding officer I feel certain that you would want to hear from me how he is. Since leaving us in October for a hospital in Amiens he has not been in the best of health. You may not have received any word from him, hence my letter to you. I can assure you that it was nothing serious, a mild fever following which he was a bit down. He has made a complete recovery by now and I am sure you will be hearing from him in the New Year.

May I send my best wishes to you and your family for Christmas.

Yours most sincerely

Raymond Drummond (Captain)

December 23rd 1915

My Darling,

Well, it has arrived and it is as terrible as we imagined. By now you will have heard of Edwin's death. The last week has been unbearable but we are learning to bear anything now, just as you have to. We have as much of a conviction of duty as you, the unfortunate soldiers, though I am still not convinced of the moral honesty of such unnatural feelings.

I received Captain Drummond's letter at the end of the week, so after the unexpected horror concerning Edwin it was good to know that you are in a reasonable state of well-being. It was kind of him to take the time to write and I appreciate his thought for you.

We had to send Hannah to the Judds' for Martha to sit with mother, she was in such a state. It didn't occur to me until she'd gone, how distressing it might be for Hannah to see Albert again. I don't think they ever see each other and he never comes up in conversation. It is sad that they could not be reconciled after the tragedy. He needs someone to love him and Hannah needs someone to care for more than a hysterical and embittered family. But who knows, maybe out of this pain some happiness might be rescued by their coming together.

I managed to have a talk with Martha before she went in to mother. She is a women full of sorrow; still bitter and hurt after all these years. But even after the distress and indignity Albert has suffered she seems, in an odd way, to want to take on all our suffering too. She kept saying over and over, 'It should not be.' She tried to get me to talk about my feelings but my reaction appears so feeble next to hers. She put her strength down to her refusal to be part of the reality. She said she moved through those weeks in a sort of amazed dream in 1901, so heady with Albert's return that she hardly dared notice his deformity. And Hannah – I know she still regrets that loss. She so much wanted a daughter and when Hannah abandoned her son (that's how she sees it, I'm sure, even though Albert insists that he was determined not to inflict his misfortunes on someone as tender as Hannah), she felt let down and disappointed for him.

Some people might dismiss her as an emotional old woman but she has had time to work through and refine her responses to tragedy, as we have not been allowed. I think the clarity of her reaction, which is a natural and human one, has come from this measured meditation. She was angry that there is no responsibility in war, moral or otherwise. Albert had volunteered, just as Edwin and you, and what occurred had to be accepted and not questioned. She could accuse no one person of having done this unthinkable thing to her son so she blamed everyone: the red-faced stuttering sergeant who appeared on her doorstep with the news; the vicar, who made a cursory visit, refusing to sit down or take a cup of tea, and whose sympathies were veiled in suspicious and cruel jargon about the honour of fighting for God. She felt pressured into believing that she should feel grateful that Albert had been injured doing his duty. She even blamed the small children who congregated in the street to snigger and whisper as her son moved past them with bowed head and empty sleeve tucked into his pocket. It was so sad that for a moment I forgot about my own sorrow.

But not for long. Today, when I thought I could not bear any more, the unspeakable happened. The parcel which Becca had so carefully and lovingly prepared for Edwin was returned. There was no message, only a bold and cruel KILLED scrawled across his name. Fortunately mother was with Mrs Judd when Hannah and I had to watch as she unwrapped it. She untied the string and wound it into a neat skein, as mother had always done. She unfolded the paper with such care that I could sense Hannah holding her breath. She took out everything and examined each item, searching for some clue behind its mystifying return. The tin of tobacco was still smooth and shiny, the sweets untasted, rattling on their bed of sugar, and the tiny scissors that she had so much trouble finding for him were sprinkled with rust. As she unfolded the socks which mother had knitted, the envelope of tea fell apart, a decaying white flower spilling its dark seeds onto the tablecloth. The saddest moment of all was when she opened the book, an exercise book filled with poems and stories and illustrations which she had worked on for hours. The cover was damp and mapped with grey smudges. She turned each page and followed each line and coloured mark, searching for something that she could not find. There were no words to answer her shock and despair. I cannot come to terms with the mindless response behind such an action. What manner of person with any feeling would be able to write that word on a parcel and return it to those loved ones who had sent it?

I have just returned from town, where the final preparations for Christmas are taking place. It began

131

to snow before we left the house and I could have cried with the beauty of it. Such beauty should not be allowed when there is so much unhappiness. It seemed that my body ached with all the tears and I wanted to close the curtains and hide away, safe and alone, until this dreadful war is finished.

But Hannah found me and persuaded me to get Becca away from the house. Poor sad Hannah, she's had so much of her own sorrow to handle as well as the handling of ours. She's called on at all hours to produce cups of tea and comforting words or inoffensive silences during our embarrassed moments as a family. She will deserve a medal as much as any gallant young soldier, when all this is over. There is a limit to how much consolation can be concocted from kind words and tonics from the kitchen.

It was a relief to see some other faces. The women in the market place with their overflowing baskets were full of chatter and even the excited children in the snow were a welcome distraction. Becca is at a singular age and I fear she is having to grow up too swiftly and carelessly. I don't recall being eleven but I am certain I was not as sensible as my dear sister.

She has taken Edwin's death much to heart but it has been good for her to have Lily and me to talk to. But I think I may have pushed her this afternoon in my efforts to help her forget. We saw Lily in Wallace's shop, smothered in a heap of delicious emerald silk that she was working on, and Becca seemed most upset at the notion of Lily's sadness. She wanted to be able to share and understand it but she felt frustrated that her sadness did not have the same qualities as Lily's.

It's difficult explaining to a child how the context of sadness has a relevance to the nature of grief. I don't want to imagine a world without those I love and I am angry that I should be expected to do so. Naturally, we came round to talk of God and his place in all this and I wasn't very much help to her, I'm afraid. Lily's faith has brought her great strength and even though she is bitter it has softened the edges of her desperation. It's hard for anyone to accept, let alone an eleven-year-old, that the power of God's love can be a force for good. How can we believe in a God who shows his love for us by taking away those we love and leaving us with a numbing frustration at our helplessness? I had to console her with the idea that if something happens to you, then I will be equally as resilient and brave. I don't believe that but how could I tell her that I could not bear to think about it.

My meagre words seemed to satisfy her for a brief time but when we were passing the church everything fell to pieces. She stopped and leaned on the wall, resting her chin on her hands. The graves were smooth mounds under the snow, their headstones powdered with white. Light glimmered through the coloured glass in the narrow windows and was snatched in gold and blue and crimson by the unmarked snow. As the voices practising carols drifted out into the still air she winced and ran off in tears, crying that she hated the place.

It was the first time since we heard about Edwin that she had let herself go. At the memorial service she had been stiff-faced and dry-eyed because she had no proof that our brother was not coming home. She had not seen his body laid in the cold ground, so she would not believe it. Her anger and confusion had finally simmered enough to allow the tears to come. As we stood there in that uncanny time between dusk and darkness, the music of the mill band playing 'See Amid the Winter's Snow' sang across the glistening snow.

We moved towards the square, where people were watching and listening with a new purpose. It was odd to see them so intent on listening to a tune that was so familiar. But that is something I have noticed since this war began; how the trivial and unsuspecting can be so moving. It no longer takes the extraordinary to rouse one's emotions. Most of the women were crying, unashamedly and without restraint, and the children were suddenly still and silent, caught in that instant of reflection between memory and anticipation. It was a cruelly magical moment that seemed to settle all our deepest feelings.

On our return up the hill, Becca complained at the injustice of people such as Henry Judd being allowed to live when everyone knew how malicious and thoughtless his short life had been. I had to tell her that life was all about our struggle to make sense of unfairness. I had never told her before about my first encounter with Albert all those years ago, so it seemed appropriate. When I stumbled on him in the park he had gone to hide from prying eyes. At six, I was totally baffled by his damaged face and body in that place that I associated with freshness and beauty. In that moment I had a glimpse of how man's impatience and intolerance can bring pain to one inoffensive and anonymous individual. At the same time I had experienced a curious warmth inside which only now can I identify as love. I was drawn to this quiet stranger. I needed to be close to his obvious suffering, hence my spontaneous giving of the flower from my hat. This story touched Becca and I knew that we both began to understand the puzzling relation between suffering and love. All the events of today – the parcel, the church, the music – although they highlighted our misery, they have in some tiny way moved us on and away from the wretchedness of Edwin's death.

Alone in my room, I feel closer to you. I had left the curtains open and the moon has risen, its ghostly light performing magic above the old town. There is ice on the window, the crystals shimmered and softened as my breath touched the glass. When I saw my face in the mirror I could not bear to look at my pinched features because I could see your face, my darling, behind mine. Your gentle hands are resting on my shoulders and caressing my hair. You, all those painful dark miles away. I want to say a prayer for you but the words are frozen in the lonely moonlit darkness. When I hear from you again I will be content. A line, a word, a sigh – if you can put that into words – to let me know that you are still alive.

Ruth

Ruth,

My darling, I must apologise if I've neglected you. Not because you're not in my mind, you're always there, but there are so few moments when I can put pen to paper. I won't squeeze you into some tiny space when you deserve the best of my time. Off-duty, all I want to do is sleep and dream of some other place. And your pitiful letters demanded a thoughtful response. I realised as I read them over and over how little we respond to each other's words. We absorb their messages, yes, we are moved by their sentiments, but how often have we made comment on them? It's as if all these words are poured out purely for our own satisfaction, a catharsis for our bruised lives.

I believe that your suffering is as valid as ours out here. You are so helplessly ignorant of the truth of events and you can only sit and wait and look for distractions in your dull lives. Whereas we are in the middle of all this – we hardly have time to dwell on what happened yesterday or last week because we are so busy preparing for tomorrow. I do feel for you but I think you are handling Rebecca perfectly. She is fortunate to have such a sensible and sensitive young woman for a sister. I recall the children I have seen over the past months and recognise the same confused incuriosity in their expressions. As to the parcel, I share your disgust at such an outrageous procedure but have to say it is no surprise. A few weeks ago I heard a young officer condemning the practice of sending letters to the families of those unfortunates shot for desertion. He enquired whether it would not be gentler to say that they were missing or killed in action. The commanding officer explained that it was the War Office's way of saving the government money by avoiding the extravagance of paying pensions to the families of those who clearly did not deserve it. And that from an individual who claims to care for his men!

These incidents are simply a measure of the sorry state we have reached, with the poor individual floundering in this morass of hypocrisy and self-congratulation at every small triumph over the enemy.

To lighter subjects. I hope you managed to enjoy a little of the festivities in spite of all the sinister shadows. It will definitely not be a Christmas to store in your memory. I made a vow that I would make the most of any celebrations we were allowed in case it was my last opportunity. I determined that if I have to leave this life, I will depart with a smile on my face. We had a splendid spread: chicken and ham and all the trimmings, and plenty of beer and wine to help it down. You would be amazed at the number of food hampers that arrived from well-wishers with cakes and chocolates and fresh fruit – it was a great lift, I can tell you. We had a few sing-songs to help us to the right mood and naturally there were a few tears when everyone brought out their presents and photographs from home. But in a cruel way that was a reminder of what we are fighting to preserve. I'm not sure the generals and the big-wigs in the War Office still see it as clearly as that, but if it helps us through, there's no harm done.

I made an early resolution to myself. You'll be glad to hear it as it was prompted by your gentle nagging. I'm resolved to spend all my off-duty in writing, even if it's only my diary. There is so much material here and it's impossible to describe it all to you – my letters would be confiscated anyway. So if you don't hear from me so much, don't despair. I'll be writing for you in spirit in my little red notebook.

Maurice had a hand in my conversion too. He says if you want to write it's no good grousing, you simply get on and do it. He's a veracious and disrespectful teacher our Maurice, there's little subtlety or metaphysics behind his philosophy.

Well, back to reality. I suppose you would like to hear about a field hospital. It's the opposite of a conventional hospital at home. Alice will have told you how they are run on strict military lines. It's impossible to keep to a daily routine. Patients are arriving and being moved at odd times. Everything must be fitted round meals and dressings which seem continuous.

Our one blessing is the setting – the largest church, apart from the cathedral. It's curious moving through the poor men cramped between stone columns in the shadow of the buttresses in the lofty roof. When I step outside for air it's as if the agonised screams of the gargoyles have been strangled by the shock of all this distress and disorder below. For the first time in its history the high altar is not everyone's major focus, although those who are conscious have a peculiar sense of the separateness of the place. They whisper to each other and I find myself creeping about and measuring my movements so as not to draw attention to myself. This will sound unbelievable to you – you know me and churches!

The injuries are mostly from shells and machine gun fire but the most terrifying are the wounds from the wire. The stuff of the devil. The enemy has refined that evil to perfection – if you dare use such a word for an instrument of such barbarity. You wouldn't recognise it, with over a dozen cruel barbs to each foot and rusty from the months of exposure. It is firmed into the ground with iron supports, almost four feet in places, and to complete the savagery, there is a trip wire on the German side. Unspeakable injuries result from the men being caught on this and then falling back onto the rusty iron caltrops behind. What a horror! The wounds are torn and jagged and impossible to clean. Infection is the dreadful follow-on to such a network of torture.

My brief medical training did not prepare me for this; men younger than myself, agonised by such injuries. But what is more harrowing and inexcusable is their terror at being sent back. When they can finally sleep, their rest is destroyed by violent nightmares of the cruellest kind. Their agitation often causes their wounds to reopen and healing has to begin all over again. This is indeed the stuff of nightmare. My greatest dread is a recurring dream of perpetual darkness. Sometimes when I try to sleep my brain is battered by the constant images of friends in pain. I have a fear of drowning in the shadows that will make up my future. But of course for shadows there must be sunshine – and where is the sun? She seems to have deserted us.

My relief from this frightful occupation comes from the half-hour walk I manage to steal at some time each day. No matter how exhausted, I force myself to take that walk away from this place. Alone, I remember you and repeat my love for you to convince myself of a world that is not all brutality. It's almost a supernatural sensation, escaping from the pain into the freshness outside, away from the stink of antiseptic and chloroform and the unwholesome air that lingers around the dying. The air is soft; there is birdsong, the ripple of water and the murmur of conversation from ordinary people going about their ordinary lives – as ordinary as they can be in the middle of all this. I often wonder if they're aware of what is going on inside their church.

It might surprise you but the locals are very suspicious of the soldiers. At times, I fear they resent our being here at all. They frown severely at individuals queuing outside shops or sitting in bars. I suppose they can't lose their centuries-old suspicion that they might not be able to rid their country of these trespassers when it's all over. The most callous thing I heard was that the French government is charging us for the use of their rail track to move hospital trains – our trains, I might add – to the ports. How does one respond to such unfeeling madness?

I don't know how long I will be here. I'm not in a hurry to return to the front and have made my wishes clear to the CO. He doesn't see a problem as they need medical men almost as much as they need fighting ones.

Sunday

The countryside was glorious today. A clear crisp morning with wisps of cloud flickering across the sky, like snatches of snow tossed into the air by a child. Even the birdsong, high above the old town, was magnified under that clean dome of sky. And a snatch of words came into my mind – the opening image of a poem perhaps – 'high up a solitary bird, dusts the dome of sky, nudges closer to God.'

I sat for a while in a sheltered copse and thought about our trips in that summer of 1914. Those simple moments seem so precious now ... that boat trip when Edwin fell into the river and Lily almost choked with laughter; early morning when we hid under misty trees to wait for the first blackbird and you shivered and shivered ... and the *Gerontius* concert in Manchester when you couldn't stop crying...

With my eyes closed I can almost forget where I am. There are church bells in the distance and voices of peasants so mild and benign under this vast sky. I can see some water through the trees, catching the kiss of the sun. Such gentleness seems out of place here. It might be England before all this began. The longer I stay, the harder it will be to go back. I have word from Captain Drummond that he's lost so many of his original lot that I'm not to hurry back. He's a good sort. I wish you could meet him some day.

Back in the hospital this evening I had a disturbing encounter with a young man who was severely injured before Christmas and sadly found his way back to us. Two nights ago he was out with a working party repairing wire when they came under shell attack. According to the doctor, he broke down and the others couldn't console him. They brought him back in a state of collapse. I've been sitting with him for the past two hours, watching and listening to his mumbling and confused attempts to come to terms with his experiences. He can't do it. I understand now why I cannot go back.

Please don't think me a coward, my darling. I'm not afraid for myself. Death would be a merciful release from all this ugliness and ferocity. Death does not hold any terrors for us, it's dying that is the greatest fear. I am afraid of my involvement in all this; it can only go on and on while we patch men up and send them back. I'm haunted by the image of individuals when it's ended. How will they pick up the scattered shreds of their lives when all this horror is still warm in their veins? How will they come back to a dullness where nothing exists but the routine and quiet and the people left behind, struggling to understand the context of their sorrow? There is the fearfully disturbing idea that this war has made it exciting to be alive and we cannot allow that sentiment to survive. War has no virtue.

Your Owen

7 Lilac Avenue
Carleton
Lancashire

January 1916

Dearest,

You are right – this was not a Christmas to remember. I long to be able to lose myself in some activity that would sap my strength and dull my frantic imagination and deny my clear thinking. I need to erase all that has happened over the last months and start all over again as a more thoughtful sister, a more selfless daughter and a more devoted lover to you. I feel I am no use to anyone, least of all myself.

It is good to see Alice when I feel like this. She has a deliberately self-conscious vigilance which I find strangely comforting. I can imagine such tender efficiency and stoicism might be irritating but I would be lost without it.

I can make believe with your sister, an amiable deceit I could never get away with at home. I can pretend that all is unchanged, that the world outside, with all its harshness and insidious suffocating shadows, has a familiar character that allows me to live as I wish. The trouble, though, is that you, my darling, are part of that other world. I cannot forget you and simply wait for you to come home. I dare not contemplate your coming home; I will believe it only when I feel your body in my arms and hear the gentle reassurance of your voice.

But I have a confession. My awkward pretence with Alice prompted me to lie about your letters. I was afraid to tell her about the horror there and the

143

subtle changes that are so evident in what you do not choose to say. Naturally, Alice accepts my mystery, she sees it as part of our necessary secret existence which must be respected at all costs. That idea has a fascinating appeal as I sense the closer I keep our secret fears, the less likely they are to take the form of reality. I hope you sympathise with this. I feel you do and I respect your need to record your private thoughts at this time. As long as I am somewhere in your tangled thoughts, I don't need your signature on a piece of flimsy paper as proof of your love.

But you must not expect me not to worry. It is clear from the last part of your letter that there are some dark coils of despair deep inside. You have torn open your heart to me in your attempts to be loyal and honest but I want you to know that your worst fears of disobedience and dishonour do not move me as much as the health of your poor tortured spirit.

I am sitting in front of my dressing table. It's littered with so many memories: grandmother's silver-backed hairbrush, the perfume spray made of amber bought by Edwin last Christmas – the first Christmas of the war – the fading bunch of violets you stuffed into my hand before you left on that dreadful day in September. I have them next to your photograph. Your smile is starting to fade from its place in the sun but I won't move it; we both need it to be there.

Even though I haven't talked about you with father, he seems to have a more alert intuition about what you are suffering than mother. He considers you as part of the family. He knows your letters make me sad but he excuses you because your sharing with me is making it easier for you, it is keeping a curb on your passions and indignation, which must not be allowed free rein. That way lies failure and despair,

144

my love. Of course I don't give a jot if you fail in the authorities' eyes, but failing yourself would be a calamity.

Mother, on the rare occasions when she does speak of the war, has this obsession with failure. I suppose it's related to Edwin's death. He wasn't allowed to fail yet she sees young men still wandering the streets here who have escaped the trauma of this war for reasons known to themselves. They may be perfectly valid, but mother can't excuse them. Any man who doesn't triumph in this war will be damned as far as she is concerned.

This seems to be her particular crusade at the moment. She sits near the window in the sitting room, without a book, without sewing, not talking to anyone, simply waiting, as though every minute were a vigil for Edwin's return. No colours are allowed to disrupt her mourning and even the spring, only weeks away, will not distract her with its budding trees and tiny flowers. She suffers this immense struggle when anyone tries to move close to her and when I want to talk, she says she can't understand why I should want to waste my time with a miserable middle-aged woman. It's so pitiful that Edwin's death has caused her such grave doubts about her own future. She feels that she has failed, that she is to blame for her son's death by not stopping him from going. And now in her inability to discuss it she feels abandoned by us all.

She has even stopped going to church. Quite right, I say, after the Reverend Green's shameful performance before Christmas. But her reasons for dissent are more mysterious. She won't have a word said against that unspeakable man. In my view, he doesn't stand for anything fine or laudable like God's love or

145

our caring for each other in this terrible time. He seems concerned only with outward signs of faith such as the abundance of flowers in church and the donations to the bazaar. He has lost touch with the people who matter. They may as well not be there; he might carry on without them and spout his heartless nonsense to the cold walls of the church. They get in his way. He has to shake their hands after the service and show his face in Sunday school when it's well known how he loathes small children with their grubby faces and runny noses. He feels power up in that pulpit, and its structure gives him an undeserved protection. If he had to walk and talk with the congregation on their level, he would soon flounder. I'm sorry for bouncing off like this but it makes me feel so much fresher inside to release these sour feelings. And it's better than squeezing it up inside and bashing old Green over the head with my umbrella next time I see him! Perhaps I've even brought a smile to your face to match the smile I'm looking at now. Let's hope so.

Keep up with the writing. I'm desperate to read some. I'm with you always.

Ruth

Who would believe that during the night, someone up there – I hesitate to call the being God – had emptied a heap of white on this pitiful place? Just when I thought we were going to see the first flowers, their tiny shoots have been obliterated and we must wait. Like all good things here, we must dream about them before they become reality. There are compensations to this white stuff; we can't see the mud, which is everywhere: on the streets, spattered on the sides of houses, carried on hundreds of boots and wheels and wretched horses' feet.

No going out today. Off-duty perched on a pile of blankets in the laundry with my books. *The Spirit of Man*, a recent treasure sent from home by Ruth, is a measureless anthology of poetry and scraps of writing collected specially for us by Robert Bridges. Words for every mood and moment. I'll never be left fumbling for thoughts again. And my scruffy copy of *Wessex Tales*, naturally. Hardy is so soothing. That gentle language and those fragile images are all I need for comfort. Astonishing the number of men who carry a book in their pockets; even the ordinary chap with little to say on life has his favourite. Maurice carries Dante and is constantly quoting lyrical snippets to anyone within hearing distance. He makes me think of Ruth and my unforgivable last letter. Too much philosophy in my art and not enough love. I've complained about those priests enough in the past, and here I am creating a theology of my own feelings when I should be listening and loving.

This weather has affected everything – mood, temperature, and the closeness of bodies which seem to have multiplied. I bumped into a corporal from my

147

old unit who came to collect supplies for the dressing station. Things are no better down there. The cold will kill the men if the enemy doesn't do it first. They can't do anything with the ground 'hard as iron' … in that sad carol Ruth loved. Captain Drummond has sent word that he hopes to get up in a few days. I wrote to him – as a warning, I suppose – of my wobbly condition. He was sympathetic but he has to be cautious about expressing an opinion in his position.

Intriguing new treatment for the terrible burns we have to deal with. Ambrene is a resin – amber – and has amazing properties to heal wounds and deaden the murderous pain. Poured into the wound warm, as it cools it sets to the shape of the damaged area. In about three weeks the wound is completely clean. Quite miraculous, but natural, there is nothing divine here!

A sudden kerfuffle early this morning in the main ward. Sad. They brought in an attempted suicide. There was little they could do for him and he passed away an hour ago. It was my young friend, the Welch Fusilier. I had recommended that he be sent home after his last experience but, as often happens, nothing was done. The insignificance of one small person amongst all these thousands makes me numb. It's futile to cry out at the needless waste of young life, all deaths are that out here. But I had hopes that he would escape.

Snow or no snow, I had to get out. Away from the town, all was still and unblemished. A few birds dotted the grey sky, a skylark, I think, fluttering high over the tallest pine trees. I closed my eyes and I might have been at home, sitting on the edge of our valley, waiting for the night to creep into our warm and secret lives.

I experienced an odd sensation while they were closed. I can only describe it as unearthly as I have no faith in the divine at present. A gentleness passed close by as though a clutch of figures from the past was moving through the countryside. Of course, there will be ghosts after all this carnage, who would doubt it? Imagine the army of spirits which will hover over this space in search of rest in the years to come. Left me with a feeling of resignation, which is a bit disturbing. I have made a decision. I cannot be sad any more. I must search for some brightness in all this – some hint behind a smile of joy remembered or dreams anticipated. Despair has become our malevolent friend but we can't allow it a place. Must focus on hope, for without hope, despair has no meaning.

I am becoming too selfish and self-obsessed. I push away thoughts of suffering because I finish up blaming myself, blaming my weakness, not only in allowing this to continue but in lacking the courage to go on as every other is driven on. It is quite without reason.

Perhaps a break from all this will help. Those who have been home on leave speak of an easier time when they return. I pray it will be soon.

I can visualise Ruth sitting at home, surrounded by the things that she loves and trying not to imagine my homecoming because it is too painful. This separation is bad for both of us but it has brought us close in moments such as this. We used to anticipate each other's thoughts and put them into words. We found it rather quaint but now it is a further example of the empathy which has flourished between loved ones...

Good Friday, April 21st 1916

A dismal day. Oppressive and grey early on, started raining heavily about eleven. Everyone seemed affected by the uneasy tension. The sergeant on duty first thing lost his temper with a couple of VADs who haven't been here long, and flung a jar of carbolic across the sluice room. Sister, normally patient and controlled, was furious and gave him a proper dressing down. She told him he wasn't fit to be in the same place with so many brave young men and warned him to keep out of her way.

Men equally tetchy. Complaints about food and damp blankets. The roof in the laundry was leaking and we now have a collection of enamel bowls spread around and all our moves are done to the accompaniment of ringing and splashing.

Escaped for a breather this afternoon but as I was leaving I was accosted by a captain who was short of a man to sit on a Field Court Martial. Of course he roped me in. No details about the case, just instructions to turn up at the estaminet at four. Made the most of my half-hour up on the hill but even up there the air was heavy with a damp despair. No skylarks today. Scores of squawking rooks darting and diving at each other in a most ill-mannered and crude performance.

Relief to get back to the relative peace of the ward, where the dull routine acts as an inoffensive anaesthetic. Since the VADs arrived the hospital is more orderly and it's easy to slip into a thoughtless and numbing round of efficiency without knowing it. Sister none too pleased with my official absence but she had to lump it. I should have known what I was letting myself in for.

I had no idea, the seriousness of a Court Martial. I expected a trivial session to decide the fate of some unimportant offender. At worst I expected a private on report for falling asleep on duty or swiping his comrade's Woodbines. Sadly, that was not the case here. When I entered the room set aside for the business, I could tell from the prisoner's expression that it was something more serious. Sorry to say, I took an instant dislike to the fellow with his shock of red hair and pallid face. Apart from the lack of freckles, he reminded me of Henry Judd. His eyes flickered round the room, studying the faces of his accusers. He had the oddest eyes – different colours – which gave him a most shifty and untrustworthy appearance.

The Captain briefly outlined the case, during which the young man shuffled his feet and rubbed his hands noisily up and down the side of his chair. Apparently, he had returned to his billet two nights before in a drunken state and become involved in a brawl. It got a bit too lively and the other man fell against the metal fire surround in the cottage. The fall was fatal – unfortunately for our restless friend.

It was disturbing, the Captain's assumption of the poor man's guilt before the case had started, but I managed to hold my tongue. Wading through the evidence was a daunting task as all of it was handwritten and almost required a magnifying glass to separate the letters from the ink blotches. There was no advocate for the prisoner and he had no friend to speak for him. Very sad – he didn't seem to understand what was happening to him.

He was asked a few terse and pointed questions about his movements on the night but from his simple answers I don't think he remembered any part of it clearly. There was no summing up and he was taken outside while we discussed the meagre evidence. The other members of the group were as junior and green as me and equally baffled by the whole experience. It was a foregone conclusion that he should be sentenced to death; no lesser punishment would be acceptable under the circumstances.

Several of us tried to protest but we were overruled by the rest, who were concerned to wind up the case as swiftly as possible so they could get back to the mess for tea! I was disgusted and requested permission to leave before the unfortunate was called back. Couldn't bear to watch his face when they declared sentence.

Back at the hospital, the belligerent sergeant told me it was nothing unusual. He'd seen more than a dozen such cases. My concern was how the decision was made but he assured me that it would be confirmed by the Commander in Chief before it was carried out. That was to shut me up. It's a mere formality. I bet the Chief doesn't even read the details before putting a rubber stamp on it. I'm sickened by the whole thing.

Later this evening I went to see the man's unit. No one thought much of him but they agreed the death sentence was too harsh. He was often drunk but normally slept it off. Some refused to talk of it, saying they had enough to think about killing Germans, without having the deaths of their own unit on their consciences. Poor chaps, what an intolerable position to be in. They rely on the strength and purpose of every individual to keep them together as a fighting unit but they all experience pressures on their stability and loyalty.

As far as I can see, their survival depends on their humour. They see the hilarious in everything, joking about things that we would consider pathetic and in plain bad taste. The sergeant had been with one group who took over a German trench littered with corpses. The men heaved them about like sandbags, plugging gaps in the trench wall and shaking hands with arms and legs that poked out. Brutal and horrific, but in such an unbearable situation the only way to keep one's sanity. These men aren't cold and unfeeling and the depth of their sensitivity for each other is unbelievably touching. If it does one thing this conflict will have united men in a brotherhood searching for a common freedom. The shame is they aren't united in some other complicity to protest against such atrocities.

Great relief that today is ended. A terrible shadow hangs over us. That poor man's fate is a mere symbol of the underlying evil that is growing like some insidious and invisible infection throughout this pained landscape. The horror of it stems from the knowledge that the people in charge of this set-up are aware of what goes on and do nothing to influence these barbaric practices. The meaning of this day has not been lost on anyone with an ounce of compassion. Everyone knows but no one has the moral strength to criticise. I include myself in that hypocritical capacity.

Mess room with two VADs sitting opposite. Pleasant enough young women but I wonder how they cope with the devastating sights they have to witness here. One is holding a skein of grey wool while the other winds it into a ball. Not much talk, just the odd remark about the day and news from home. They are both aware that someone close may be missing or dead, a brother or cousin or neighbour from home, but this knowledge seems to carry them through the drudge of each distressing day.

Alice must be like them. Soft Alice, who wouldn't raise her voice or wear a blouse that bore the smallest stain on it. How does she cope with all this uncertainty and ugliness?

What a day! First the young Welsh boy's death, then that other inexcusable fiasco. My mind starts to play tricks with its jumble of images and sounds colliding with each other; bloody dressings, soiled bedding, bits of body that have been cleared from the operating room and have to be stuffed into pillow cases to be burned; disjointed phrases flung as advice and not meant literally; the murmurs of the sad and the desperate and the idea that hope is gradually losing its privileged station in this place. Without hope we are lost.

Maurice's sacramental motto:

> *Who in that land of darkness and blinde eyes*
> *Thy long expected healing wings could see,*
> *When thou didst rise,*
> *And what can never more be done,*
> *Did at midnight speak with the Sun!*

It's time for the healing to start; God, if there is one, must recognise that.

I must write to Ruth to let her know what decision I have made...

7

Clarity

I turned my face towards the sun as it slid over the roof of the cottage. I did not know why I had gone there except perhaps that I might rediscover some part of Owen's spirit where we had been so secretly happy, in this place where we had talked of our growing love in uneasy whispers.

If I closed my eyes the last months might vanish and I could be anywhere. But the sun had disappeared and I could only shiver in my uncertainty. I clutched at the folded sheets of paper in my pocket, drew them out and looked at the words through the anger of tears. It must be the fiftieth time I'd searched these lines since I received them this morning.

Owen described it as 'giving in' but I prefer spiritual acquiescence, for he hadn't capitulated in any physical sense. Persuaded by Captain Drummond and the sister, who had been keeping more than a professional eye on him over the past weeks, he was going to apply for the Non-Combatant Corps.

There was a touching relief in his words. He was terrified of his decision but the notion of a more peace-orientated regime gave him the necessary courage to carry it through. He sent his apologies for the untidiness of his emotions recently. I approve of that word, it's more gentle than confusion and does not convey such abject loss of purpose. It brings what he intends to do within his grasp. He can sort his feelings away from the distractions of the battlefield without fear of being sent back.

He was afraid that I would think him self-indulgent and irresponsible. But for his commitment so far, to his duty and his companions, I cannot find fault. Some will accuse him of ignoring his responsibilities, of holding misguided aims of self-preservation, but I can never think of him in cowardly terms.

The Reverend Green's words still punched in my head. That apocalyptic rhetoric flung at his congregation represented a moral challenge that now made me uneasy. I had to be sure that my devotion to Owen was not a misguided response to someone who had undoubtedly suffered but who had decided that enough was enough. It was clear that Owen was aware of reality. He was not one of these absurd pacifists I had read about who are convinced of their own infallibility and impatient with a world which refuses to live up to their expectations. He had shown in his humble and self-effacing way that he was not indifferent to the sufferings of his comrades. He turned away from them reluctantly and with the most conscientious and honourable of motives.

I am no longer able to smother my horror at all that I see and know to be going on in the name of justice, freedom and Christianity. Having become involved, though, I cannot abandon them completely. I will put all my efforts into relieving the suffering and consider it merely as an extension of my medical training... Please don't think me weak and useless. I will try to be worthy of your love and respect in all that I do. Don't think any less of me because I can't kill for you. I'm sure you will understand it is far more difficult and painful for me to take this route than to continue in this blind and senseless pursuit of misery and death... I can't feel detached about actions done in God's name which have nothing to do with God's will. I am not a traitor to my country and I will never be a traitor to my family or myself...

My tears dropped onto the last words. I sniffed, refolded the letter into my pocket and searched for a handkerchief. When I looked up a face was peering at me through the trees. It was a stranger, unclear through the tears, but when I wiped them away there were the disjointed features and smiling mouth of a man.

'Ruth Cleery, is that you there?' The gentle voice was familiar and I realised that I had nothing to fear from those macabre features.

'Albert Judd, come out here where I can see you.'

He shuffled forward, moving the lower branches with his arm and bending his face slightly away from me to conceal the scars. 'I wondered who it was, I've never seen anyone else down here.'

'I don't know why I came back, it only made me unhappy.' I dabbed at my cheeks and sat down beside him with the good side of his face nearest.

He was good-looking without the deformity, his face smooth and honest except for the frown that never lifted. I could not decide whether it was concern for me or for himself but as he began to speak I knew that I had misjudged him, he thought only of my distress.

'Don't be unhappy. It's so sad to see women cry. They should smile and make themselves busy with pretty things.'

'Albert.' I leaned closer to him but he turned his face away. 'You're almost a poet, where do you learn such words?'

He looked down at the spread of faded grass and weeds

157

under where we were sitting and crumbled some dry leaves between his fingers.

'I read. Can't do much else but read and walk in the sun.' He glanced up to where the sun was peeping over the roof once more and closed his good eye.

I watched his eyelid flicker, his long eyelashes touching the soft skin under his eye and the smooth rise of his cheekbone. If it were Owen here beside me, so close ... I bit my lip to force back the tears.

And then I thought of Hannah. All those years running round after the Cleery family; wiping up after them, guiding stubby fingers over awkward stitches, cooking and clearing up after endless meals, polishing silver, changing hundreds of beds and scrubbing the red tiles in the scullery. Did Albert know all this? Had he ever imagined her doing such things instead of smiling down at her own babies and making herself pretty for him?

She had told me once of the afternoon when he had told her he was going away to that other dreadful war. When he left she started to snip the crisp heads from the roses. In her angry clumsiness she had caught her thumb on a thorn and beads of bright blood had dripped onto her white apron. Swishing it in the basin, the flushed pink water had reminded her of the gully from the pig house when her father had killed a sow, and that made her tears more furious. She held up the dripping cotton to search for stains and struggled to hold in her tears. She knew she was not crying for the apron and her carelessness. She was haunted by the image of her dear Albert lying lifeless on some dusty plain, pierced by a native spear, flies buzzing round his damaged body. She knew that she could not bear it so she had walked away from him in the lane and kicked at the gate as the geese rushed at her, flapping and hissing. She had decided that she would not go and wave him off. If Albert Judd wanted to waste his life as a

158

soldier, in some war on the other side of the world that was no concern of young Englishmen, he would do it without her blessing. So he had gone, and returned nine months later a damaged man, no longer the Albert she had known.

Those words had thrilled me when I first heard them. I found the idea of true love a fascination which I longed to experience. The pain of separation was all part of that fascination. I was sure that one day Hannah's love would re-emerge and captivate Albert again. But when I was old enough to understand and the fear of Owen's leaving became more than a recurring nightmare, I saw Hannah's suffering for what it was.

'Lost your tongue today?' He let the brown curls of leaf fall onto his outstretched legs. 'What are you thinking?' He rubbed his hand along the brown corduroy and I saw it for the first time; sensitive fingers, made for some gentle occupation, not for wielding a rifle or a bayonet, not for taking people's lives. I put out my hand and gave his a squeeze.

'Do you remember Owen, Albert?'

'Of course. In France, is he?'

I felt my fingers loosen in his and I drew my hands together across my knees. 'Yes, he's in France.'

'He didn't seem like a soldier, your Owen.'

'No, he didn't.'

'Henry is in France. Haven't heard from him for months though. We don't know where he is.'

'Your mother will be worried.'

'He's no letter writer. Lucky if we get a field postcard from him.'

'Does he mind soldiering?'

'I don't suppose he likes being told what to do but he's no choice out there, has he?'

'Not really.'

He looked at me with his head on one side. 'You're sad. Nothing happened, has it?'

'No, I'm fine. Talking about Owen makes me serious.'

'It would be good for you to see each other, he must be due for a spot of leave.' He smiled and put his fingers under my chin to raise my face. 'Smile for me.'

'Albert, can I ask you something?'

'Go ahead.' He dropped his hand.

'Were you and Hannah...?'

He turned away and nodded uneasily.

'Poor Hannah.'

He tried not to look at me but he could not resist the pull of my curious eyes. 'It was my doing. I didn't want her to feel obliged to go through with it after what happened. It wasn't right to load her with an invalid.'

'But there has never been anyone else, Albert.'

'I know.'

'Have you thought of asking her again?'

'No.' He shot up and plucked at the branches above his head until they caught in his hair. 'I couldn't ask her now. She's made her life with you, she's quite content.'

'Is that what you believe?'

'It's true, isn't it?'

'Come up to the house and see her.'

He shook his head and peered up towards the roof of the cottage. The sun had slid behind it. The air was suddenly chilly. 'Are you going home? I'll walk you.'

I gave the garden a final look and he caught my arm. 'Was it Owen who brought you here?'

I flicked at the dry leaves on my skirt and nodded without looking up.

'I can understand why you're sad.'

'How could you bear it, Albert?' I stopped him with my hand on his empty sleeve tucked into his pocket.

'I could only bear it, what else could I do?'

160

I walked ahead of him and as we reached the top of the slope to the woods I turned and offered my hand to help him up. Suddenly I did not care what Owen had done, I knew only that I must have him back.

Stern daughter of the voice of God! O Duty!

William Wordsworth (*Ode to Duty*)

Carleton Gazette, Friday 28th April 1916

At a recent meeting in Carleton Town Hall, the notions of duty and responsibility formed the core of a Tribunal held to consider the appeal of Mr Matthew Parker, 22, of Riverwalk, Carleton, against military service on the grounds of a conscientious objection.

Under the direction of the War Office and as a result of the Military Services Bill of January this year, Tribunals have been established to consider the status and fate of individuals who refuse to engage in military service.

On this occasion the Tribunal, chaired by Alderman Percival Jones, a respected local businessman, proprietor of Jones and Son, builders, convened in the council chamber at 3 p.m. on Wednesday 26th April. Members of the Tribunal were: Mr Anthony Braine, solicitor, Mr Malcolm Wallace of Wallace Drapery, Mr Jeremiah Adcock of Adcock Textiles, Mr Alistair Grove, manager of the Lancashire Bank in Harbury, Councillor Albert Morris of Morris Engineering, Mr John Read, Headmaster of Harbury Church of England Aided Junior Mixed and Infant School, the Reverend Oliver Green, Vicar of St Oswald's Church, Carleton, and Colonel Harold Smythe representing the Lancashire Regiment.

Alderman Jones opened the proceedings with an invitation to Mr Parker to explain as fully as possible the reasons for his position. The young man stated that as a Christian he considered the taking of life as incompatible with the teachings of Christ. He was asked about his affiliations and gave St Oswald's as his church. When asked if he would be prepared to undertake military service of a non-combatant nature, Mr Parker, without hesitation, answered that he was unwilling to participate in any kind of military service because he saw that as an indirect support of the war.

The examination was taken up by Mr Anthony Braine, who suggested that an involvement in some medical support might be a suitable way to demonstrate Mr Parker's Christian responsibilities. But Mr Parker refuted this argument on the grounds that any work of this kind would be merely making men fit and well in order that they could be sent back to the Front more quickly. This he said was 'unforgivable and wrong'. At this point it became clear that Mr Parker, who had started with a certain unease, was beginning to feel more confident in his presentation to these strangers whose sympathies were a complete unknown to him.

But Mr Braine refused to let his refusal rest without further challenge. He insisted that by such supportive actions would not Mr Parker in effect be helping to shorten the war? '... the more able men we can provide, the quicker this conflict will be brought to an end...'

Mr Wallace, noting the young man's agitation, attempted to create a more gentle approach. He turned the discussion to questions about Mr Parker's conduct as a boy and wondered whether he had taken part in fights. Mr Parker's prompt response was that he 'kept clear of trouble like that'. Colonel Smythe immediately interrupted, expressing his dismay that any boy who had gone through the school system in England should have been allowed to develop such 'cowardly values'.

Mr Parker's annoyance at such a remark was clear when he reaffirmed that 'nothing justified violence and murder'. The Colonel was quick to respond by explaining that 'killing Germans is not murder. It is our Christian duty to wipe them out!' He followed this with an appeal to the young man for his definition of duty. His answer clearly stated references to obligation and respect but he was somewhat confused when the Colonel pushed him on the nature of moral and legal obligations. Our readers will be familiar with this particular argument, which has been aired in these pages over the months since the introduction of the Derby Scheme in the autumn of 1915.

However, Mr Parker gave a good account of his particular interpretation of duty, giving examples of his family, the church and the children with whom he worked. But this did not satisfy Colonel Smythe, who went on to emphasise the legal position as set out in the Military Services Bill: '...any man between the ages of 18 and 41 years of age should fight to defend his country...' and Mr Parker could not deny it. According to the Colonel, this highlighted some serious inconsistencies in the young man's personal philosophy and he warned the other members of the Tribunal to be vigilant.

Alderman Jones chose this moment to invite the Reverend Green to present the religious aspects of the case. With his usual dedication to Biblical authority, the Vicar of St Oswald's gave several instances from the Holy Book that refer to war and man's response to a challenge in conflict. Mr Parker seemed bemused by the cleric's allusions to Moses's warrior

God and St Paul's urgency that man 'put on the armour of God'. However, Reverend Green continued to present an excellent justification for the present war. He attempted to comfort Mr Parker in his reassurance that 'God is on the side of right and justice'. He appealed to him to remember all the other young men who had gone without question to France in Christ's name, '...young men with families and responsibilities but they do not hesitate to answer the call of their country ... they are carrying the flag for Jesus with pride and selfless courage'.

Mr Parker had little to say in answer to the Vicar's appeal, so Alderman Jones called for any other questions from the members. Mr Adcock wished to know if Mr Parker was a member of any political party and if he had attended meetings of the Independent Labour Party held in the council chamber. With some amusement, Mr Parker explained that his work with local children took up all his time and that he had none to spare for 'the trivialities of politics'.

The final question came from Mr John Read and concerned the hypothetical situation so regularly cited in these cases: that of Mr Parker's reaction if a German soldier were to threaten a female member of his family. Mr Parker stated that he would do his best to protect the victim of such an attack but he would be unable to use violence, as violence was no solution in such a situation.

Mr George Cleery was called as the first witness to represent the appellant's character. Mr Cleery is a respected member of the community, the Headmaster at the Board School in Carleton for the last eighteen years. He had known Mr Parker since he was a pupil at the school in 1903 and had always found him to be a reliable, sensible and sincere individual. When questioned further on the young man's sincerity, Mr Cleery defended him as a devout Christian who gave his time unselfishly to the church and the community. Although a quiet, unassuming character, he was well-liked by the local people and known for his valuable voluntary initiatives and inspirational energy with the poorer children of the town.

Colonel Smythe thanked the Headmaster for his 'glowing tribute' but suggested that perhaps there was something sinister in Mr Parker's eager involvement with impressionable young people. He went on to ask, '...was it not dangerous for him to be a part of the process which instilled moral values in our young?'

This uncompromising claim was denounced promptly by Mr Cleery, who added this tribute to the young man in question: 'Matthew is nothing if not tolerant. He possesses the integrity to respect the independence of an individual and would never deliberately set out to influence others with his own opinions. As I understand it, he has taken this present position to safeguard the freedom and sacred nature of the human personality. It is totally against his honest nature to insult an individual's integrity.' These words, so eloquently presented, left the Tribunal stunned. Then the Chairman invited a surprising witness to come forward.

Father Fortune is the parish priest of St Theresa's in Carleton and has known the young man for more than four years since he became involved in a boys' club run by the Roman Catholic parish. The priest began by questioning the Chairman about the doubt expressed over Mr Parker's motives. Colonel Smythe resented the priest's approach and immediately asked him, had he not wondered why Mr Parker was not away fighting for his country. Father Fortune stated that he was satisfied with the young man's justification and that he respected his conviction and his right to interpret the Lord's teaching in his own way. Had he volunteered for military service, he feared the young man would have been betraying not only his faith but himself.

These remarks gave the Colonel the opening he needed to return to the young man's response to the nature of duty. He was eager to know which was more terrible – betrayal of country or betrayal of oneself? Mr Parker showed no hesitation in affirming his loyalty to himself, thus confirming the Colonel's opinion that 'selfishness and self-preservation were at the root of this young man's problems'. However, the priest countered with a further illustration; he believed that most young men at the Front, if they were asked to examine their motives and beliefs, would come out with similar or even conflicting views. 'The truth is,' he proclaimed, 'that most of our soldiers do not know why they are there and I see that as a very dangerous and unacceptable position. But those individuals with a strong faith have made it their aim to understand and respect themselves and consequently will show a respect for their comrades beyond that required by military law.'

Colonel Smythe was eager to know how Father Fortune had gained such enlightening knowledge and the priest was able to support his views with evidence; he had spent several weeks in France in 1914 and 1915 attached to a Red Cross Hospital. The Colonel was sceptical of the validity of such exposure, claiming that a hospital was not the front line, and that where men are sick or injured they are not necessarily in control of their feelings. 'War is an emotional experience. It may weaken their sense of reality.'

Father Fortune claimed that on the contrary, he believed that suffering heightened men's feelings and allowed them to display great honesty – a quality which he considered to be 'sadly lacking in so many areas of authority and accountability today'.

At this point, Alderman Jones attempted to rescue what was becoming a debate on the situation in France. The other church representative was asked to contribute one final question with direct relevance to Mr Parker's situation. In response Reverend Green asked for a statement of the Roman Catholic Church's view on the war in case the young man in question had been 'unwittingly influenced by his contact with such an institution'.

'The Roman Catholic Church,' began Father Fortune, 'is very clear on this matter. It follows the conditions established by St Thomas Aquinas; a just war must fulfil the following conditions: it must be fought with the authority of the sovereign, the cause must be just and the military actions taken should bring beneficial results.' The Chairman accepted this explanation and went on to say that he could not see any conflict between those conditions and Mr Parker's statement of conscientious objection. But Reverend Green insisted that the term 'just' was ambiguous and 'dangerously open to individual interpretation'.

By this time everyone was becoming restless and the cleric's point fell on deaf ears. Alderman Jones called on the members to consider some satisfactory conclusion to this problem and suggested to the priest that perhaps he might find some useful role for the young man in the community through which he might contribute to the war effort. This was readily endorsed by Father Fortune and the members retired to discuss their conclusions.

It will be several days before the final fate of this young man is known. It is to be hoped that whatever the outcome, no slur will be levelled at the loyalty of the citizens of Harbury and Carleton in the conduct of their response in this dreadful conflict. As is our usual policy in such contentious matters of interest, we invite our readers to comment on the progress and the outcome, when known, of this disturbing case.

April 19th 1916

Mrs S. Judd
4 Catherine Street
Carleton
Nr Harbury
Lancashire

Madam,

I am directed to inform you that a report has been received from the War Office to the effect that 443610 Private Henry Judd, 2nd Battalion, Manchester Regiment, was sentenced after being tried by Court Martial to suffer death by being shot and his sentence was duly executed on April 11th 1916.

Captain Ryder-Jones

for Officer Commanding

April 30th 1916

My Dearest,

This evening I returned from the country. Aunt Vi
and Uncle Edmund send their love. They made us
very welcome and for a few days we managed to talk
of something other than the war. It is sad to see older
people distressed by what is going on. They appreciate the devastation on our generation more than we
do; we're too close to it.

Poor Edmund, he's lost so much of his lively manner. No more little jokes or digs at Violet's fussiness
or scolding. And Violet seems to consider before she
opens her mouth.

Becca even forgot for a while. The last few months
have been so dark with Edwin gone. She doesn't possess the experience to see beyond the hurt and imagine what might be round the corner. I think we would
all benefit from seeing you come home on leave. To
be in your company and know that some of you will
be kept safe and returned to us. Pray God, it won't
be much longer.

I had a long talk with Alice about you. I'm glad
there has been some resolution. A prison hospital will
probably suit you, you'll be able to feel you're doing
useful work without being directly involved. Alice
made me feel so much easier; she knows you so well
and tiny snippets of memory were a reassurance.
Images of you chasing Alice through the snow or
studying butterflies or stomping the hills with your

father helped to blank out my picture of you alone and brooding on all you might have to do for the sake of duty. Alice was so confident of your good sense and control but I don't think she understands as I do the risk to your soul of all this.

You'll be cross with me but I spoke with Father Fortune. I needed to seek the opinion of someone objective, someone who does not know you and who recognises the spiritual side of existence. That is the part of you that is in peril. He was very sympathetic although he has not heard of anyone declaring a conscientious objection once he is in military service. Your one course seems to be the NCC, an option you mentioned in your last letter.

Father had to appear as a witness at a Tribunal for a CO – you'll remember the young man involved, Matthew Parker. He won't talk about the details but he seems very upset and confused and it has certainly shaken his attitude to the war. Since Edwin's death he has never questioned the motives of those involved; popular notions of duty and responsibility were far removed from his view of what good citizenship was about. Since the unfortunate experience he has been reading all the literature and has discovered the No Conscription Fellowship, which has been running since the start of the war. Initially it was a pacifist group, set up to oppose conscription, but after the law was changed in January they switched their opposition to one against military service and other services that might prolong the war. There was an article about it in the local paper along with a report of Matthew's case. There is an address if you need it. Let me know if there's anything I can do, it seems so little but I'm here waiting with only your well-being to occupy my thoughts. I pray for your safety and ease of mind, for a relief of Lily's loneliness and mother's sadness and poor father's endless patience which seems constantly under pressure.

It's Lily's afternoon off and we usually meet and walk if the weather is fine. She is so brave she makes me ashamed. She has to work so hard and her life at home is not easy. You'll be glad to hear that she and mother are great friends once more. I've prayed for it since Edwin was taken away. They have been a great strength to each other, sharing snatches of memory and recalling how happy he made them both. It is sad to consider how many other such friendships have been strengthened or lost by the torture of separation and uncertainty that is the touchstone of this war.

Write to me soon. Every day you seem further away and I can't get your bewilderment from my mind. It stretches like some grey shadow between us and I feel, in spite of all that is happening, that I am in some dreadful limbo. I have stopped growing up. I'll still be a girl when you come back a man. I understand why you find it difficult to write but your last few notes, although short, have been a strange comfort. A blank piece of paper would be acceptable; you would still be thinking of me. Above all, my darling, don't be ashamed of what you are compelled to do, I will love you always.

Ruth

Prison Hospital, Boulogne

May 18th 1916

My Darling,

This letter is a sad one. I promised there would be no more like this but this is unavoidable. By now you will have heard about Henry Judd. I hope you will be able to offer some comfort to Albert and his mother. I have little to offer but I feel you should know the manner of his unfortunate end.

When I arrived at the Military Prison Hospital I didn't know what to expect. There were gruesome tales of the brutality and the appalling conditions. In a way this was welcome as some sort of punishment for my failure to continue at the Front. Everyone was reasonable but underneath I could sense their disgust at what I was doing. No matter what my justification, I was a coward, plain and simple.

The establishment at Boulogne is a Field Punishment Barracks – in layman's terms, a prison. When I was introduced to the CO, a savage and arrogant chap, he left me in no doubt about the consequences of my action. It was clear that he had no time for shirkers who denied their responsibility. He did not approve of the Non-Combatant Corps and made use of its members only because he was short of men. It was his belief that prisoners were privileged to have a hospital; they did not deserve it and should be allowed to die and save the army a great deal of unnecessary expense and bother.

You can imagine my state after meeting a man like that and I was determined to make myself as indispensable as possible. The men are cramped into cells of only 11 by 11, three or four to a cell. In some I noted as many as five. There is no sanitation and beds are basic, with the minimum of bedding. Rations are almost starvation. Most of the men have committed what in civilian life would be considered serious offences: robbery, violent attack or even murder – they are criminals. However, there are some unfortunate cases of persistent drunkenness and failure to carry out orders. These inmates are treated as severely as the tough criminals.

Henry Judd was brought here in April after an incident in the Support Line where he left his sentry post and made his way back to the Reserve Line. He claimed he didn't know what he was doing but naturally no one believed him and he was arrested to await Court Martial. A young man who landed up in the hospital with a nasty infection in an old wound mentioned this red-head with an aggressive manner who had upset the sergeant and whom everyone expected to get the death sentence. I saw him after sentence had been passed but his mood seemed as defiant and provocative as I remember all those years ago. I will never forget him standing over Edwin after he'd thrown his books into the gutter. Somehow I could never quite forgive him for that meaningless act. I saw his punishment as a punishment for that as well; after all, Edwin died – what right had this careless and insensitive person to live?

Forgive my words. It would be no surprise to hear that people were saying the same about me after what I have done. As long as it is not you, I can bear anything. Still, it was a shabby affair, conducted hastily. According to the sergeant, the CO had recently received an order from the Chief of Staff that all cases of cowardice and desertion were to be punished by death. No excuses and no medical grounds to be accepted. This is what we have come to, my love. Killing our own, for what? Even the thousands on the Front Line would probably not be able to tell you why they were fighting the Germans, let alone why they were expected to execute their own comrades.

There seems little doubt in the authorities' eyes that Henry deserved his fate. He never had the make-up of a good soldier and his death in such a place might be used to effect as immediate discipline on other prisoners. But not all of them. The saddest are the conscientious objectors who have started to arrive here since March when the Tribunals refused to recognise appeals. You may not realise it but once a case has been dismissed by the Appeals Tribunal, an objector is called upon automatically and is deemed to have enlisted. If he refuses the call he is liable for prosecution for desertion and is handed over to the military authorities. Of course, under military law, the penalty for this is death. I don't think there have been any deaths yet but it can only be a matter of time. Don't tell your father any of this, it would upset him after his involvement in that Parker business.

Most of the fifteen COs here are sober, unassuming men who are content to blend into the background but there are a few who have refused from the start to obey the simplest of orders. They will not sign their paybooks and refuse to put on a uniform. This disobedience means that they have to appear on parade without clothes – a most degrading performance. At night they are allowed one blanket but during the day it is uniform or nothing. Persistent resistance results in a diet of bread and water, but only one cup a day, any other water is doctored with soap to prevent consumption.

I have found great strength in the fellowship of these men. They have a unity of purpose and share a mutual respect that is refreshing in these selfish times. They are not the unpatriotic and self-indulgent individuals that the government cites as a danger to law and order. In truth, they appear to be doing much good here by encouraging the real prison element to settle. Discussions are held and even the worst types join in a sing-song each evening. It's quite a sight, those ruffians chanting 'Soldiers of Christ' as loud as their lungs will allow.

There are a number of Quakers in the group who seem to have an odd mystical influence on the rest. They inspire serious talk about the possibility of peace as a result of Christian action – Christian in-action, the sergeant calls it! He's a dedicated man with no time for their ideas but deep inside I suspect that he feels a great sadness for their position. This is no place for the mild and inoffensive.

As for me, well, I'm here and I will make the best of it. Talk is a marvellous palliative and has the benefit of keeping everyone's mind off what is going on down the road. And there is always work. I'm becoming quite hardened to the squalor of what we have to deal with. Most is the result of inadequate hygiene – boils, skin conditions and stomach disorders. Not the most challenging of work but who am I to choose or complain? And it gives me the opportunity to watch and listen and capture all that goes on and store it away in my mental notebook. Not much time to write except for my diary but the experience does not need embellishing with too many literary terms so it's just as well.

I shouldn't expect you to write. I'll try not to be

177

disappointed if you can't bring yourself to do it but I will miss your tender and amusing letters. And who knows – one of these days you might even see me back home. It'll happen very swiftly so you won't know until I arrive. Perhaps that's for the best.

Think of me a little.

Owen

8

Regrets

'You're wearing that dress,' said Lily, running her hand over the smooth material.

'It's for Owen. If I dress for him I feel in some strange way that I may help him through this terrible time. He loved this dress.'

'It makes you seem quiet.'

I giggled. 'Lily, what do you mean?'

'Edwin.' She swallowed. 'Edwin called you wild once but in a white dress it can't be true.'

'Dear Edwin. He was too perceptive to be in a stuffy office. He was a thinker, a watcher of people. He loved to imagine their secrets but he could survive without them.'

Lily was twisting a piece of grey ribbon on the front of her dress round her finger. She didn't look up.

'Oh Lily, don't be sad, I didn't mean you. He needed you.'

'It doesn't matter now, does it?' She tugged on the ribbon and it came away in her hand. She clicked her tongue and stuffed it into her pocket. She ran ahead of me up the slope, swiping at the branches that grew close to the path. Her great fear was being a burden to another. In quiet moments the tension of clasping her emotions was noticeable. Her eyes became clouded with some secret grief that she refused to share. She feigned a brightness for those around her but underneath every action was a measured seriousness that jarred against her youth and seemingly carefree disposition. At such moments I found it difficult to approach her yet these were the moments when she needed me more.

'How is your mother, Lily?'

'She's quite well, thank you.' She was grasping at her old formality as a means of protection. Talk of Edwin had made her feel afraid for her position.

'And Harry?'

She frowned. 'He's still very angry. He feels bad about being here when all his friends are over there.'

'It's natural that he should feel upset.'

She paused and turned to look at me, her brow now smooth, with the beginnings of a smile, as if a reassuring thought had suddenly come to her. 'Odd, isn't it – he can't wait to go and Owen can't wait to come home.'

'Lily, does it bother you, Owen wanting to come home?'

'Bother me? Why should it?' She flicked at the dress where the ribbon had come off and pulled at some loose threads. This was the closest Lily would come to disapproval. 'Because of Edwin, you mean?'

I nodded, taking her hands. Those hands, once so perfect, were thin and red, the tips scratched and sore from all the work with a needle. 'Dear Lily.' I smoothed the inflamed fingers.

She pulled her hands away. 'I think Owen is right, if more people made a stand it might be over soon.'

'I doubt if the politicians and the military are aware of awkward individuals like Owen.'

'They must be,' protested Lily in her charming innocence.

I gave a sigh and put my arm through hers and we continued up the slope. 'Sadly, men like Owen do not make a fuss. They don't want to draw attention to themselves. It might be easier if he were more sociable and belligerent.'

180

'Can we stop here for a moment?' She pulled on my arm as we reached the top of the hill. She turned her face to the valley below, where the lake sparkled in the afternoon sun. 'Have you seen the swans? There were two pairs last year, one pair had four babies.'

'I never came up here.' My eyes were drawn to the other side of the valley and the clump of trees where Owen and I had strolled and laughed together.

Lily was searching the lake below, her hand held up to her forehead. 'I wonder where they've gone. They live for years with the same partner, did you know that? It's beautiful, isn't it?'

'Yes, Lily.'

'Edwin knew so much about birds.'

'Lily...' I tried to hold her close but she swung away from me.

'He was special, wasn't he?' There was a shiver in her voice as if she feared her original tender convictions about him might evaporate with time.

'Of course he was.'

'I wonder sometimes what would have happened to us if he had survived the war.'

'He would have married you, Lily. And you would have lived in a perfect little house in Harbury with lots of babies.'

'I'm glad you think we would have married. Sometimes ... I believe that after the war he might not have wanted me any more. He would have met so many exciting people. I'd be such a dull little dolt, wouldn't I?'

'What nonsense.'

'But it doesn't matter now.'

I took her shoulders and wanted to squeeze some confidence into her tiny body. 'Don't keep saying that, Lily. There will be other young men. Wait till Owen comes home, I bet he'll bring some smart handsome engineer for you.'

181

She laughed, shaking her head. 'Your mother says as much but I would be hopeless with anyone new. What would I say?' She turned towards the cinder path and I had to run to keep up with her. The grass had grown and handfuls of wild flowers were scattered under the trees: primroses, celandines and pale buds of pink campion.

'Everything goes on,' I whispered, stooping to pick a primrose. I studied the yellow petals and pushed it into the top of Lily's dress. 'You can begin again with Edwin's love to make you strong.'

She stroked the flower and looked at me with a sad smile. 'You always know the perfect words to make me feel better.'

'That's what friends are for.'

'I'm glad you went to see Father Fortune,' she said suddenly.

I put my arm round her shoulder and we continued down the path. 'He knew exactly what to say. He understood about our distress. I felt that he knew Owen; it was strange.'

'He's very perceptive and he has been over to France. I don't think anyone can forget that.'

'Yes, he told me about that little church where he found the picture of the Sacred Heart. He seemed so sure that the Germans would not destroy a picture of Christ.'

'Don't you believe that?'

'We don't know our enemy, do we? Owen says there is little place for the spiritual over there.'

Lily paused and bent to fasten her shoelace. When she looked up there were tears in her eyes.

'Lily, I'm sorry. Why do you let me go on like this? I only upset you.' I led her to a nearby seat and we sat with our hands twisted between us.

After a few moments she spoke more firmly. 'It's very sad to hear that but Owen has given you the truth. We

182

need that. If everything were left to our imagination, we would never understand.'

'I don't expect Owen to have anything to do with the church when this is all over. He's grown so cynical. Religion has become sterile to him, cold and detached from the warmth of any life that we know.'

'It gave our lives meaning once.'

'This war arrived at the wrong moment. We might have shaken the dull institution that called itself our church, rid it of all its petty doctrines and suspicious bigotry which have nothing to do with humanity. We had so many hopes and our needs were so urgent and seemed so right. Let's pray that enthusiasm won't be lost for ever.'

Lily's eyes were wide at my outburst. 'You sound like Owen.'

'He's been so wound up, I suppose I've been infected.'

'What will he do? Could Father Fortune help?'

'He read some of his letters and he feels Owen knows what he must do next. He's not a coward, he assured me of that.'

'Of course not.' She squeezed my fingers reassuringly.

'And he won't let himself be destroyed, I know that.'

'But what can he do?'

'This hospital may be his salvation. I know it's a prison but he could be useful there and he'll be with men who think as he does. He won't have that terrible dread that he is the only one. My fear is that he may be accused of disobeying orders or desertion because he's already volunteered. It's not usual to declare a conscientious objection once you've joined up.'

'What would that mean?'

'A Court Martial.'

Lily gasped. She understood the implications of such a move. She held onto me and closed her eyes. 'I will pray for him,' she whispered, 'I will pray for both of you.'

We were soon on the path that led across the middle of the park. A couple were playing tennis on the grass, the young man trying to show off his skills while his partner giggled and swiped awkwardly at the ball. Lily watched the young man as he took up his position so carefully between each service and prepared to receive his partner's wild balls. As he bounced sideways his hair flopped across his brow and he flicked it away with a toss of his head. Edwin had done that.

'Lily, are you all right?'

Her eyes were sparkling with tears and she brushed them away with the back of her hand. 'Yes, I'm fine. Come on, mum is expecting us for tea.'

'Are you sure?' I had to run to keep up with her.

'You cheer her up.'

I tossed my head to release my hair from my collar and laughed. 'I don't know why.'

9

Despair

Mother was wearing a bright yellow dress, the colour of spring. I wondered if it were part of a concession to the new season or perhaps it meant a fresh start with all the horrors of the old year pushed away. I was sure Lily had a part in it; she was so clever at persuading people to be optimistic even though she was not so easily bright herself any more.

A piece of tapestry lay across mother's knee, her long fingers working at the colourful stitches. She had gradually become absorbed in this activity, never allowing herself a moment of idleness. She feared unoccupied hands and a mind without focus lest the tragedy of Edwin's death find its way back into the routine of her life.

'How is Lily?' She looked up and selected a fresh length of scarlet wool.

'Tearful at times.'

'We must be patient. They knew each other so long.' She dug the needle into the canvas and bent lower over the petals of a pansy.

'Another cushion cover?' I lifted the corner of the material.

'For Violet's birthday.'

I moved round the room, touching things. Mother was watching me. The photographs on the piano needed dusting. I picked one up and studied the uncomplicated features of my brother, so protected and innocent of all that was to happen in his short life. He had rushed away to that awful place full of energy and blind enthusiasm for something he was not supposed to understand. It was evident that he had never imagined his death or the effect his absence would have on those near to him. But then if all those young men had imagined, none of them would have gone.

'Is father all right? He's very quiet.'

'That Tribunal business upset him.' She paused with the needle halfway into the canvas and rolled it up. 'Has he spoken about it?'

'He's avoiding it.'

'That's understandable.' She stared at me with a preoccupied expression and fumbled the tapestry into its bag.

'Because of Owen, you mean?' I was trying to be less defensive. I turned over the picture and examined the name of the photographer. What a strange occupation, recording a person's features and expression in that one instant. It was a serious responsibility, holding onto that moment. It could mean the difference between happiness and forgetting.

'Had things been normal, he would have discussed it with you. You know how he respects your opinions and you're such a good listener.'

I replaced the photograph on top of the piano and ran my fingers along the keys without depressing them.

'You haven't played for a while.'

'No, I can't.' I lowered the lid with a thud and was forced to attend to mother at last. 'I often felt you might resent it, our getting on so well.'

'Nonsense, I was glad. We needed to share the responsibilities of a daughter.'

'But we don't talk much, do we, you and I?'

She was thoughtful for a moment then she leaned

towards me. 'Not as much as I would have liked. Perhaps with Edwin not here ... we may grow closer.' She stroked my sleeve and drew me to sit down. 'I want you to know how much I appreciate your patience with me. These last months haven't been easy ... for any of us. I feel very fortunate to have you, and Becca, of course.'

'You should tell her.'

'She would find it embarrassing. She has no time for emotions.' She rolled the edge of her workbag, tracing the clumsy stitches. It had been Becca's hardest work during one of her rare practical phases.

'So what happened at this Tribunal, did he tell you?'

'I had to squeeze it from him. It seems the local worthies gave a confused account of themselves. They weren't familiar with their role, they misunderstood their powers and deliberately misrepresented the instructions they were given to suit their own personal convictions. To quote your father, "it was an abortive and fumbling attempt at justice and a total disgrace to our community".'

'Surely, they were supposed to be impartial?'

'In theory, yes. But with councillors and a cleric, how could you expect anything but bigoted confusion? I've never seen your father so bewildered. He didn't know whether to be angry at their ineptitude and suspicious hostility or upset for the young man's hopeless situation.'

'I met him once, Matthew, he was a harmless young man, rather sad. Owen knew him better.'

'And did he sympathise with his ideas?' There was a tone of gentle suspicion behind her question.

'No, not at the time. He expected his doubts to be satisfied when he arrived in France. He was willing to keep an open mind.'

'I see.' She curled her fingers round the bone handle of her workbag as though suppressing some painful reactions.

187

'Couldn't father protest at the way things went?'

'It wouldn't help Matthew. His real fury was with the military and the church. The whole performance seemed a gigantic indulgence for their benefit, especially Reverend Green.'

'Don't mention that man.'

'He does his job in very difficult times; you forget he represents the community's interests, and many of our young men are out there doing what Matthew refuses to do.'

'I can't see what is so Christian or representative about his attitudes. After that blustering speech last year I think he's betrayed anyone who has Christian feelings. And from the newspaper account it appears all he did was fling biblical insults at poor Matthew and imply he was indolent and insincere.'

'According to your father, it was his duty to refute the heresy of the pacifist. Unfortunately, no one could identify the heresy so there was no true case. Even that Smythe chap could only complain about Matthew's disloyalty as a citizen.'

'Disloyalty, when he spends all his time with those poor children? Is that to be a crime now?'

'He wasn't on trial. But they saw him as an insidious influence on the young. How do we know their suspicions aren't correct? Because his objection was unpatriotic they assumed he must forfeit the right to justice and a fair hearing. Even though they could not accuse him of anything criminal, he was made to feel a guilt that your father thinks was totally inappropriate. They implied that he shouldn't expect the basic needs of food and shelter from this community if he wasn't prepared to defend it.'

'I wish I'd been there. I would have told them a few truths, narrow-minded bigots. I suppose he's in prison now?'

'I think the Appeal Tribunal have upheld his application providing his work with the boys is supervised by a responsible person and he reports to the authorities. He won't be allowed to sit around doing nothing while all that goes on out there.'

'Do they trust him with those boys?' I sneered and flopped back into the chair. 'I don't know whether I should tell Owen any of this.'

'Why not?'

'It might upset him ... when he knew Matthew.' I sensed the change in mother's mood as we had discussed the case and I knew that she was undecided about the whole process. Her natural instinct for justice and fairness was still present but it was overruled by her unease about the acceptance of such individuals in our community.

'Is everything all right between you?'

I felt the tears behind my eyes. 'Things are pretty bad.'

She touched my cheek with the tips of her fingers and drew it round. I knelt at her feet and clasped her shaking hands to steady them. 'Mother, I wish you could tell me that Owen will be all right, but you can't.'

She smoothed my hair and kissed my forehead. 'Owen would never do anything reckless, he has you to come home to when all this is over.'

'What if he can't wait until it's all over?'

She snatched away her hand. 'That's foolish nonsense. Owen knows his duty, he's a serving soldier. Put that thought out of your silly head.'

'Mother...'

'I won't listen to such talk. He could never leave his friends ... especially after what happened to Edwin. You must tell him how you feel about it.'

'But I don't know.'

'Talk to your father.' She stood up and crossed to the window. The sun had risen above the tops of the trees in the park and a patch of sunlight had squeezed into the room. She closed her eyes.

'Help me, mother. You were always so wise.'

Her eyes snapped open. 'Wise! Was it wisdom that lost my son and pushed my daughters away? And my silent husband, I wonder sometimes how he sees my wisdom now.' Her eyes filled up and she was unashamed of surrender. She recognised that it was only one more pathetic symptom of her weakness. 'We should stop this conversation.' She wiped her eyes on a lace handkerchief.

'Mother, what am I to do?'

'Not another word.' And she put her finger to her lips.

I paused to catch my breath. The heat had made me weary and I longed for a drink but inside the trees it was cooler. I was glad I had put on my muslin dress – Owen's favourite dress – the scent of violets still clung to the chiffon bodice and gave my memory a gentle nudge to remember his closeness. I was puzzled why I had been led to this place. I had not seen Albert since my last visit and Hannah told me that he had not stepped outside the house since Henry's death. It was strange, the bond between those two brothers; they were different but they were drawn together by the unfathomable thread of their experiences at the hands of authority.

The cottage had the same neglected appearance and I did not go in. Someone had been clearing the garden; the lawn had been trimmed and the neat flower beds, stripped of weeds, were bright with the rosettes of primroses and buds of bluebells. I made a seat by the apple tree and unfolded the red square that Maud had given to me and which now cherished her son's letters. So many words, such tragic joyless moments, yet an insignificant drop in the ocean of sentiments that must have poured from those pitiful and graceless trenches.

I flicked through them, all in order, still in their buff envelopes. I wondered how many had not squeezed through. Were they kept back because of the unpleasant and unfailing detail they contained? It did not matter. Once Owen's words had been composed and written, he had as good as told me.

I opened the top envelope and unfolded the sheets. As I read his words again, I wanted to conjure up his presence but the fear of disappointment made me resist. And if he were to appear I did not know what I would say.

My eyes were closed but I felt the warmth from the sun weaken as someone stepped in front of me. For a moment I could not see clearly the faceless figure, then I knew. I had no words of greeting or comfort for him, only my tears. I stared through brimming eyes and he bent to kiss away my tears. His face was pale and his eyes heavy with lack of sleep but their complexion had not changed. All that he had gazed on, all that he had been compelled to witness; the horrors reflected there could not extinguish their intensity or expression. They might be the same eyes in a different body sent to torment me. At last a whisper fluttered from my lips in between the kisses but I could only murmur his name over and over.

As the sun was gathered lower in the still air, we stirred. Owen had drifted into a light and dreamy sleep, his head across the folds of my dress. My fingers stroked the sandy hair, afraid to lose contact in case he was taken from me. The shadows of early evening began to take shape and I tried to free myself without disturbing his rest. I whispered his name, still not believing that he was truly there. He opened his eyes and gazed up at me then clung on as though he would never let go. I slid away and offered a hand to help him up. For a moment we were still; a ladybird flew into his hair and I let it crawl onto my hand. We watched it scrambling between our fingers before it flew back onto the collar of his coat.

'She won't leave you,' I whispered, putting out a finger. 'She feels safe.'

His eyes grew cloudy and he turned away, pulling at the collar of his great coat; then, clinging onto it with his arms around his chest as though he were reliving some awful moment from his experience, he leaned against the tree and closed his eyes. He had still not spoken and I didn't know if it was truly him or his ghost come to tease me.

'Owen.' I touched his arm and he cringed away. 'Don't be afraid.'

He found it hard to look at me. After all that had passed between us in those letters; all the pain and terror, the helplessness and the bravery; here he was close to me and he was fumbling for words.

At last he looked up. 'I'm sorry. I didn't know what to expect, I had no right to expect anything.'

'What do you mean?' I could not understand his lingering confusion.

He held my hands and drew my fingers to his lips. 'You didn't let me know how you felt about what I was doing. I didn't know if you would ever speak to me again.'

'Owen.' I brushed his lips with the tips of my fingers. 'How could you think that?'

'After Edwin.' He let my hand fall and reached out for the tree and stroked the ridges on the trunk as though he were reawakening his senses after a long sleep.

'You didn't think I would desert you because Edwin had been lost?' I asked incredulously. 'Oh Owen.' I ran across the grass to hold him close. Now the sun had weakened, his face was white and he was beginning to shiver. I started to fasten the buttons on his coat. 'I loved you when you went away. How could that change when you were

192

suffering so much? You could never be a coward to me. You were strong because you had faith in your own ideals. You had the resolution to turn away when it would have been simpler to accept in silence and carry on, watching more of your friends being slaughtered. If there is one things I will never forget, some words of that man – that cleric…' I spat out his title. ' "self-sacrifice is proof of love…" but for what purpose and for love of whom?

'You were not proving anything watching your companions suffer. Your sacrifice was to deny yourself the complacency and self-satisfaction that the rest of fighting Britain wallowed in.' I stopped, breathless and feeling my cheeks colour. 'Are you amazed that your delicate flower has found a true voice?'

He pinched my nose. 'You were never a delicate flower, my love.' He ran his hand down my dress, feeling the shape of my body under the thin fabric. 'And now I must get you home before I ravish you.'

'Owen Webb, have you no control?' I laughed.

'It must be something to do with the approach of darkness.'

I clutched the bundle of letters wrapped in the square as he led me away from the garden. 'Why are we going this way?'

'You'll see.'

We left the trees behind and there was the lake below with the hills in the distance like reclining shadows. Owen pointed at where the water was tinged with mauve from the shrinking sun. On the edge of the water were the swans, bobbing expectantly at the approaching figures.

He saw my eyes fill with tears and squeezed my arm. 'Why are you sad?'

'Those swans were Lily and Edwin's.'

He nodded. 'I think I need to apologise.' I tried to interrupt him but he held up my hand. 'No, let me speak. I

193

haven't long to make up to you – five days at most before I go back – I have to be certain that what I have chosen is what you expect from me.'

I sat on the grass and leaned back on my arms. He ran his fingers down the bare skin and I shuddered. We had not been physically close before he went away. Our fondness for each other extended only to holding hands and a kiss on parting. It had seemed natural to keep our desire for love under control as a measure of our respect for each other. But now I wasn't sure. If he were to be taken from me, I wanted to have experienced love with him so I would have some joy to remember.

'You must be strong for both of us,' he continued.

'Nonsense.'

'It is not nonsense. In some things I am weak. I can only be strong if I know that you understand and support me.'

'I know I couldn't write about it, somehow I feared that if the words were written down you might be lost, your choice might be snatched away. There was so much I needed to say to you but I couldn't even remember how to say "I love you". It should have been easy enough but the words wouldn't come. And you are here and the words are still out of reach. I've found you again and all my fears were groundless, you are still the same Owen. You have my blessing to do as you must.'

The sun was melting behind the hills, its rays touching the water for the last time that day. The water was stained with pearl, and the slim necks of the swans picked up the pink from the sky.

'What do you want most in the world?' I asked, searching for the violet from the sun in his dark eyes. 'Peace? An end to the war?' I was suddenly impatient for some promise, some resolution that included me.

'My love.' His words fell in a whisper.

'The return of joy?' I gave a sigh. 'Those are blessed

creatures, those swans. Do you think we will ever be blessed with their freedom?'

He frowned uncertainly then smiled. 'Freedom,' he repeated the word, his lips almost kissing the gentle sound.

1919

10

Truth

When I stood outside the sitting room I could hear father's voice, brighter and more buoyant than he had sounded for months, recounting some amusing incident with one of his more notorious pupils. Everyone laughed but Violet's giggles were the loudest and most irreverent. I could imagine Edmund's wince of disapproval as he tried to hide his embarrassment.

Dear Edmund, at a time when many had turned away from us, he had become an unexpected ally. He possessed an unrefined good sense that was refreshing when those around were struggling with the last desperate threads of a sickening patriotic fervour. He had found the time to take me aside and reassure me that his loyalty would not be shifted by snide remarks or inept accusations. For this understanding I had blessed him.

Mother was less fathomable. She approached each day with a mixture of muffled resentment and shadowy bitterness, though Lily's comfort had sweetened her temper. She was able to distract her from her eternal notion of the fragility of life. At last it seemed probable that there would be good things to anticipate and with every challenge she accepted she became stronger. One such challenge had been a terrifying argument before Christmas, terrifying to me as I saw for the first time a strange and alarming aspect of mother's nature.

I had been baking in the kitchen when she came in with a letter. She had been suffering with neuralgia for a few weeks and I was ready to excuse her black face but the letter was from Owen. She tossed it onto the table close to where I was rolling out pastry and sat down to wait.

'I thought you wouldn't be able to wait,' she said in a voice that was husky with unkindness.

'Mother, please don't.' I accepted these brief but sharp outbursts in the hope that she was working through them in preparation for her acceptance of Owen's tenuous and unsteady position.

'Aren't you going to open it? It's probably taken weeks to get here.'

I finished the pastry, cleared away the flour and rinsed the cloth under the tap. Mother's face grew more agitated at the deliberateness of my delay. She took a clove from the jar and started to suck on it noisily, like a precocious child who is being ignored. This behaviour was new and I despaired of ever being able to bring Owen into the house again.

I opened the letter carefully and laid the three sheets of closely written paper on my knee.

'What does he say? I suppose he'll be home soon.' She took out the clove and stared at it as though she did not remember what it was.

I ignored her disapproval and tried to respond normally. 'He's very busy clearing up at the hospital. There are still a lot of men too injured to move. He won't be home until after Christmas.'

'Oh, shame.' She popped the clove back into her mouth. 'Still, I didn't really want him over Christmas. It wouldn't be right, would it?'

'Mother,' I pleaded.

'Well, Edwin isn't here. Why should Owen take his place when he's done so little to deserve it?'

'That is cruel and it's also untrue.' I folded the letter and thrust it into my pocket.

'How do you know what he's done or hasn't done? You only have his word for it.'

'I believe him, mother. I trust him. Why would he lie to me when the truth is painful enough?'

'Is it indeed? I should have thought turning away from the fighting was easy. Skulking secretly in some hospital must have made a pleasant change.'

'I don't want to hear this, mother. You don't know what you're saying.' I rose from the table and put the pie in the oven, slamming the heavy door with my foot.

'I know perfectly well what I'm saying. I don't want that man in this house again. I don't want you to see him again. You owe it to Edwin's memory.'

I turned away, anger and disbelief flooding through me so that I wanted to hold her shoulders and shake her until the pain came away from her. How long had she been storing up all this bitterness, like some fine wine that had turned sour and become vinegar at the first sip? 'You can't say that to me, not after all that he's suffered.'

'My loyalty is to Edwin, as yours should be.'

'Least of all in Edwin's name. Owen was Edwin's friend. He would have been the first to offer Owen support if he had been given the chance. He respected an individual's freedom to follow his conscience.' I shook my head and knelt close to her chair, examining her face, trying to find some change in the features that would explain this unwarranted callousness. For months it seemed she had been settling to a more judicious and passive state of mind, this unthinking cruelty in her tongue was bewildering.

'You didn't know your son very well, did you? Perhaps that's why you have grown bitter. You've realised how little you knew about him and now it's too late.'

She shuddered and twisted her hands up to her chest.

She tried to turn her face away but I held onto her chin and made her look at me. 'Edwin had no time for hypocrites and that is what Owen would have been if he had carried on. Do you understand what that is, mother? Do you?' I almost spat the words in her face. 'Owen would have betrayed himself and been the worst coward imaginable, a moral coward. I respect him for his strength. Do you hear? I love him.' I flicked my fingers across her chin in a desperate gesture of frustration. I had no other way of explaining my feelings when Owen was far away.

I poured water from the kettle into the sink and heard her behind me, shuffling uncomfortably in her chair.

'You can't truly love him, not when he left his friends to die.'

I swished at the soapy water and stared out of the window. 'I've told you, mother, I love him, no matter what. I will be with him, no matter what you or anyone else thinks. I can't love anyone else.' I plunged the dishes into the sink and when I turned back, mother was sobbing quietly but desperately.

'You shouldn't speak to me like that,' she gulped, 'you've never done that before.'

'You've never insulted me like that before. Do you think I don't care what happened to Edwin? I feel furious and helpless about it as you do but I'm not going to let it haunt the rest of my life; neither should you.'

'He was my son, my dear son.' She leaned over the table and appealed to me to understand but I would not be drawn into some sentimental reunion that excluded the man I loved above all other.

'And he was my brother, but he wouldn't want us to live the rest of our lives brooding over his death. His memory should be our strength, don't you see?'

She shook her head and struggled from the chair. At the door she paused as if to add some thought but when I turned a stony face towards her she bowed her head in a gesture of desperate helplessness and left the room.

When I was around her now she put up a courageous facade; secret half-smiles curled her lips whenever she thought I was watching her. She deliberated over simple activities to assume a thought and attention that were out of place and she tried to show fine feelings that she did not truly hold. I was mystified by this good-hearted deceit when mother, although she had never expressed her emotions with enthusiasm, had never concealed her true fears before. But as the time for Owen's return approached I had to put her strange behaviour down to one thing – mother was afraid. She did not know how she would greet him. Her feelings were flimsy and unreal, like delicate flowers that shattered at a touch, and the pain of that alarming day when she had nearly lost her daughter was always present, an ugly shadow near her shoulder, forcing her to look ahead and never behind.

I opened the door a fraction and peered into the room. The scene gave me a warmth I had not felt for a long time. Father was standing with his feet apart in front of the fireplace, running his fingers over his watch chain. His face was fixed on nothing in particular but I knew that he was listening from the keen expression across his dark eyes. Although he looked older, the lines around his mouth and his eyes gave his face a reassuring quality, a settled 'grandfather' look, as Becca called it.

Violet was chattering about the journey home, which Edmund hated. She accused her husband of not enjoying it on purpose to add to her annoyance. The words came out with an odd slightly amused emphasis, so that if you did not listen carefully it was easy to lose their meaning. I could only smile at the way Violet deprecated her partner while at the same time moving closer to him on the sofa. For all their outward disharmony, they were as close to each other as ever.

Mother had learned to treat her sister's importunate words with caution; they may have sounded harsh and scathing but their true implications were harmless. In her present unsteady state she preferred to listen to that than be swallowed by her own inner uncertainty.

Edmund saw me first but kept quiet until I had slipped into my seat near father. He opened his sharp eyes wide in approval of my new dress. I could count on his support for any slight change to my appearance or personality. I had become the daughter he and Violet had never had.

Violet finished her little speech neatly, rounding off her words with a delicate cough as though filling a tiny space around her head so there would be room for no other words. 'My dear Ruth, what a pretty dress.' She leaned across her husband and rolled the silky fabric of the skirt between her fingers. 'Why have you never worn that colour before? It's such a striking pink and so perfect with your hair.' She turned on her sister as if about to accuse her of some mortal sin. 'You had a dress that colour, didn't you, Fay? I hated you in it, you were so slim and pretty.'

Mother smiled uneasily as her sister squeezed her arm. She did not enjoy being reminded of the past, even mellow moments seemed to impart to the future a grey inconstancy that was too painful. 'Ruth wears it much better,' she began, trying to please me. 'It lifts that pinched quality from your cheek, my dear. You look quite flushed.'

'Getting excited?' Father gave a most uncharacteristic wink and pulled out his watch. 'Ah, supper time. I'll see what's happened to Hannah.'

'She's out for the evening, father. I'll deal with it.' I moved to the door but he called me back.

'Don't run away yet, dear, we've been waiting for you.'

I sat down and felt their eyes as if they were expecting some memorable announcement.

'Well dear, aren't you going to tell us about Owen?' Violet's face was oddly serious as though, in deference to her sister, she treated his return as a matter of cautious celebration.

I glanced at mother but her features were impassively mysterious. 'There is little to tell, he should be home tomorrow, about noon.'

'Splendid.' Father rubbed his hands together and shifted his feet to a fresh position in front of the fire.

'You'll be relieved to see him,' said Edmund kindly, 'after all your trials...'

No one had expected such a remark from Edmund. Only I understood what he was trying to say and I loved him for his directness. He had the courage to hint at what everyone else thought but dared not say, that Owen's homecoming would be a terrifying ordeal for both of us and that we should be left alone to deal with it in our own way.

'Yes, uncle, we'll need our strength.'

Father was suddenly conscious of the direction of the conversation and to save his wife from any involvement he made a move to the piano. 'How about a little tune before supper, clear the lungs and so on?' he sat down and started to sort through the pile of music. I was aware of his straight back and broad shoulders, so like Edwin's as he had coaxed Becca into practising.

'Where's Becca?' I tried to banish the image from my head.

'She's out walking with Alice,' said mother.

'In the dark?'

'Alice wanted company. I didn't think you would want to go out tonight,' explained mother. 'Did I do wrong?'

'No, no. You're right. I couldn't go out tonight.' I

thought about Alice and Becca striding through the woods or across the hills, gazing at the winter sky and listening for the night sounds, and I longed to be with them instead of here with all this embarrassed distraction.

Becca had explained to me that afternoon how confused she felt about Owen's return. She couldn't imagine my feelings. She had given up hope of ever seeing Edwin again long before news of his death had arrived. And with his loss had come a blanking out of all those eager young faces that she had known and never counted on seeing again.

But this did not diminish her sense of loss. She envied Alice and her affinity with her brother. She had thought she was close to her brother but now she found it impossible to recall the shape of his face or the exact colour of his eyes; his features were an annoying concoction of all the young boys she had known.

I had tried to reassure her that Owen's return was confusing for all of us and that she mustn't be afraid to ask questions and involve herself in the difficult months ahead of Owen's rehabilitation. Then I remembered Alice and her optimism about everything and I recognised that I would not have to cope alone.

'What will it be, Violet? Come on.' Father held his hands over the keys.

She slid to the end of the seat and closed her eyes. Taking a deep breath, she folded her plump hands in her lap and began to sing in a deliberately subdued voice:

> *If I were the only girl in the world*
> *And you were the only boy,*
> *Nothing else would matter in this world today,*
> *We could go on loving in the same old way...*

11

Secrets

Hannah had come in late. Blushing and tongue-tied, she had told us about Albert's proposal. It seemed a fitting end to so many frustrating and empty years. I had known that it would happen from the moment Hannah had revealed her secret. Her love for Albert was so certain and her faith in the future so enviable.

I sat in front of my mirror and glanced at my few cherished things with a peculiar panic, as if I would have to snatch this moment to hold the memories associated with them. There were only a few drops of Edwin's violet perfume and I should keep them, fearing when they went that his presence might finally be lost. Tucked away behind Owen's photograph was a tiny wooden horse. I held it to my cheek and it was warm on my skin after the coolness outside. Hannah should have it; Albert had meant it for her but in his good nature had allowed himself to be badgered by a small girl with a voice that was too demanding. It was such a tiny gift but it signified a bond between them which Albert had feared; a mystical challenge to Hannah's good sense.

I picked up the hairbrush and began to smooth my hair. It was beginning to tarnish but I had turned away from meaningless tasks such as polishing during the war. Suddenly I was angry with myself and flung down the brush. My emotions were so muddled but I should be dizzy with happiness. I had seen Owen only once since our meeting at the cottage, a few hours wandering the damp streets and sitting in a gloomy public house before he boarded his train back to the coast. It had been a hurried and distressing visit which had given no sweet hope for the future of our relationship. Since, there had been a scattering of tangled letters, the words formed out of a sense of obligation to a sad friend rather than to a lover. That final letter was the source of the greatest soul-searching.

In it Owen was an older, sadder man. He had suffered as so many had suffered but he seemed unable to accept his moral weariness without question. But queries about death and defeat put in jeopardy the essence of why he was in that unfortunate position. He appeared to be growing in weakness rather than strength. Those who did not know him as I did would see him as self-obsessed and concerned with only his emotional well-being and moral survival. I knew that this was wrong but could not account for the dramatic change in his personality. Once these seeds of doubt had been planted they grew insidiously until I was beginning to doubt the most familiar aspects of him, like his physical strength or his ability ever to concentrate on a job again.

Far better had he arrived home unannounced. Imagine my joy had he come upon me in the garden while I was tidying a flower bed or while I dozed over a favourite book. I would have been ill-prepared but I would have accepted him as he was. That letter was like a splinter of wood which refused to be drawn out, persistent and mildly painful, a nagging distraction which refused to leave me.

I had thrown it away. At six one morning I had left my bed, sick and light-headed from lack of sleep, and run up the hill to the memorial. There, standing with my face to the wind, I had torn it into a tiny mosaic of pieces and flung them into the damp air. It was a childish prank, flippant and without meaning, but it made me feel some hope. Perhaps the man I was to meet would be the same gentle man who had been my comfort and support, my friend before all this uncertainty began. That was the man I loved and I dared not contemplate any other.

Becca and Alice had been longing to come with me but feared to intrude. I was sorry, I might have had someone to chat to on the draughty station. As the clock ticked away each long loud minute, I wanted to scurry away and hide, a nervous creature who did not understand fear.

The train lumbered into the station, hissing and groaning, impatient to disgorge its load. Everyone spilled out like terrified insects leaving an overturned stone and I wondered why I had not thought before now that I might not know him. He might be a stranger.

Stupidly, I had assumed that he would be the only serviceman on the train and that we would fall into each other's arms on the lonely platform. But here, smothered by all this soot and steam, hidden amongst blank colourless faces, I was suddenly filled with a new panic; he would miss me, he would not know me in my new coat and he would probably be looking for Alice and his mother and father.

As I tried to suppress this terrible ache I realised that I was not looking at any of the figures as they passed by. Most of them ambled until they recognised loved ones then broke into an uneasy trot, but none of them displayed the eagerness and excitement that should have been.

The entrance was ahead of me, drawing me from this place of confused emotions, leading me to the bright freshness outside where I could be myself, when out of the corner of my eye I sensed a hesitant shape, weighed down by a greatcoat and a kit bag. He paused to swing the bag onto his shoulder and, as he turned, the sunlight from the noon sun shone through the waiting room window and caught the top of his head, picking out the gold in his hair. He stopped, dropped the bag and called out, 'Ruth, is that you?'

'Of course it's me, you goose, come here.' And I opened my arms to reclaim him.

That first moment of closeness seemed to go on for ever yet it seemed over in the blink of an eye. I could not let go but wanted to push him away so that I could look at him. We did not kiss, I could not bear the thought of touching those lips until they were purged of all they had to tell. Others had drawn close, mothers and sons, husbands and lovers; soft broken shadows of people, made one shape by their love and joy at being together again.

'Let me look at you,' he said. It sounded like an expression of Aunt Violet's and I found myself giggling, which served to break the uneasy tension between us.

'I'm older, that's all,' I said glumly, allowing myself to be pushed to arm's length.

'You're more beautiful.' He squeezed my fingers up to his face and peered at me with his head tilted. 'but there's something different, I can't quite identify it...' He twirled me round before drawing me close. 'You've lost some of that mystery,' he announced. 'I always suspected you were holding some of yourself back from me. It's gone. You're not afraid of me, are you?'

'Of course not.' I snapped my hands together and put them under my chin, making a brief but necessary prayer. 'I've nothing to be mysterious about, have I? You were my only mystery and you're home.' I studied his features as he watched my movements. I had been right to expect a change. He could no longer pretend to be a fresh-faced raw youth, secretly amused at life's little turns. He was a man; cooler and more suspicious, the softness smudged

210

from his features as though an artist had worked away at his flesh with cruel, sensitive fingers.

'Say something,' I pleaded, disarmed by his stare.

'I was thinking how I imagined this moment.'

'I hope I'm not a disappointment to you.' I gave a pout in an attempt to be a provocative woman and not a girl.

'You could never be a disappointment.'

'Owen?' I wanted to ask him so many things but he wouldn't allow it. He was leading me away from the people, out of the steam and commotion as the train made ready to leave. 'Where are we going?'

'Does it matter?' He threw off his coat and slung it over his shoulder. He was leaner under all that bulky uniform and I guessed that, like most men, he would be looking forward to a decent meal. But he was eager to be out and after stowing his bag in the left luggage he raced ahead into the bright day.

'This was the only thing that saved me, the thought of escape into some fresh air and sunlight.' He squinted up into the trees and smiled at me. 'And your fine letters, of course.'

'I'm sorry they were so scrappy. I thought you would want to hear what was going on but when I tried to string it together, it seemed simply a list of names and silly events. Quite pointless.'

'Not at all. It was important for me to see Lily's new hat or Becca's new shoes or hear about Violet's little disagreement with the greengrocer. It confirmed that there was a life outside that war.'

'Maybe I could have helped more. I didn't realise how important the ordinary was.'

'Shush.' He silenced me with his fingers to my lips. 'It's all over now. Nothing matters but us. Relax, enjoy the air. Tell me when you get tired, I can walk for hours.'

We did not walk for hours. In the first village we

211

stopped and bought some bread and cheese in a little shop. When the old lady saw Owen's uniform she gave us some fresh baked scones wrapped in a napkin and a bag of sugared almonds. We struggled up the hill behind the village and sat under a chestnut tree to eat, feeding the crumbs to a bunch of hungry sparrows who dived from the trees.

'We must be mad, a picnic in January!' I laughed. I was beginning to relax, no longer measuring every thought which came into my head. I allowed myself a few blank moments of bliss without the inevitable apprehension of what was to follow.

'We don't need warmth, look at the sun.' Owen pointed up through the branches, suddenly aware of how much comfort that sun had given him over the months. 'You're not cold are you, darling?'

I was shivering. 'No, I don't know what it is.' I snuggled up close and he wrapped his coat around my shoulders.

He gave a sigh and looked out across the pattern of fields below. 'I hope you won't expect too much of me for a while, I'm so weary.'

'Don't think about it.'

'I have things to tell you, Ruth, such things you could never imagine.' There was an agonised thickness in his voice, like emotion swaddled up tight to protect it.

'There will be time for that,' I comforted. 'Plenty of time, now rest.'

He stretched out beside me and presently he was asleep, a deep peaceful rest that revealed nothing of the agony of his poor battered spirit. I could examine his features without fear of intrusion. He seemed changed in a mysterious way, indefinable and illusive, but I sensed from his earlier exuberance at being free in the country air that he was clutching some immense sorrow and disgust deep inside. It was as if it was not only a reaction to what he had been a part of but a greater one, to the sins man had committed in the name of duty and justice and freedom, and for which there could be no swift or decent redemption.

Owen stared at the food on his plate and the rest of the family looked at him. His father coughed, reminding them of what they were doing, and they started to eat once more, heads discreetly lowered over plates.

He glanced at me as if to excuse his lack of interest in food. He supposed they all expected him to relish a fresh-cooked meal, hot and well-presented and in the company of those he loved, but he had already told me it hadn't upset him, not being able to eat fresh meat or rich puddings. He had learned to enjoy the dry insipid flavours, the lack of fresh fruit, and tea like sweetened sump oil. He had made a sport of enjoying it as a means of reminding himself that he was fortunate to be alive. But he did not wish to upset his mother when she had so obviously taken care to make this meal special.

'This is splendid, mother.' He took a forkful of beef and creamed potato and dipped it into the horseradish on the side of his plate. The hot sweetness bit into the top of his mouth and he took a gulp of water.

Alice was laughing at him across the table. 'Owen, don't you ever learn?'

'Pass the water please, Alice.' He gave his sister a smug smile for his mother and father were too engrossed in their food to notice what was going on.

'When I watch you doing that, it could be yesterday,' whispered Alice.

'Nothing has changed here.' He nodded at the room and I followed his look as he took in the comforting clutter of nearly twenty years of occupation: books perched on the ends of shelves waiting to be put away, Maud's

213

sewing on the arm of her chair and his father's tobacco pouch in the corner of his, and family photographs dotted about on tables and cupboards.

'Doesn't it feel odd?' Alice was bursting with curiosity but she hesitated. She knew from her contact with men returned from the Front how reticent and mysterious they became. She looked at me for encouragement.

'It's almost as if I've never been away – apart from Alice grown up, that is.' He smiled and grasped her fingers across the table. 'Poor hands. Have they got you scrubbing floors up there?'

She pulled them away and started to clear the plates.

'It's terrible what they expect young girls to do. I don't know how she stands it.' Maud was suddenly interested in her son's opinion.

'Now Maud, Owen doesn't want to hear all that. We need to be bright and cheerful, isn't that right, Owen?'

'If Alice wants to talk about it I don't mind.'

'Alice doesn't want to talk about it. There.' She set an enormous fruit cake studded with golden skinned almonds in the centre of the table and offered Owen the knife. 'Please cut it for us.'

'I say, did you make this, Alice?'

'Of course.'

He measured its top thoughtfully with the gleaming knife. I recalled his account of how he had broken such cakes into hearty chunks for his companions to help down that dreadful tea and wondered if he was remembering too. How they had laughed at his fastidious manner of opening the brown paper parcel; untying every knot and winding up the string, folding each piece of paper into a neat strip and pushing it inside his boots for extra warmth. Not everyone had been so particular, most had ripped open the mystery shape, straight up the middle, as though attacking the belly of the enemy...

214

Owen gasped and found that he had hacked the cake in two and I leaned across the table and squeezed his arm. Alice helped him to divide half into more manageable pieces, her hand firm but gentle on top of his.

'I'm sorry, I should have done it. I didn't think. All those cakes we sent you,' she said with a shaky voice.

Maud rose from the table and hurried from the room.

'Shall I go after her, father?' Alice listened for her mother's steps in the room above.

'No, she'll recover in a moment. It's all been a little overwhelming.' John looked down at his half-empty plate and pushed it away. I sensed a quiet turbulence about their situation as though they were preparing themselves to hear and accept whatever Owen had to tell them. And until that moment John could not think of Owen as his son but merely as another unfortunate casualty of the war.

'Shall I go to her?' suggested Owen, watching his father's expression for some clue to the way things were moving.

John shook his head sadly. The change in his father must have been a surprise to Owen; his fine hair had thinned almost flat to his head and his flesh was paler and more solid around his neck. He had the same open expectancy around his eyes that had come from his years of listening to others' troubles but this would make Owen uneasy. He was not ready to divulge what he had experienced to this man or any other yet.

On our walk from the station he had apologised to me for the long silences and the lack of anything substantial or sympathetic to say. He found it difficult to understand that we expected nothing more from him, just to have him home was enough.

'Eat your cake,' ordered Alice with prim efficiency. 'I'll make some tea.' She left the room with the rest of the dishes.

215

A thick silence surrounded both men. Owen crumbled the golden crumbs of cake onto his plate and bit into an almond.

'You mustn't mind your mother. She's been very emotional since the end of the war. I think she squeezed it all up. We hardly had a tear while you were away.'

'I understand. Alice told me how brave she was.'

'We've all had to be brave.' He cut his cake into tiny squares and arranged them round the edge of his plate. 'Ruth especially.' He held out his hand to me and I clasped it across the table.

'We must all be patient with each other,' I said.

John nodded and popped a piece of cake into his mouth. 'Have you any plans, Owen?'

'I thought I might go walking for a few weeks.'

'Alone?'

'Yes, alone. Does that seem strange?'

His father thought for a moment. 'It's not for me to say how you behave after what you've been through; I've never experienced war or the strains of living closely with a bunch of strangers for three years. If it's what you need to do ... but how does Ruth feel about it?'

'I'm happy that he's safe.'

John piled up the squares of cake until they fell over the edge of his plate. 'Just as long as he doesn't take you for granted, young lady. It's been an ordeal for you too.'

Owen's eyes flashed. His father would think it was anger but I realised it was resentment at being told something so obvious.

'I'm sorry,' began John, 'I shouldn't have said that, it was unnecessary.'

'I want Owen to be happy, Mr Webb, more than anything else. So if a few weeks alone is what he needs to settle, I don't mind.'

'He's very fortunate to have you, my dear.'

216

'Nonsense.'

'Any plans for afterwards?' He turned to Owen.

'I'll write for a while, there's so much that needs to be said.'

'And can you make money at this writing? I hate to bring it up but if you and Ruth want to settle down...'

'Don't worry. I have something waiting when I'm ready.'

'That Major Burgon chap you mentioned?'

Owen nodded. 'He wants me to write a history of his family. I can take as long as I like.'

'Generous chap.' John seemed to have some doubts about Owen's commitment to such work. Owen had told me that his father was suspicious of anyone offering money for notional services. As a scientist, he was concerned only with facts and evidence; ideas were a confusing irrelevance to most of his work.

'I can see you're not easy with it, father. We'll discuss it when I get back.'

Alice came in with a tray and set it on the table. 'Mother is asleep.'

'That's a good thing.' John pushed away his unfinished cake and poured milk into the cups. 'Owen has been telling me of his plans. He's going to do some walking.'

Alice raised her eyebrows and glanced at me.

'I thought the Lakes,' Owen said quietly.

'That will be good for you. More men should do it.' She poured the tea but left them to take their cups. She sat by the window with her arm on the sill, staring out at the dim street. 'I hate January, it's so dismal and undecided. Christmas has been forgotten and spring is too far off. But this January will be special. Dear Ruth.' She turned to me. 'It's special for you, isn't it? Tell me, how do you feel about your lover toddling off to amuse himself with Wordsworth's ghost?'

I smiled and rose from the table to stand behind

Owen's chair. I put my hands on his shoulders and bent to kiss his hair. 'As long as he comes back refreshed and happy, he can take as long as he needs.'

'You must meet Stanley before you go, Owen. I've told him so much about you.'

'I should love that.' Owen leaned back and held onto my face.

'I've asked him tomorrow, I hope you don't mind?'

'Not at all.'

John was watching us and there was a deep expression of sadness in his pale eyes. He might have lost all this. Owen might have been killed. Alice might have gone to France had the war continued. I wondered if those thoughts had ever passed through his mind.

'Why don't you help me clear away, Alice? Let these two lovebirds have some time together.'

'Yes, of course.' Alice jumped up but before she started to clear the table she put her arms around both of us. 'It's lovely to see you together again. I didn't dare imagine this day.'

When they had gone Owen sat in a chair beside the fire and held out his arms for me to sit on his knee. I leaned against him and closed my eyes, so happy yet afraid in case something should snatch away my euphoria.

'You really don't mind about the walking?'

'Haven't I said?' I kissed the side of his neck and took in the warm mustiness of his skin. He had a different smell, a smell of uncertainty and pain; it was bleached into his skin and only time and perhaps the wild damp air of Cumberland would dilute it.

'Alice looks well.'

'Yes, it suits her, all that hard work.'

'And Stanley?' he smiled.

'Yes, and Stanley. Poor man. They've kept him on at the hospital, did I tell you, to manage the garden? It's the least they could do, considering how they messed up everything for him.'

'It wasn't their fault. Some injuries call for drastic remedies.'

'It's not the amputation – it's the way they expected Alice to tell him about it. It was so cruel and unnecessary.'

'Perhaps she was the right person – if she loves him?'

'She was concerned that a love grown out of pity might not last, although she's quick to claim that "an incomplete body does not mean an incomplete spirit".'

'But is he bitter? I would hate my sins to remind him and sharpen his anger.'

'Don't talk about sins, my darling.' I pulled myself up and looked at him sharply. 'Don't you dare call yourself a sinner, I won't have it.'

His brow creased then he pulled me close and stroked my hair. 'My love, what have I put you through? I am so sorry.'

12

Joy

It felt wonderful to have Owen home. Even the most ordinary actions like walking down a familiar street held a certain magic and I was conscious of a permanent smile on my face, so obvious that I think poor Lily thought I had been touched by the spring sunshine. There was a strange excitement in the town that infected everyone. As I walked back up the hill beside the park people who passed said 'good afternoon' with bright smiles. Some of the young men had a weariness about their grey faces and hunched slow movements but the women had taken trouble over their appearance and some were wearing new hats. I wondered how long the novelty of peace would be safe from the tarnish of real life which still had to be lived.

As I let myself into the house the quietness was oppressive and I hoped that I wouldn't find mother in one of her uncommunicative moods. She was in the sitting room with a book in her lap but she wasn't reading.

'Ruth, you're back early?'

I flopped on the sofa and pulled off my hat. 'Lily's very busy. Everyone is wild for new clothes.'

She tutted to herself. 'I hope she's not overdoing things.'

'She loves it, mother, and it gives her something to think about.' I watched her across the dim room. She still held herself like a young woman, erect and confident, physically in control in spite of her pain. Many admired her strength when compared with the helpless women who had capitulated so easily, ignoring the family they had left, but I wondered secretly if it wasn't all a charade. Her self-possession was beyond question but underneath I detected a trembling shadow of a woman, terrified to let go.

'Of course. Is she still coming tomorrow?'

'Yes, and I reminded her about the scarlet wool.'

'Good. And did you have a lovely tea?' She was indulging in small talk to keep me from talking about Owen. She knew that since he'd gone away I longed to do nothing else.

'Splendid. I had three cakes and Lily hardly managed a half. But I'm in sympathy with Owen up there in the hills with his dry bread and berries, so I had his share as well.'

'Are you still angry with him?'

'Angry? No. I'm disappointed. I suppose my happiness and enthusiasm were too much for him to bear. He needs stillness. I'm bored with three years of meagre miserable thoughts – I want to laugh and forget about the past. Mother, we should talk while Owen is away.'

'I've wanted to... I've had time to think and I want to help you if you'll let me.'

I couldn't answer, I simply stared at the tiny buttons on a blue dress I hadn't seen before and wondered if this was part of her charade or a genuine attempt at reconciliation.

'All those things I said,' she continued, 'they were said in anger. You know that, don't you?'

'It was very cruel.' There, I had come out with the words that Owen had advised me to forget and replace with more understanding.

'I know,' she replied quietly, 'but I'm not angry any more. If he'd come through that door during those months after Edwin's death, I could not have spoken to him, but that frustration has gone now. Of course I'll

221

never forget but I am trying to forgive. And if I've still seemed strange, it's because I'm afraid for you.'

'Afraid?'

'You don't understand what you'll be taking on.' She plucked at the front of her dress, distracted by her admission and uneasy at my possible response. 'I think sometimes that you don't want me to forgive him, in an odd way, it would be a betrayal of Edwin and you don't want that.'

'Is that what you think? You're wrong. And I do understand.'

'You seemed so obsessed with Owen, but it was more than love and a longing to have him home again. You wanted to give him some sort of heroic quality which I am sure he wouldn't want. You wanted to exclude everyone from his moral victory.'

I could not believe what I was hearing. Never before had mother spilled out her thoughts and feelings so savagely. Her honesty made me feel vulnerable. She was correct, of course; I had cloaked Owen in a mystical valour which was totally undeserved and out of character. My brief time with him since his return had allowed me a glimpse of his nature, which was not as disturbed as I had feared, so I should work at refining my myopic view of him while he was away.

I knelt before mother's chair and clasped her hands. 'Thank you for that. I know it wasn't easy for you.' I swallowed, my mouth dry with emotion. 'But you are perfectly right. My vision has been totally flawed. I focused on the good things that might have resulted from Owen's actions. He wanted me to see him for what he was and not build him into some virtuous character returning from some personal moral crusade.'

'Don't be too hard on yourself, he wouldn't want that either.'

'I wanted to keep his triumphs for myself. I enjoyed the

struggles with my emotions and you're right, your disapproval gave them more validity. But I didn't care about his dear mother and father or Alice. As far as I was concerned, Owen came back for me and that was all that mattered.'

'Ruth...'

'It's all right. I need this. His absence gives me a chance to redeem my misguided feelings.'

'Wait until you have been with him for a while before you talk about modifying your feelings – you may not have seen the true Owen yet. You said yourself – he wasn't ready to talk about it. You both need time to adjust and to learn to love each other again.'

'I've never stopped loving him.' I looked towards the window where the dusky shadows were touching the glass. 'We're very similar, you and I. That's why our relationship hasn't been smooth. I should learn from this and take reality as my guide, not a dream.'

'It won't only be Owen you have to cope with. People around here may be critical and suspicious. It's going to be very difficult for you, both of you. Everyone will be watching and waiting for Owen to make mistakes and crumble under the pressure of disapproval.'

It was clear that she had been preparing these words but I was relieved they had come when they did. They were hard but they served a double purpose: they prepared me for the ordeal ahead and they brought me closer to the woman from whom I had drifted but for whom I still had a need.

'Ruth...'

'I'm all right. With you and father to support us – and John and Maud – we'll survive.'

'Don't forget Lily.'

'And Lily. It did cheer me up being with her, she is so happy now.'

'How do you account for that?'

223

'Has she mentioned Billie Judd to you?'

'No.' Mother smiled with relief.

'It's good for her, isn't it,' I suggested, 'to have a new friend?'

'Oh yes, Edwin would be pleased that she is happy at last.'

'It was quite funny how it came up. We were sitting in Walker's tea shop when there was an almighty commotion outside. A runaway horse from Jackson's delivery yard came careering round the market place, terrified by a length of rope caught in its tail and slithering after it.'

'Good heavens, what happened?'

'The door of Wallace's shop flew open and Billie Judd flung himself down the steps and into the path of the frightened animal. He clung onto his neck and managed to steer him towards the wall of the Rose and Crown. It was uncanny – he suddenly stopped with his nose touching the bricks. Billie ran one hand down his trembling neck and fondled his ears with the other. We could see him whispering towards the horse's lowered head. Eventually he was calm enough for Billie to remove the tangled rope from his tail and fasten it round his neck to lead him back to the yard.'

'Well, well. What an adventure. I wish I'd come with you now.'

'Lily was secretly proud of him, I could tell. Her face had a lovely flush and her eyes sparkled.'

'I'm so pleased. She deserves to be happy.'

'Yes, she does.'

'And so do you, my dear.'

13

Stardust

It is a little stardust caught, a segment of the rainbow which I have clutched...
Henry David Thoreau (*Walden, or Life in the Woods*)

'That's beautiful.' I stood under the apple tree and pressed my cheek to the grey-green bark. My eyelids closed and I waited for more but Owen snapped the book shut and slipped it into his pocket.

'Too much Thoreau will upset your digestion.' He smiled. 'We mustn't spoil it.' He nudged his face into my hair.

'Words become so important, don't they? Physical things are almost nothing.'

'Some physical things.' He pushed his body more firmly against mine and for perhaps the first time I acknowledged its urgency. I had not thought about desire very much. Of course I had wanted Owen to be there, to feel his hands clutching mine, his head relaxed on my shoulder, his arms protecting me, but that was all. Only since he had returned and abandoned me again had I recognised the ache inside that would only be eased and comforted by the closeness of his body.

I moved my face to see him more clearly. How many times had I longed to see that wide-eyed expression as I collected and organised my thoughts together for him? 'You're not disappointed, are you?'

'Disappointed?' He blinked, spoiling the softness of his look. 'In what, for heaven's sake?'

'Me, what else? I thought with you dashing off like that you weren't sure about me any more.'

'You silly goose.' He folded his arms around me and I felt the rough skin of the tree pressing into my back. 'It was myself I was disappointed in. It was to be wonderful, our coming together.' He touched the top of my head with his lips. 'But I was like one of those invalids in Alice's ward, feckless and dithering. You should have been ashamed for me.' His head flopped onto mine and I felt the heave of his chest as he drew in a confused sigh.

'Owen, my darling. I would never be ashamed of you. How could I, when I loved you more than my life?'

'I prayed to hear you say that but I dared not hope for it. You see how my confidence has been butchered by that place?'

I felt his arms tighter and more desperate around me and my own small body shrinking and becoming fragile under his gentle insistence. 'I can help you – I want to help you. Will you let me?' I tried to free myself to see his features, to guess what he was thinking, but his limbs had grown heavy and unresponsive as if he were hovering on the edge of some bitter lethargy that was out of his control.

I helped him onto the patch of dry ground under the tree, smoothing away the few curled leaves that had been blown there. He was a child, pliable and trembling in my arms. I began to recognise what I had feared: his vulnerability and his total dependency on someone apparently stronger than himself. 'We will build our courage together, my darling. It won't be easy but we will fight this together.' I clutched the collar of his coat and rolled it up round his neck. My fingers glanced the skin there and its warmth sent a burning thrill down my fingers and my arms. I knelt

226

beside him with my hands inside his coat and held him close, rocking him like a baby.

'You are an invalid, my love, but you have no wounds, no sickness that tells people to excuse you or to be sympathetic. Your bruises are in here, in your heart and your head. You must think about them and tell me about them so that I can help them to heal.'

He fumbled for my face and gazed long and sad into my eyes. He had tried to imagine these words but the dream must have been pale and spiritless compared with the reality.

'Kiss me, darling, the way you kissed me the first time, at the Morris' party, do you remember?' The sweetness of that kiss had stayed with me through all those grim months, warming my despair like the memory of honey and flowers long after the summer has burned away.

We kissed and it was as our first kiss; expected but still with the hint of something radiant to follow. I pulled away. His eyes were closed beneath the fine curls that had grown so long since his return more than a month ago. I stroked them back and shuddered with a tenderness that was frightening. That moment marked the trembling height of something intangible, like Thoreau's star-dust or the blushing rainbow that was always out of reach or Vaughan's healing wings.

'Oh bother.' I pressed my fists to my eyes. 'It's so silly to cry when I'm so happy.'

He pulled out a stiff white handkerchief and dabbed at my eyes. 'Tears for dreams,' he whispered, and cuddled my head to his shoulder. 'Do you think if we stay here long enough Albert and Hannah will think us part of the garden?'

'We're a little conspicuous, don't you think?' I smiled at the idea of Hannah stepping over us to peg out the washing or Albert working round us with his hoe.

227

'How much longer have we got?' asked Owen.

I glanced up at the little sparkling windows of the cottage with their pretty yellow curtains, the neat, newly-made path round the side where Albert had started to stack logs for the fire. I sighed. 'Soon they will be here. A few days, I think.'

'We must say goodbye to the old place then?' Owen stood up and pulled me after him. His eyes swept the garden, already laid out for flowers and vegetables.

'We can come again. They will love to see us,' I said, trying to cheer him.

'We mustn't intrude on their happiness. They've waited for so long.'

I nodded. 'We won't wait so long.'

'You mean that?'

'Owen, of course. I want to be with you always.'

'Thank God.' He pulled me close again, snatching at my arms as if I were about to fall away from him.

'Do you think God has much to do with it?' I said doubtfully, refusing his kiss until he gave an answer.

He shook his head. 'I don't know why I said that. I lost God a long time ago.' He looked bewildered. I knew that he felt it was wrong to deny God, unforgivable to allow himself to sink into that joyless state that brought nothing but despair.

'Did you?' I started to walk into the trees that sheltered the cottage. He followed with hesitant steps, not wishing to leave this place.

'It was after meeting the boy in the church – I told you didn't I? He had such unconditional faith. He accepted the existence of some benign power that would take care of his ducklings, and the simple act of lighting a candle satisfied him that his wishes would be carried out.'

'But you were moved by that place, surely that holiness stayed with you?'

228

'I left it there. I couldn't hold it with me – not when I had lost trust in what was happening around me. Bewilderment killed any faith I might have had. I couldn't live with the uncertainty of God as well as the uncertainty of life.'

I put out my hand and our fingers touched. 'I won't let you go again. I will be your faith until you're sure of yourself.'

'Thank you.'

As we climbed the slope through the trees I told Owen about my talk with mother. He was surprised at her change of heart but glad that she was showing some concern for me as a daughter.

'It's not only me,' I continued, 'she wants to forgive you too.'

'And when I see her again, do I behave as if I know all this and play the penitent would-be son-in-law or the ignorant shirker who should have known where his responsibilities lay?'

These sudden shifts in mood were characteristic of Owen's slow regeneration and I would have to support him through them. 'You must not talk like that, you've nothing to feel guilty about.'

'I'm afraid that's how it is. That's a taste of what is to come. I have to work through these feelings. Do you think you can handle them, my love?'

I stopped his lips with my fingers and frowned. 'How many times do I have to reassure you? I love you. I will love you. That love will be our strength in this. Now I don't want to hear any more of your doubts about me.'

14

Sunlight

I put my face to the warm glass and felt the sun on my head. I realised that I had never imagined this day. I hoped that was not a gentle omen that all would not be smooth, that there might be some blissful turbulence ahead. Immediately, I was angry with such unsavoury superstitions. This was my wedding day and I ought to feel ecstatic.

As a distraction I reviewed the advice that people had been offering all day, most of it flippant and amusingly meant but a fraction of it wise. I needed to hear any views of marriage as I possessed few of my own.

Violet's 'little word' had been succinct and not a little serious. 'Keep some part of each day for yourself ... a moment only, when you can clear your mind of any untidy clutter and prepare for the next round. And never, never let your husband see your tears.' I agreed with the first – indeed, I already practised it – but having already broken the second, I wondered how practical it was to include it in my list of dos and don'ts.

I had been quite touched by John Webb's youthful embarrassment. Poor man. He had taken me to a quiet corner and plied me with a drink before urging me to be confident and true to myself. 'That's what Owen married you for, my dear, just that.' It smacked of self-absorption but he understood our relationship and knew Owen perhaps better than anyone else. I had to hope that Owen appreciated the struggles of his father when he had turned his back on a medical career; it had caused him to re-examine his own particular motives and make allowances for his son's individuality.

Lily's advice, uncharacteristically, was offered with a hint of smugness. She hovered closely, on the arm of Billie Judd, until she had the courage to speak. 'Dear Ruth, you won't mind if I say something? Have lots of babies but don't love them too much, remember your poor husband.' I wondered how long it had taken Lily to put the words together; so apt and such good sense, they might have been made by my own mother.

I felt proud of that lady today. I had expected more agitation, a measure of taciturnity along with her disappointment at our decision not to hold the marriage in church. But she had disregarded everything but our happiness and secretly she had admitted that she was relieved they did not have to entertain that dreadful vicar to a reception. She let herself be carried along in the enjoyment as though this occasion was what she had been waiting for, her chance to demolish for good her guarded approach to life.

Only my father had been sad. His face was perplexed as though there was a struggle going on inside him, a puzzled denial of the sudden relaxed surrender of his wife. Perhaps his certain faith in me was a trifle shaky, knowing what shadows still lurked around us. But mother scolded him, exactly like her sister, urging him to throw away his miserable mask and adopt a bright positive one, the sort he had always wanted his children to wear. 'Shame on you, George. I never thought to see you so dull and pathetic on your daughter's wedding day. She will never forgive you.'

This made him sit up but I comforted him. I knew that

he could not so easily dismiss the past but I was determined not to begin this phase of my life heavy with shadows. Soon there would be so much to do, so much to
think about, there would be no place for shadows.

The ceremony had been simple and touching and so
soon over that my nervousness did not make me hesitate
in my responses. We had refused the offer of a carriage,
the spring day was so glorious; we had strolled up the hill,
a strange, slightly comical procession in all our frills and
smartness.

Lily had excelled herself, designing and putting every
stitch into the wedding dress of cream satin trimmed with
crocheted lace. I felt conspicuous in such finery, my first
new dress since the war, but I suspected that Owen did
not notice much of what I was wearing, he was so particular about the order of the ceremony. In spite of this,
I understood what people meant when they gushed about
the enchantment of the wedding day for I had felt it, like
a snatch of magic, with a charm that made me breathless
and set my feet walking on air.

Although I sensed Owen's fascination with what was
happening I was not sure that I could explain to him
about my feelings. He was suspicious still of any religious
feelings and his claims about losing God were not something that could be lightly forgotten.

I pulled the curtains across the neat little windows and
the sun squeezed through the yellow cotton and spread a
warm glimmer across the bed, as if those moments of gold
we had experienced apart had been rolled into one for us.
Perhaps it was fear that I had not seen this moment; fear
initially that Owen might not return and that if he did he
would be so transformed that we would not relate to each
other and that even our love would not save us from the
trauma of separation.

I sat on the edge of the bed, my hand resting in the

pool of yellow, and I was reminded of all the simple beauty in that colour; dancing buttercups, fresh butter, sweet golden honey and the wide faces of sunflowers. Everything joyful and pleasing was held in that colour.

It had been kind of Hannah and Albert to let us use the cottage; it was the best wedding present we could have hoped for. It seemed perfect, this place whose memory we cherished through those dreadful months, a place to come back to. By chance Owen had discovered the true owner through his meetings with Major Burgon. They had been pleased to see the place restored and lived in for a nominal rent. At first Albert had insisted that we should have it but Owen had refused and I agreed. All the hours they had put into repairing, cleaning and planting, without question it should be theirs, and it became our present to them both.

I wished Owen would come up before the sun dropped away from the window. At that moment, as though he had been listening for that wish, he stood in the doorway, so tall in that small room. I patted the bed beside me and he sat in the sun. His breathing was uneven, as if he'd run up the stairs, and there was a tremor in his movements but nothing mattered except our closeness. I started to undress him, carefully folding his clothes at the foot of the bed, and when he finally stood naked before me I felt my eyes fill with tears at the sad beauty of him. I had never imagined a man's body could evoke such tenderness and I was surprised by my reaction. He knelt in front of me and kissed away each tear with the tip of his tongue. I slipped my arms out of my shift, and dropped it to the floor.

For several languorous moments he looked at me, exploring each gentle curve and shadow of my body. I longed for him to touch me but before he did he crossed to the window and drew back the curtain so the generous sun bathed us both.

'I could never have imagined this,' he said softly, 'you are so perfect.'

'And you.' I ran my fingers down his back and traced the curve of his thigh until his pale flesh began to tremble. 'Come to me, my love,' I crooned and lay back, holding out my arms for him. He kept the sunlight from my body but its warmth was still around us, a blessed intoxication.

After our lovemaking Owen had told me how he had glimpsed this day during the grim dreariness of war. It had been the bright star behind every shadow, the tiny bird that seemed to flutter our of sight before he could catch its perfection; his hope and his comfort. Many married men had intrigued him with their gentle and generous pictures of sharing their lives with another. They had spoken of the warmth and calm of companionship and the special quality of self-assurance that came with caring and being cared for.

Naturally, he had seen it in his own family; that kindness and secret empathy that kept his parents close even through his mother's stiff determination and his father's intensity focused on his career. Without that distraction Owen hoped that we would be able to share something close to that harmony; an implicit acknowledgement both spiritual and physical, which would bind us together and ensure our future happiness.

It was too early to know how Owen's commitment to writing would affect the adjustments he had to make to his personality. He had only dabbled in brief sketches of his comrades, idealised romances of non-heroes, and some poetry to capture rare and inexplicable moments, not the type of material that was a focus for close or earnest discussion. But he knew that he must guard against it taking over his physical nature and draining him of the desire to be normal emotionally again. I sensed that he had discovered a sweet release in our lovemaking but he could not risk tarnishing or devaluing that with a senseless preoccupation with dreams that were unobtainable. We were not seeking perfection in our intimacy, we would grow together, and that gentle flowering would draw us closer to that essential mystery that all lovers searched for, that intangible that was beyond dreams and perfection.

I woke in the early hours, the breeze from the open window playing on my skin. I rolled over but the space where my lover should have been was cold. If I had imagined this it might have been hurtful, but after the tenderness we had shared I was unconcerned. I closed my eyes and tried to doze, soft contentment thrilling through my limbs. In a moment I sensed a movement beside me. Owen was looking down, a strange smile softening his even mouth.

'What is it, my darling?'

He knelt in the hollow where his body had been and touched the crease of my elbow with his lips. 'Such happiness, I didn't know it was possible.'

I rolled towards him but his face was in shadow and I could not read the message in his eyes. 'Do you think we've caught the star-dust?' I whispered.

His mouth against my neck made me tremble. 'I think I've caught the star.'

1922

15

Clouds

Like a child dreading the change in the weather that threatens to spoil carefully laid plans, I had stayed in bed, the covers over my head, until Owen described the day outside. Then he pulled me giggling from the sheets and watched as I dressed.

'No one would suspect you for a mother,' he said, playfully stroking my thigh as I fastened the tiny buttons on my blouse. I slapped his hand away.

'You look so trim and bright and pleased with yourself. It agrees with you.'

'He's a good baby, it's the father who is difficult.' I rolled onto the bed and held my arms out to him. He pressed his mouth on mine and laughed as I struggled to break free. 'Owen, we must get ready, they'll be here soon.'

'So what? They're in love, they'll understand.'

'I have to see to Joseph.'

'Hannah will do all that, and he's asleep.' He slid from my arms and crept over to the crib under the window where the baby was sleeping soundly in spite of our amorous disturbance. 'Look at him. There's never been such a contented baby.' He held out his hand for me to join him.

'That's because he has such a contented mother,' I smiled.

'Truly?'

'Yes. I am happy.'

'No regrets?'

'None at all.'

He leaned against the window, staring up at the sky, clear but for a few wispy clouds hovering above the blue distance. 'It's going to be a perfect day,' he announced.

'Perfect.' I tucked the blanket more securely round the baby and finished dressing.

'Have you been to Llandudno before?' asked Lily, moving closer to Owen, full of excitement at the prospect of a train ride.

'No, it's all new to me.'

'Ruth has been lots of times, haven't you, Ruth?'

I nodded, recalling the school outings when my father had been in charge; the stifling carriages bursting with noisy children, the relief as they tumbled out and the feeling of exhilaration as they were allowed to run on the beach.

I had not enjoyed it. Father was always too busy to spend much time with us and Edwin had wandered off on his own, leaving me to amuse Becca. I had loathed the sand between my toes and on the rug. It had found its way into our food and our clothes, even father's newspaper, so that when he opened it on the way home, a shower of it covered his grey suit. We had taken Lily once but I thought she would not want to recall it.

'Edwin didn't care for it,' she said suddenly, tossing her head towards the window as the train started to move.

I glanced at Billie for some reaction but he appeared his usual genial unruffled self, perfectly accustomed to Lily discussing Edwin as though he were some long-lost brother who had popped out to the corner shop and never returned.

'He dragged me on some terrible walk.' She screwed up her face. 'My poor feet were blistered for days after.'

'He never said he didn't like it. What about you, Billie? Have you been to the sea?'

'Only once. A Sunday school trip to Blackpool. I don't remember much about it except that Henry ate too much ice-cream and was sick on the way home.' He laughed and we all groaned.

'Well, today is going to be different,' exclaimed Lily, lifting the hamper onto her knee and opening the lid. 'Everyone will have a splendid time.' She lifted napkins and peered into little pots with widening eyes at the array of foods Hannah and I had prepared. 'It's very special, isn't it, Billie?' She grinned secretly at him over the lid and patted her stomach.

'Lily!' I had been expecting this news. 'I'm so happy for you both.'

Lily bobbed her head ecstatically and reached across the carriage for Billie's hand. He gazed at her with pride, as though no one else had ever achieved what they had.

'Congratulations, Billie.' I gave him a delicate kiss on the side of his face.

'Well done!' echoed Owen, squeezing Lily's fragile body until she squeaked breathlessly to be released. 'We'll be celebrating now,' he added, linking hands with me so we were all united in our joy.

'I'm ravenous!' chirped Lily, delving into the hamper. 'Anyone for a sandwich?'

I collapsed beside Lily on the sand. 'Oh, I shouldn't have run, it's too hot.' I took several gulps of air and put back my head and closed my eyes against the sun. How many times had I rejoiced in that revitalising comfort on my eyelids?

241

'What are you thinking?' Owen flopped beside me, rolling up his trousers to keep them out of the sand.

'That sun,' I whispered, 'it was so precious to us once, wasn't it?' I spoke quietly, aware that Lily might be listening, but she had fallen back onto the rug and was drowsing.

Owen stroked my neck where the sun caught it. 'So long ago, we should forget that now.'

'Not all of it, surely?'

'Everything is mixed up together, it's hard to make sense of the fragments.'

'When I read your letters again, it's almost as if they were written by someone else. I can't believe that you are here, bouncing Joseph on your knee or digging the garden where I can see you from the kitchen window.'

'You still have those letters?'

I did not know why he was surprised. I had always considered him a romantic, deeply attached to tiny pearls from the past. I thought he deliberately preserved them so he could recall their precious virtues. 'What else would I do with them? They're still a part of my life with you.'

'I had hoped you would have had more interesting and more palatable things to take their place.' He moved close and the sun was stolen from my face.

I rubbed my eyes. 'Of course I have. My life is wonderful and I'm not dwelling on the past all the time, but I like to remember.'

'It's an unhealthy occupation.' He smudged the soft skin under my eyes with his thumb.

'What's that?' Billie stood over us with a bag of sweets and the largest ice-cream I had seen.

'Three guesses who that is for,' I giggled.

Billie grinned and knelt beside Lily and dabbed a blob of ice-cream on her nose. She licked it off with the tip of her tongue and opened her eyes.

'Billie Judd, you spoil me.'

'I've got to look after you – both of you.' He pushed the ice-cream into her hand and she started licking it like a child pretending that no one was watching.

'Shall we walk?' Owen helped me to my feet. 'Leave these two lovebirds to their games.' He gave Billie a wink as he squatted beside the preoccupied Lily.

'I'm so happy for Lily, it's what she wanted more than anything else.' I said, taking his arm.

He was silent for a moment, distracted by his thoughts. Then he put his arm round me to keep me close. 'I was remembering Edwin. They would have been happy together too.'

'Do you believe that?' I'd had my doubts since seeing Lily with Billie Judd. They had so much more in common.

'Why not?'

'I wonder if she would have been enough for Edwin – he was very demanding. There has to be more than love. Billie loves her, of course, but he cares for her too. There is a difference, isn't there?'

'You are so expert at sorting other people's lives into neat and satisfying compartments.' He smiled. 'But you should think more about your own life. You have a family now.'

We had reached the end of the sand and had to clamber over stones and rocks to reach the next bay. I paused and looked out across the ocean, silver-grey and shimmering in the midday heat.

'Perhaps I'm afraid. I'm too much like my mother. She was too involved with her children, and look what it did to her. Edwin's death nearly destroyed her, and our relationship gave her more than a few sleepless nights.'

'So what is a mother to do? She can't keep herself cold and separate from her children for fear of being hurt.'

I put my hand up to my hair where the wind had

loosened the slides. Owen leaned towards me and pulled them out. 'I don't know. It's so easy to feel trapped.' I shook my head away from his fingers. 'It's something I have to learn. My memory of mother's despair may keep me from making the same mistakes.'

'Hardly mistakes.'

I strolled ahead, shaking my long hair free from my collar and it streamed behind me in the sudden breeze from the headland. I turned to him with a sense of relief. 'No, I'm too harsh. But it frightens me, this certainty of youth. We're too proud and self-assured. We don't listen to those who have gone before, wiser and more experienced. If we had more caution we might not inherit so much misery.'

'What's brought this on? I thought we were going to be happy today.'

'I'm sorry. It's seeing Lily like that. I've never told anyone, but I have the most terrible dread for her, it's ridiculous.'

A commotion suddenly spilled round the next cluster of rocks; people were shouting and a woman's screams throbbed in the hot air. Owen ran on, stumbling on the uneven rocks, but before I could catch him up he returned and held me back. His face was white and stiff and he could not look me in the eye.

'What is it? Has there been an accident?' I struggled to pass but he held me round the waist.

'There's nothing you can do, don't look.'

But I had broken free and was peering round the edge of the rocks. A group of people was leaning over a dark bundle on the shingle. Several women were weeping silently and the men were shouting for someone to get help. One person, a young man about Owen's age, with creamy brown hair falling over his face, was bending over a small body, rocking it in his arms.

I moved closer and the women turned to stare in

244

silence, resenting my intrusion. It was a child, a girl of six or seven, perfectly still, her smooth pale face relaxed as though she were sleeping. Her wet hair clung to her face and neck, as did her thin blue dress with its dainty lace collar. I swallowed the sick pain that flooded through me and backed away from the pitiful group. Owen caught me from behind, pressing his hands into my belly, protecting my womanhood from such unexpected ugliness.

'Take me away from here,' I whispered, my voice almost failing.

We made hurried steps over the stones, slipping on the damp rocks and tangles of rubbery seaweed abandoned by the tide. Where once Owen might have paused to search for shells and stones, we saw nothing, only the haunting face of that unfortunate child. I gasped for breath as though the air were stifled with the anguish of that group.

'Hello!' A child's voice addressed us across the thick air and we stopped. 'I've caught three crabs, do you want to see?' A small boy was crouching over a rock pool in the shadow of the cliff, dipping his hands into the crystal water. Beside him was a metal bucket which he kept peeping into.

We peered over his shoulder and he held out the bucket. Three tiny crabs were trying to scale up the smooth sides but their efforts were hopeless.

'I should put some water in there,' Owen advised, 'they'd be happier.'

'That's a good idea,' the child agreed.

'Take care on the rocks, they're slippery,' shouted Owen as we left him but the child was too absorbed to answer.

Our steps became more urgent and I kept my hands stiff by my side, refusing Owen's offer of support. He considered it prudent not to speak of what we had seen and I dabbed at my damp eyes with a handkerchief from his

245

pocket. Before we joined the other two I hesitated, looking back the way we had come, but the group of people had dispersed. There was only a shuddering heap of pewter clouds growing out of the sea and moving towards the bay ... and the little boy hunched over his bucket.

On the journey home Owen tried to maintain the mood of busy cheerfulness but I slumped in the corner of the carriage in glum silence. Lily sensed that something had upset me but remained uncharacteristically self-contained, respecting my need for secrecy. Perhaps the new life inside her made her wary of unpleasantness, gave her that divine good sense that protects.

'You were very unkind to Lily. I think you might have tried to talk to her on the way back.'

I looked up, surprised at the severity of Owen's tone. Since our arrival in the cottage he had not been able to settle, and while I was preparing supper he stomped around the garden, taking out his distress on any tired-looking plants that fell in his way.

We were seated at the kitchen table, with the moon sending a wedge of creamy light between us. He stopped me lighting the lamp and I suspected that he was ashamed of his anger. For several long minutes, heavy with silence, I stared at the table then plunged my hand into the moonlight to pick up some bread. He grasped it until the bread fell from my fingers and I was forced to look at his face.

He had been wise to hide in the darkness; his face was gaunt and colourless in the shadow, as though he had been dragged back from some place that he had long forgotten.

'Have you nothing to say?' His voice trembled and I had a sudden impression of my mother's shaking head, the tears of warning in her eyes and the despair across her hunched shoulders, and I knew that this was what we had been moving towards; this unknown, unpredictable reaction to a disagreeable mood.

'What should I say?' I was surprised by the firmness in my voice. I had shut out the haunting picture, determined to unravel any difficulties, free from my mother's unwarranted advice. 'You're making a fuss over nothing.' I snatched up the bread and dropped it onto my plate, rescuing it from the moonlight. 'Lily knows me well, she didn't need an explanation. I will give her one when I'm ready, and better still, when she's ready to hear such disturbing things.'

He was watching me spread butter onto the bread, shocked at my apparent disregard for Lily's feelings. 'Stop doing that!' he snapped, and I felt my chest and throat tighten. He had never raised his voice to me before. I swallowed and put down my knife.

'I don't know what you expect of me, Owen, but I will behave with Lily as I've always done. Because I'm married to you it doesn't give you the power to censor my behaviour.'

He rose and stood in front of the window, and the table was in darkness. Waiting for him to speak, I looked at the food; different shapes with no colour and no clue as to what they were. The table had come from mother's kitchen, it was where mother had flung down Owen's letter and over which she had spluttered those harsh words. I rested my hands flat on the edge of it, afraid to let the words take shape in my head.

It was not the first time I had sensed my mother's presence; a cool shadow half-leaning over my shoulder, hovering too close, suffocating any careless actions I might be tempted to make. She had tried so hard at first to accept and like Owen but when she became ill her resolution seemed to evaporate, and now I could only remember her in that dying state.

247

Owen was leaning on the window sill, staring into the garden. I felt he was deliberately pausing, holding his breath, measuring his response, and I knew that the longer he hesitated, the less challenging would be his voice, calmed by that milky soothing glow from the moon.

'Owen,' I whispered, hoping to make it easier for him. 'Owen, please don't be angry with me. I can't bear it if you're upset.'

He ran his fingers over the glass, tracing the outline of the lilac tree against the dusky sky. 'I'm not angry.'

I could feel the desperation and disappointment in his voice. 'Then what?'

He swung round and clasped my body to his. 'I'm sorry. I shouldn't be so sensitive. You're right about Lily, she knows you and your moods.'

'Of course she does. But tell me why you were so upset. You know it was the child who made me sad.'

'Yes. Perhaps it was the child who made me angry.' His grip loosened and he leaned away from me. 'I thought all the pain was behind me. I was silly, wasn't I? There is hardship in life apart from war.'

'If only I were more help to you. I am too impatient. Every day I want you to be the Owen I knew before but that can never be. I must accept you as a different, a better Owen.' I held out my arms to him.

'I'm afraid I'm still very selfish. I don't want to be excluded from any experience. I was angry that you couldn't share your grief over the child with me and Lily, who is your friend.'

I longed for a time when I had not known the detail of his ordeal, when I could comfort him without the words of his letters at the back of my mind. But knowing it all, I could never separate him from his experiences and it was unfair of him to expect me to behave as though his past was an inconsequential dimness.

248

'Owen, we must never make the mistake of groping in the darkness alone when we have each other.'

He nodded and picked up a felt rabbit which Joseph had flung under the table. He sat in his place again, holding the soft creature to his cheek.

16

Shades

I was fascinated by the care he was taking. He had been sitting at the table for almost an hour, his brown leather boots in the centre of a double sheet of newspaper, his cloths, brushes and polish set out around them like arte-facts for some sacred offering. I wondered at his absorp-tion in such an ordinary task. Perhaps it helped to scatter the painful images from his memory, repeating the clean-ing that must have been a part of his ritual of living, almost like breathing, out there.

'I've been speaking to Lily.' I turned back to the sink, where I was washing some of the baby's clothes.

'Oh yes, how is she?' He did not look up from his pol-ishing and I considered, in spite of his concern for Lily previously, that he could not possibly care about anyone else. That other was all some show to draw attention to himself, to ensure that he was the only individual allowed to reveal distress or react to pain.

'We must talk, Owen, about Joseph.' I listened to the words, surprised at my courage for coming immediately to the point but remembering our vow to keep nothing to fester in secrecy. The silence that followed was thick and unbearable and I wrung out the tiny clothes until the drip-ping water sounded like a torrent in the hush.

'What has Lily to do with this?'

'Owen, please stop for a moment.' His constant buffing

with the meticulously folded cloth was irritating. I needed him to be still.

'I'm listening.' He set down the duster and peered at his face in the gleaming toecap.

'Lily thinks we should have Joseph baptised.' I sat at the table and folded my wet hands in front of me. The skin around my fingers was crinkled and pale like an egg custard that had been overcooked. 'If anything were to happen to him...'

'Nothing will happen to him,' interrupted Owen, breathing onto his boot and rubbing at it with his sleeve.

'Yes, but if... He wouldn't go to Heaven, he's not prepared. He'd go to some dreadful limbo place, perhaps for ever.'

'Do you believe that superstitious nonsense?' He reached for my hand across the table but I snatched it away.

'It's not nonsense.' I said desperately. I could not banish the picture from my head of that pale child dragged from the sea... Was her soul still wandering dazed and lost in some unfriendly half-world? 'Lily says...'

'Lily is a lovely girl. I'm glad you have her for a friend but I don't think she's in a position to advise us on our son, do you? When he's old enough to make decisions he can do what he wishes. I won't choose for him, it's hypocritical.'

'It may be too late then,' I appealed.

'That's a risk we have to take.'

I dabbed my fingers in the pool of soapy water on the table. 'So you won't see the priest? He'd like to meet you.'

'Whatever for?' He picked up his other boot and smeared it with polish, keeping his eyes averted from mine. The stinging memory of that other disagreement was still fresh in his mind and I knew that he did not want to hurt me again. 'What does he know about babies anyway? I doubt he's married.'

'Of course not,' I snapped, 'he's a priest.' I jumped from my chair and turned on the tap as hard as it would go until the water thundered into the sink, splashing the window and the front of my dress. I submerged my hands in the icy water, relishing the ache that slid up my arms, and bit into my lip until I could taste blood. I would not cry. He would not see me give way on this.

I turned off the tap. I could hear him rubbing furiously at his boot and I wanted to fling the wet clothes at him to make him stop. I should have known he would react like this; all that business of confidence and being open with each other, it was all nothing when it came to religion. He closed up and became disdainful and unpleasantly introspective, almost as if he resented his inability to face up to its challenge. Intellectually, he was quite capable of questioning fundamentals but he shied away from it. Perhaps he was afraid of what he might discover, not only about religious matters but about himself. He held it up as a capitulation to convention, an undesirable weakness of the spirit, a lamentable imperfection to be ashamed of.

'Father Fortune knew France in the war,' I said suddenly. 'He's not completely insensitive.'

'I believe you but that doesn't change things.'

'You won't see him for me?' I turned with the dripping clothes in my hands and felt the cool drops of water on my feet.

For an instant his face suggested a change, a helplessness that was driving him to compliance, but something deep inside, an impotence of spirit, held him back. He shook his head and banged his boots on the stone floor. Carefully he folded up the newspaper, collected his materials and returned them to the drawer in the dresser. For a moment he stood with his back to me, his hand resting on the brass handle of the drawer, trying to form the

252

words I longed to hear, but finally he ran from the room and into the garden and I heard the little gate snap shut.

'He'll come round. Give him time.'

'I know him, father. He's stubborn and nothing will persuade him to change his mind.'

'I never thought him so implacable.'

'I suppose it's fear. He still feels the guilt of what he did. Some called him weak; he might see this as a sign of weakness.'

'Surely, shying away from responsibility is weakness?'

I gave a faint smile and shook my head, clasping father's hand in my lap. 'You don't know him. He takes his responsibilities as a father very seriously. Religion is no part of it.'

My father sighed. 'It's a pity your mother isn't here, she might have been a lead for him.'

'Mother?' I smiled. 'I hardly think so.' I realised my words were sharp as I saw the change in father's face.

'Don't be harsh on her, she had a great deal to put up with.' This new tenderness was a surprise after his efficient practicality with his wife. Perhaps his inevitable clear thinking had distorted mother's imagination.

'What are you trying to say?' I encouraged.

He looked at my white fingers in his and I remembered how I had always gone to him as a little girl and never to mother. Perhaps he had let us both down in some way. 'I might have done more,' he said regretfully. 'I didn't give her enough support with Anthony and Edwin, she never forgave me for that.'

'She was not bitter, that wasn't her way.'

'Your memory is short, isn't it?'

'You mean Owen?'

He nodded and a few strands of hair, now turning grey,

fell across his face. He pushed them away and the action was reminiscent of a young man, reticent, struggling for some coherent course of action that would be acceptable to those close by. 'She never forgave herself for that outburst, you know.'

'I forgave her – I thought it was all tidied up.'

'She couldn't believe it. She carried that wrong with her for the rest of her life.'

I slid my hand away and played with the tassel on the end of the cushion beside me. The house was quieter since mother had gone. This room seemed less cluttered with only father's essentials scattered around: his pipes, a few books stacked neatly on the table. He had banished all the photographs to one corner of the room where a tiny posy of flowers made it almost a shrine to the memory of all those lost faces: baby Anthony, schoolboy Edwin, my own defiant grin with an impetuous Becca looking over my shoulder. He had added his own, baby Joseph in the arms of his father. I hardly recognised the uncompromising smirk on Owen's face. Strange, clustered together like that, they didn't have such an overwhelming aura of sadness. They seemed to be listening and absorbing the words that flitted about the room.

'If only she had come back to me.' I punched my hand into the cushion and pressed my knuckles into the pale hollow.

'We leave things until it's too late. It's a human failing. I was equally to blame, wrapped up in other people's children instead of my own, impatient with her superficial worries. There is too much fear of the truth.' His words came rapidly as though he'd been saving them up for this moment. 'Most of all, we judge others too hastily. We only live to regret it.' He looked at me, a sad shadow across his dark eyes. 'You don't mind me talking like this?'

'Oh father.' I clung to him, and all the flimsy

unimportant memories flooded back to remind me how fortunate I had been in this man. Perhaps without his guidance and preparation I would never have risked my life with someone as unlikely as Owen.

I knew all at once what I must do. Only I could lift my husband from his confusion now; my own selfish wishes would have to be suppressed to leave room for our love. I would show him the importance of our love for each other and for Joseph. God, if there was such a power, would watch over Joseph in the event of some unthinkable tragedy...

17

Friends

I spent more time by the kitchen window than any other part of the house. There I felt in touch with the seasons; watching rain spatter against the glass and flowers burst out of the ground; listening for the careless thrush who sang out a plaintive chorale with such energy and desperation from the top of a mulberry tree that it brought a lump to my throat every time I heard it.

This morning I had discovered the first shy snowdrops nestling under the lilac and there was a tiny bunch on the kitchen table. I didn't expect Alice to notice them; she'd become such a practical person since she'd married Stanley, and her organisation infuriated me. She set aside special times for her children, and others for her husband when the two little boys had to be quiet or out of sight.

I enjoyed Joseph because he was there all day; chattering to me while I worked in the kitchen; sticking his fingers in the cake mixture and rubbing at the polish with his own tiny duster and making feeble attempts to draw when I read a book in the afternoon. When Owen was there it seemed right that Joseph should be there too. He giggled at conversations he did not understand and pushed his plump little body between us if we became too amorous. I could not imagine shutting him out of that part of my life with Owen.

He seemed fascinated by the growing baby inside my

body, stroking it with such tenderness and putting his ear there to try and catch the tiny breaths. I didn't know how much he understood but the thought of another child in the house didn't appear to trouble him. I doubted that a being so young could feel resentment, but if it wasn't a part of life, why would Alice have been so particular about the way she introduced Paul to his new brother?

I put the finishing touches to the table, folding the freshly laundered napkins the way Violet had shown me all those years before and ensuring that Alice's two were at separate sides of the table. A twinge of cramp in my legs made me wince and I sat for a moment before finishing the soup. Sitting there, looking out on the garden where Owen was digging, I realised how lucky I was to feel content. Owen had never mentioned the business of the baptism again but I sensed if it arose with the new baby that he would reconsider. There was a resignation about his manner since I had become pregnant again, not a hurt resentful resignation, but a measured contentment that was easier to live with.

He had been more relaxed, with no nightmares for over twelve months, and Major Burgon was pleased with the progress of his research and writing. He had relented over his attempts to keep Lily and me apart, ignoring what he suspected was an unhealthy religious fervour on my part. We met at least once a month but he insisted that Alice should be the one to stay while the new baby was born.

I was trying to overcome my discomfort with Alice's efficiency and her insistence that everything be done in an agreed way. But Joseph worshipped her and showed that uncanny respect that small children cannot hide from well-intentioned authority.

'Alice is coming!' Joseph ran into the kitchen and

leaned across my knee like a dog waiting for loving attention.

I ruffled his dark hair and held his head in my lap. 'You're not tired, are you, darling?'

He shook his head and stood up near the table, his chin on the cloth, peering curiously at the arrangement of cutlery and glasses and fancy napkins on the new white cloth. 'Where am I sitting?' He trotted round, tapping each place with his finger until I called 'there' and he was satisfied that all was in order.

I could hear excited voices and the children laughing as they helped Owen with the potatoes. I might relax now, it would soon be over. I was not one of those creatures who found pregnancy tiresome but I would be glad to put on a pretty dress instead of these awful wrap-around smocks with their smudged flowers.

'What can I do?' Alice had removed her coat and was searching for an apron.

'Everything is under control, Alice. Sit down and I'll make some tea. How will Stanley cope with the boys while you're here?'

'His mother will have them. She loves it. Makes her feel young, she says. I can't imagine how.'

'Alice, they're not that bad.'

'No, they're not, it's me. I want everything to be as it was before they came along and of course it isn't. Tell me how you are.' Alice had found an apron and was washing the potatoes which Owen had left by the door.

'Never better. I enjoy being a mother.'

'You're mad.' She speared a potato and began to peel it quickly and efficiently, collecting the peel on a sheet of newspaper on the draining board.

'I suppose it's something that I can manage myself. It's under my control, more or less, and I don't have to depend on anyone. That's refreshing.'

'You wait until they're both rushing around, you'll feel different then.'

I laughed and put a pan of water on the hob and turned up the heat under the soup. 'I won't mind. They'll be company for each other.'

'They'll squabble like hell.' Alice swung round with a pert smile on her lips. 'You haven't changed, have you?'

'Oh but I have. When I first had a family I was terrified of the responsibility but after a while I decided to enjoy it. Fortunately Owen feels the same.'

'I wish I could do that.' Alice plunged her hands into the water, searching for another potato.

'Do you know,' I began, 'I used to envy you? You were so meticulous, you had everything under control. I spent the whole day with Jo sometimes and when Owen arrived home I would have forgotten to do anything.'

'He's lucky to have such a devoted mother.' Her expression was almost one of misery as if she could not imagine the possibility of such a relationship with her two.

'It's probably been very bad for him. He's not very independent and he'll be madly jealous of the new baby.'

'Impossible in such a loving house. Look how well he gets on with those two.' On the other side of the window the three children were playing together on the grass. Joseph was showing something to Paul, and the younger Peter was looking at him with unquestioning admiration.

'I'm so glad, he doesn't see many children out here.'

'Don't you get lonely?' Alice glanced round the little kitchen for some clue as to how I filled the hours when Owen was up at the Hall.

'No, I love it. There is so much to do, and the garden. We go for long walks. The Major lets us tramp all over his land.'

This didn't sound very interesting to Alice, who had forgotten her wild walks on the hills with Becca. She

259

preferred her amusement to be more thoughtfully organised now, like trips to the Picture House in Harbury or
the sea. She never enjoyed the uncertainty of walking out
of the house and not knowing where she would be in half
an hour.

The potatoes began to bubble furiously and the water
ran down the pan and hissed on the hob. Alice slid it off
and raised the lid to release the steam. 'Do you think
they'll be long?'

'Owen gets carried away when he's out, they could be
hours. We can start lunch without them.'

Alice looked surprised. She was used to a routine that
revolved around mealtimes which her husband was
expected to attend. As I carved the cold meat from the
ham I grew thoughtful, wondering how I would tolerate
Alice for several weeks. We had been good friends but
marriage had changed things for both of us. I didn't feel
any different except for the freedom to choose what I
wanted to do. I held no resentment for the time lost caring for Joseph and Owen.

I looked down at my hands resting on my swollen body
and was glad that I didn't know anything about the baby.
It was unbearable, the thought of seeing into the future;
it would take away the sweetness and purpose from spontaneous action, squash the thrill of the unexpected. I
pushed the notion from my head, along with all the other
unanswerable questions and my odd feelings over Lily and
Alice.

'Here they are!' Alice was relieved. Pleased, I thought,
that she didn't have to spend the meal making polite conversation with a batty pregnant woman.

The men bustled into the kitchen with the children
clinging to their legs, eager to see the treasures they had
found on their walk. There was a jay's feather, brilliant as
a jewel, a tiny skull of a vole and a few early celandines.

Owen gave the flowers to me to add to the snowdrops but when he offered the skull to Joseph, the boy passed it to Paul. Even as a child he sensed how fortunate he was to be close to the countryside. There would be other skulls.

'That was a fine walk,' said Stanley, sitting down at the table.

'I hope Owen didn't wear you out, he forgets himself sometimes in the fresh air.'

Stanley threw back his head and grinned. 'Don't worry about me, I'm used to hopping around.'

'Stanley!' Alice grimaced at him and nodded towards the children. He apologised and picked up his soup spoon impatiently.

'That's all right, Stanley, don't apologise.' I set a bowl of soup before him. 'Help yourself to bread.'

'Ruth's right,' Owen smiled, 'I do get carried away. The air seems to have an effect on my brain.'

'It must have been the hours you spent as a boy in the wind,' said Alice. 'Mother was quite frantic if he wasn't in for a meal.'

'Poor mother, she did like things just so,' Owen replied.

'Sounds like Alice,' I said with a grin, giving Stanley a wink.

'Well, there are no complaints, are there, boys?' she said with good humour.

Peter and Paul looked up at her with puzzled expressions and everyone around the table began to laugh.

18

Heartache

It was strange to see Violet standing by the kitchen window neatly cocooned in her flowered apron, washing my meagre collection of ornaments in a bowl of vinegar and water. She had one eye on the garden where Owen was amusing baby Liza on the grass. It was refreshing to see her enjoyment of simple tasks when so many young women complained about the amount of chores they were to do to support a house. I felt inclined to remind them how much they had longed for a life without uncertainty, any life with a healthy young man and children to raise, when they were struggling through those dreadful shadowy years of the war.

'I knew he would make a good father,' announced Violet, rubbing at a particularly stubborn mark on a tiny porcelain bell. 'He has honest eyes, nothing shifty about them.'

'Oh Violet.' I was in my chair near the window, mending a pair of Joseph's breeches and not enjoying it. I would have preferred to be out in the garden with Owen and the baby.

'I trust my instincts.'

'And they're usually right,' I agreed, wincing as I dug the needle into my thumb.

Violet turned to me with a frown. 'Didn't Fay teach you anything? You should be wearing a thimble.'

'It gets in the way, I can't be bothered.'

'There.' She placed the few ornaments in the centre of the table and rubbed her hands together with satisfaction at a job well done. 'You don't realise how grubby they are until you see them clean. Marvellous what a spot of vinegar will do.'

'Thank you, Violet.'

'It's nothing. What shall I do now?'

'You can sit down and put your feet up, you're supposed to be here for a rest.'

'I've never taken to rests. You know your old aunt, dear.'

'I insist. The children will be in soon, you won't have a moment to yourself after that.'

'I love them.' She leaned on the sink and smiled at the scene through the window. 'She's such a happy little bird.'

'Why are you so surprised?'

'I'm not, it's just...'

'Well, go on.'

'With Owen the way he is, I feared that the children might be rather a burden.'

'Owen is better.' I said the words with conviction so she would be left in no doubt.

'Is he?' She rolled her eyes, weighing up the hunched figure in the grass leaning over the baby.

'Yes he is. No more moods, no more nightmares.' I rolled up my sewing and pushed it into the workbox.

'I'm glad to hear it.' She turned round, her arms folded across her ample chest. She really did look terrible in that apron with its bright red and green petals and fruit, shapelessly stretched across her lumpy body, but I didn't have the heart to tell her.

'You don't believe me?'

Violet smiled, that enigmatic smile that only her husband understood. 'You should be happy but you're not. I don't know why.'

'I'm trying so hard,' I began, 'the children are so good and Owen is so helpful ... I...'

'You try too hard. He doesn't mind the children though, does he?'

'No, of course not.'

Violet shook her head and stayed close to me. 'You remind me of your mother. She was so concerned to do everything exactly right. I don't know what she was afraid of, she never made a mistake in her life.'

'She might have thought so,' I said quietly.

'You mean Anthony and Edwin?'

I nodded but kept my thoughts secret. Violet was too perceptive, an expert at appraising other people, and with no children of her own, she made everyone else's her prime concern.

'That was nonsense. Babies were always dying in the first few weeks and lots of people lost sons in France.'

'I wonder,' I said mysteriously.

'Don't you dare start thinking like your poor mother. You have nothing to blame yourself for.'

'Oh, but I have.' I was too eager to answer. I'd been saving it all for this moment. 'What about my arguments with Owen over Joseph? I think it has driven him away from his son. He's nervous of showing his feelings in front of the boy and he spends more time with Liza than he ever did with Joseph.'

'I do believe you're jealous,' Violet smiled.

'Rubbish!'

She settled herself more comfortably over the table and twirled a trim china figure between her fingers. 'I had hoped you would avoid all this. You're too involved with your children, you told me with great glee once how you were going to enjoy them.'

'I know, but it's happened because I wanted to be close to them.'

264

'Is there a problem between you and Owen?'

I shook my head but thought about the weeks since he and I had spent time alone or had an intimate conversation.

'Is it still the baptism?'

'No. I'm reconciled to that now. I didn't understand how long it would be before Owen would be normal again.'

'He seems so much better. He was telling me how well he is sleeping.'

'But he's not the same man.'

Violet put down the figure and leaned towards me. 'He can never be the same man. Not after going through all that.'

'But it wasn't totally destructive. He used to tell me in his letters how strong he'd become through experiencing others' suffering. I think he wants to forget all that – all the positive things – and cling onto the horror to give a reason to his uncertainty. But life has to go on. We have a family to care for and prepare for the future.' I leaned close to the window and looked at him. He was cradling Liza across his knees as she chattered and pointed at the birds in the trees above her head. If he realised how vulnerable she was, I thought... 'His behaviour appears so selfish. He pursues his own satisfaction in spite of us. He'll have to face up to what he is eventually, and that includes us.'

'What he is?'

'He'll have to tell his son, won't he? One day Joseph will want to know about the past, he'll need to know.'

Violet sat up and frowned towards the garden. 'He's no right to be discontent and dissatisfied with all that he has,' she said sharply. She rifled through my workbox. 'Here it is, I knew you had it.' She pulled out the silver thimble and tried to push it onto my finger but I pulled away. 'And all that you've given him.' Suddenly, she tapped the edge of the table with the thimble. 'You must be patient a while longer. When the children are more independent, he'll come round.'

'I hope you're right.'

'Of course I'm right. Now, let me make some tea, I'm sure Owen will be ready for one.'

I watched as she busied herself with the tea. I hoped I was not growing too reliant on her support. I still felt that I should be able to stand alone and be self-assertive regardless of my married position. I had a dread of making use of the kind people around me and needed to repay the smallest kindness with some tangible gift. My good fortune seemed too good to be true but I could not appreciate it.

Owen was trying to persuade Liza to come inside and I felt that queasy feeling that had been there on and off since Alice had put the baby in my arms. For this silly reason alone I had wanted to call her Elizabeth, recalling how in the Bible, Elizabeth had been blessed in her old age by giving birth to John the Baptist. I had some strange notion that this would bring good fortune and a long life to my daughter.

'You mustn't mind me.' Violet was conscious of the silence and thought it the result of her tactless advice, too eagerly offered.

Owen waved and pointed for Liza to wave too. The tiny child tottered a few hesitant steps before crumpling onto the path outside the window. Owen held her up to the glass and she pressed her chubby fist up to feel my face. I could identify with my mother's unnerving feelings; that stirring of the heart by a child, your own child; the pain and elation all rolled into one puzzling incomparable experience. It was unlike any other powerful sensation, even the love of a man.

I hadn't seen Owen laugh so freely for a long time. His daughter was already an accomplished little actress who was learning to provoke and react to an audience with her hilarious manners.

'No Liza, put it down,' Owen roared as she picked up Joseph's dish and tipped the contents onto the table.

Joseph made a face as she pattered her hands into the spilled custard before sucking her fingers with a malicious grin.

'She's naughty,' he announced, disgusted at the mess on the cloth.

'No Jo, she's only a baby, babies do such things,' excused Owen. 'You did the same.'

The boy shook his head, not believing he could have been so disagreeable.

'Oh dear.' I reached the table with a cloth and pretended a severe smile in the baby's direction. 'Would you like some more, Jo?'

'No thank you, I'm all right.' He slid from his chair and settled near the window to watch the starlings that were squabbling over the bread he had put on the grass before lunch. 'Come and see, Liza. Look at the birds.'

Owen lifted her down and knelt close to the glass so she could lean on him. At the sight of the three dark heads an immense and unaccountable sadness rose in my throat. Owen clasped the baby to his chest and Joseph had his arm across her head, clutching his father's jacket. At moments like this I was ready to forgive Owen anything. When he behaved like a proper father, tender and thoughtful, not losing his temper because he was tired or worrying about his work, I could almost forget the heartache he had caused.

I took my place behind him and gently fondled his hair. He took my hand and held it to his cheek. There were intimate moments of stillness like this when I believed in some magical affinity of the spirit which had nothing to do with physical love, a beautiful potency about the closeness of another; to sever it would be devastating.

Liza chuckled as the starlings fought over the last piece of bread, then lost interest and buried her face in Joseph's hair. He laughed with her and they tumbled to the floor while Owen and I looked on.

19

Fragments

It had not been a wise idea, coming up here. I had thought to be nearer to the sky, nearer to the sun and perhaps closer to God. He was my God now. But it was too bright and cloudless. I could not bear the joyous insistence of the birdsong, willing me to listen and be cheerful when all I needed was to be alone with my sadness. I might have obeyed my first impulse, to hide away in the quietest shadows under the pine trees, away from the light, far away from the sun. Instead, I ran, peering at the sky between the trees, not caring where I put my feet and eventually I tripped and sprawled into the body that was moving towards me.

For some moments Albert would not let me speak. He let me nestle close to him and soothed the sobs with his hand on my head.

'I must tell you,' I trembled, 'I have to tell someone.'

'In good time. Calm down, sit here.' He led me to the shelter of a stone wall where sheep escaped the wind. I noted the soft locks of wool clinging to the grey stones and automatically pushed some into my pocket for Joseph. When I looked up, Albert was watching me, curiosity and alarm across his face. I recalled his saying before how he hated women's tears and I made an attempt to tidy my features.

'I was on my way to see you,' he said gently. 'Hannah thought there was something wrong.'

'It's Elizabeth.' My voice stumbled over her name, that name that I had thought so fortunate. He squeezed my arm to give encouragement.

'Take your time.'

'She's gone. Drowned.' The words were out and it did not feel so bad.

Albert hung his head and considered the words. Was there no end to the sorrow one family had to suffer? 'Did you . . . ?'

'Alice and Stanley. They took her to the lake.' I was describing it as though it were someone else's child. I could see it as though I were there, close to the dark water, watching, interested but unconcerned as the child was another's responsibility. 'She was so excited with those swans. There are three cygnets this year, you know.' My voice was becoming lighter and out of control. 'She loved those swans.'

'Was there nothing they could do?'

I swung my head away from him and caught the full warmth of the sun as it squeezed over the wall. I closed my eyes. 'It was too deep. Stanley . . . with only one leg . . . it was hopeless.' My tears had stopped. I was surprised how easy it was to talk, how it gave me a sense of control, a feeling that perhaps I might alter what had happened, perhaps banish events from my memory.

'Where is Owen? You should be together.' Albert, ever conventional. He probably thought me odd coming up here alone at such a time. 'You need people round you, people who love you,' he added, trying to help me up but I could not move.

'I like it here with you, Albert. I can talk to you; with Owen it's so difficult. I'm always trying not to upset him or disturb his ordered existence.'

This was a surprise to Albert. From what he had seen and from what Hannah had told him Owen and I were very happy.

270

'You don't get upset, do you, Albert?'

He shook his head. 'It's a waste. You only end up hurting someone.'

I leaned against the wall. The rough stone pierced my back through my coat. The birds were filling the air with music, several were wheeling and chirruping above but I no longer minded their insolent interruption.

'If only I were strong like you.' I looked on Albert with a new and peculiar admiration.

'You're bound to feel unsure of yourself, I would feel the same.'

'Would you? You always seem so in control of all that you do. I bet when you were injured you didn't complain, am I right?'

'It's a long time ago, I've forgotten.'

His resilience, his resolution and lack of bitterness made me suddenly ashamed. He was right, I should not be inflicting this on anyone but my husband.

'Tell me, Albert, I want you to be honest with me.'

'I'll try.' He crouched beside me and the complete side of his face was close. It was healthy and smooth from the sun, I wanted to reach out and stroke it but thought he would be appalled by such an action.

'Violet accused me of jealousy. She said I wanted to hurt Owen for what he had done and for his attitude to Joseph. Am I very wicked?'

'What a terrible suggestion. I think your aunt doesn't know you any more.'

I was not satisfied by his assurances. I needed his condemnation, to punish me for my disappointment and insecurity with Owen, his friend.

'And now he has been punished. Little Liza was everything to him.' I wanted to cry as I pictured them together, busy with some scheme in the garden or preparing some benign joke on Joseph. I didn't try to hold my tears back any more.

'Where do you learn all the quaint notions of punishment and payment? Is it from that priest of Lily's? I'm glad I don't know him.'

'But what other reason could there be for taking the life of a small child, an innocent who knows nothing of wrong? Perhaps my wishing harm on Owen led to her being taken away.'

'Oh no.'

I was not making sense. He had heard all about my weird notions of a grand design with every event mapped out by a God with no compassion, but perhaps my emotions were fuddled by my distress.

'Does it make it easier to accept if you think of it as a punishment?' he asked.

I thought for a moment and lowered my eyes from his face. 'Perhaps it does, I don't know.'

'You're too hard on yourself.'

'And you're too good,' I snapped. 'Why are you so good, Albert Judd, when your brother Henry was such a tyrant? Nothing makes you angry, does it?'

He looked away, uncomfortably conscious that it was not the first time he had been contrasted with his unfortunate brother. 'I try to see everything from the other's point of view, like looking at a picture, fresh and for the first time.'

'I can't do that, I become too involved.'

'You shouldn't think that.'

'It's true. Not even Joseph will want me now I've allowed his sister to be taken away.'

'In time he'll understand. He's special, your Joseph. He won't blame you or anyone else.'

His words made me tearful again and he moved nearer. I was surprised how easy he found it to be physically close, to show warmth and sympathy without feeling embarrassment.

'I should have married someone like you, Albert,' I said stupidly.

He blushed, not wishing to know why I'd made such an unlikely suggestion. I might have been happier with someone so selfless and undemanding. Albert found it simple to accept the inevitable without raising destructive and wicked questions. Owen had a manner of breaking down everything that was hopeful into uneasy fragments.

Why had I been drawn to someone as complicated as Owen? I considered myself ordinary; I was not bursting with ideals or desires that needed instant gratification. I had wanted what every woman needs – love, comfort, security and companionship. But since his return from France, Owen had been merely a lover. He seemed incapable of friendship except with someone like Stanley, in truth, another man, and I wondered how much of a friend Albert was to my husband.

As if reading what was in my mind, Albert spoke, his voice quiet and unruffled. 'I don't know how I can help you, Ruth. What has happened is unjust and cruel and totally beyond reason. Perhaps if I had been more of a friend to Owen, I would know...'

'No, don't blame yourself. It's time Owen learned to grapple with decisions in his own way. I'm sorry I've distressed you with this, it was wrong of me.'

'No.' He held my arm, fearing a hasty departure. 'Whenever you need to talk, about anything, you know I can listen.'

His sentiments filled me with self-reproach; they were completely without condition and reminded me that my contrition should be with my husband, with my son ... poor Joseph. In my despair I had forgotten the anguish he must be suffering. He would be in darkness without the benefit of experience to add light and hope to his sorrow. He wouldn't understand why I rushed from the house

273

in that way, leaving him to his father, who was already locked in his own grief. My rashness had been brutal and illogical. I had left him to Owen deliberately, expecting him to make the dramatic gesture which had been expected of him for months.

'Thank you, Albert, you've been a good friend to Joseph. I think he'll need a friend now.' I remembered Joseph's visits to the little cottage, his tales of time in the woods with Albert, trapping rabbits, watching birds and building a shelter which they were going to sleep in during the summer.

'I loved it. It meant a lot to us to have the boy.'

'Hannah should have had her own babies instead of caring for other people's.'

Albert didn't answer but his face became stiff as if he wanted to speak.

'I'm sorry, that was unkind and thoughtless.'

He squeezed my hand. 'That's all right. Hannah is quite resigned now. And she has Charlotte to care for...'

'Ah yes, Charlotte. Oh Albert, how can you forgive me? I'm so selfish. It was you Billie came to, wasn't it, when Lily...?'

'Don't, Ruth.'

'How can God allow these things to happen – so much pain in one place and to one family – your mother and Henry and then Lily – the daughter your mother always wanted. I can't bear it.'

'Sh. No one knows why these things happen. All we can do is accept them.'

'Hannah will hate me for this,' I said, crying. 'Putting one more burden on your poor shoulders.'

'How could Hannah ever feel angry with you?'

'She doesn't think me very strong, the way I've dealt with Owen – she told me after Lily died. She said I was too ready to accept the blame for everything, even Owen's stubbornness over Joseph. She thought me too loyal to my husband. It was time for him to come out of his self-satisfied hibernation and be a proper husband and father; everyone had been too accommodating of his fancy ideas about freedom and self-sacrifice and now that I had lost my dearest friend in Lily, I would need him for a friend.'

'Ruth, don't upset yourself any more.'

'And what now? I've lost not only my friend but my daughter. Will that make him a more attentive husband? Only God knows that and I don't think God is paying attention to us.'

'Come on.' He helped me to my feet. 'I'll see you home. You should be with Owen and Joseph.'

'Yes, I should.' I looked into Albert's face and gave thanks. He was an honest man who demanded nothing except that people return his friendship. He had none of Owen's puzzled charm which concealed so many un-expected flaws, and his existence, though disordered by trauma, seemed smooth and uncomplicated. 'Thank you, Albert.'

'I'm sorry.' My voice came out as a whisper, weak and repentant. I thought he hadn't heard. He appeared to be asleep, his eyes closed, his head resting on the back of the chair, his elbows tense on the kitchen table. I watched and his fist opened and closed. Was it anger or frustration or simply mindless activity to guard him from the horror?

'Where have you been?' He spoke without looking at me and his fists continued to flex in front of him.

He wants to hit me, I thought. Lash out at someone who might have saved his child from this cruel accident. Then it struck me how stupid that was. He was a gentle man, a pacifist, who never raised a hand or voice to any-one and who turned away from the threat of disharmony.

'I had to be alone for a while. Do you understand?' The tone of my voice, growing louder and more impatient before he had a chance to answer, alarmed me.

He nodded and relaxed his arms on the table, then reached out for me, needing my comfort. I could not go to him. It was too soon. I drew away, stiff and uncertain, and flopped into my chair near the window, the chair where I had nursed my babies, where I had watched them playing in the garden, curious and excited by the living things around them. The window where I had touched Liza through the glass last summer.

I tried in vain to shut out that round face, those rosy cheeks, the wide brimming eyes full of questions, exactly like her father's. My fingers plucked at the arms of the chair. 'Where is Joseph?'

'Hannah took him. He doesn't know.' His voice was flat and without emotion and I wondered whether he understood what had happened.

'You didn't tell him!' I shouted. It was the first time for months that I had raised my voice to him but my anger was the only feeling that was giving me any life at present.

He leaned over the table, his head in his hands, his shoulders hunched in despair. 'I hadn't the courage.'

A coward again. I almost spat out the words. 'You must go now and tell him.' I moved over towards the clothes basket where several of Liza'a dresses lay on top. He had not even thought to remove them. I spread one flat on the table between us, smoothing the creases in the tiny skirt and rolling the white collar around my fingers. 'How can they keep him there and not tell him?'

Owen reached out a finger to stroke the dress and a sob shuddered through his body.

'We have to get over this,' I said firmly, folding the dress and placing it in the bottom of the dresser with the baby clothes I no longer had a need for.

He shook his head.

'She was my daughter,' I added.

'You have Joseph,' he said without looking up.

'Joseph is your son too, he needs you as much as a mother.'

'He will never be the son he could have been, I saw to that.'

'Owen, what are you saying? Go to him now. Your telling him will make it right.' I could hardly believe what I was saying. How would the unthinkable give the intimacy and trust with his son which they both needed? I had failed to give him the confidence that was indispensable in such complicated but natural relationships. But if he couldn't carry this out, he would be as nothing in his son's estimation. There was the measure of his failure.

20

Doubts

'Come on, Jo, we'll miss the bus,' I shouted up the stairs but he didn't reply. I could imagine him lying on his bed staring at the ceiling. I entered his room pulling on my hat and he laughed at my round face peeping out from the untidy fur. I reminded him of baby Liza last winter when she had insisted on borrowing her father's big muffler.

'Coat, Jo, come on.' I held it out and he slid in his arms.

'Is father coming?'

'No darling, he's busy this afternoon.'

He was accustomed to such replies. Owen spent hours shut up with his books, more than he did when Liza was alive. 'He never comes with us now.' He climbed onto a chair and took something from the shelf and put it in his pocket.

I took his hand and led him from the room, fearing to comment on the odd or unsociable behaviour of my husband. But when we were safely on the bus I thought a word of loyalty was appropriate. 'Your father is very busy at the moment, Jo. He's almost finished a book and there's a great deal to do.'

The boy squinted at me sideways, perhaps wondering what it had to do with him, needing a father to talk to and walk with in the snow. 'It's because of Liza, isn't it? He liked her better than me.'

I felt the tightness and pain of realisation in my chest but it was hard to contradict when his words held a measure of truth. We had raised him to incautious honesty, to say what was in his mind, and now he had to deal with the sad truth. He would be growing up more speedily than we had hoped.

'Losing Liza upset your father very much but he loves you just the same – perhaps he will love you more because you are all he has.'

He turned to stare out of the window with a serious expression. He had been so happy and carefree, excited by the simplest things around him, but recently, pushed to spend more time alone, brooding in his room or slumped in a corner while I was busy in the kitchen, he was becoming more solemn. If Owen offered to take him somewhere he responded with glum assurance that he was all right, he wanted to stay inside.

I felt the sadness, heavy in the house. I believed that Owen was suffering twice over: for the death of his daughter and being abandoned by his son. In part it was my doing; I had been hasty with careless recriminations, unforgiving over the matter of the baptism and impatient and irritable with his slowness to come to terms with the loss, our loss. Joseph was a sharp little boy, his perceptions caught the hints of hostility between us and, sadly for Owen, he was ready to side with me as his mother.

'I wonder if the tree will be up in the market place.' I tried to cheer him.

'Hannah said Saturday,' he replied and thrust his hands on his pockets.

'Didn't you bring your gloves, darling?'

He shook his head but I stopped before I scolded him, he was on the edge of tears.

'Did Hannah take you into the church?'

'No.'

'Then we'll go. You won't remember the crib from last year.'

'Do we have to?' He had been looking forward to a visit to the market, not a fusty old church.

'You'll have plenty of time for your shopping.' I had promised to let him walk round on his own to spend the small amount of money he had saved for presents. 'It'll be more fun when there are more people.'

I looked out of the window. It was strange weather for December. The beginning of the month had been unusually mild and for the rest of the week it had rained almost relentlessly; dull silver drifts of rain that obscured the hills and brought a heaviness to the air and to everyone's movements. This was the first day when I had managed to persuade Joseph to come out and I was trying too hard to raise a spark of enjoyment from him.

He was silent for the rest of the journey and when the bus pulled up at the bottom of the hill I expected him to refuse to get out.

'Why are we going to this church?' He looked up at the cross over the doorway and shivered as it began to rain again.

'This is Saint Theresa's, I thought you might like to look inside.' I held out my hand and he followed with slow steps.

The main altar was lit with several pairs of candles and the arrangements of holly and white and gold chrysanthemums glowed against the claret and white altar cloths. The small side altar was ablaze with tiny candles in an iron stand. Joseph crept forward, wrinkling his nose at the musty smell of incense and wax, and leaned over the rail to look at the woman in her long blue and white garment. She held a smiling baby and seemed to be staring directly at the boy with a mysterious glint in her eyes.

'Is that Jesus?' he said, pointing, and I nodded and pushed down his hand. 'Is that his mother?'

'Yes dear, that is Our Lady.'

'What is her name?'

'Mary.'

He stared at the candles glimmering against the deep blue carpet and picked one from the box on the end of the stand. 'Can I light one?'

'You must put a penny in the box. Then you can say a prayer and wish for something as you light it.'

He dropped in a coin from his pocket and took great care with the candle. As he set it in the stand, I noticed his lips moving. 'Shall I tell you?'

'No, it's a secret between you and Mary.'

Suddenly, he moved away, bored by the stillness. 'Where's the crib?'

I pointed to the other side altar, where the nativity figures were arranged on the straw-strewn steps. He sat on the bottom one and stared with wide eyes. I was longing to tell him of the hours I had sat in front of the holy figures when he was a baby inside my body. I had prayed for some of that sincerity and quiet resignation to be mine when I became a mother.

'Has father been to see them?'

I shook my head and he looked disappointed.

'He would like it here, it's quiet. He doesn't like noise, does he?'

'No darling, he doesn't.'

'When we were walking once, there were lots of shouts and bangs over near the Hall. We had to come home.'

'It's nothing to worry about, he gets upset sometimes.'

'I'll tell him about this place, perhaps he'll bring me again.' His prosaic manner made me yearn for the little boy he used to be.

He clambered to his feet and took my hand, no longer interested in the odd surroundings. As we strolled between the pews I sensed his thoughtfulness and wanted to ask him what was in his head but I knew he would tell me when he was ready. At the door, he turned and ran back towards the crib. He crouched down, pulled something from his pocket and set it next to the porcelain cow which breathed over the baby in the straw.

'What was that, darling?'

'A horse. The baby will like it. It's all right, isn't it, only a small one?'

'Where's it from?'

'Hannah gave it to me.'

I hugged him, relieved that his despair over his sister had not turned completely inward and become a destructive preoccupation that would exclude anyone else.

Outside rain was still falling. Little rivers of water gurgled between the cobbles and washed the dust and leaves down the hill. Joseph turned his face to the dripping sky and opened his mouth. 'It's sweet,' he said, 'like honey.'

His sensitivity made me catch my breath. I should not have been surprised; after all, he was Owen's son, and up to Liza's death, they had tramped the woods and fields together, chattering and composing little verses to amuse each other.

'Hurry, we'll get wet.' I urged him up the hill and as we entered the market place a solid figure hidden inside a dark green coat almost walked into us. Her head was bent against the rain.

'I'm sorry.' I pulled Joseph out of the way and she looked up. The grey hair was pushed under a shawl and her creased face and deep-set brown eyes were vivid against the dark wool. 'Mrs Judd, how are you?' I held out my hand and the woman stepped forward and peered into my face.

'Is it Ruth? I'm sorry, my eyesight isn't what is was.'

'Of course. This is my son Joseph, Mrs Judd.' I nudged the boy forward and she bent down to smile at him.

'I would have known him anywhere, he's exactly like you, my dear. Such lovely dark hair.' She stroked the curls, no doubt recalling that other dark head, bent over a bowl of bread and milk in her kitchen all those years before.

'Owen is there somewhere,' I added, eager to show my loyalty.

'I'm sure he is. A kind man. I remember him at Albert's wedding.' She looked up, a wistful expression in her eyes. Suddenly, she grasped my hands and squeezed. 'But you've had a loss, how cruel of me to forget. Your little one.'

I nodded, pushing down the anguish that swelled inside whenever the child was mentioned by a stranger. 'It's several months now,' I said firmly, determined to be strong and feeling the comfort of her kindness. 'We've all been very brave, haven't we Joseph?' I gripped his hand and he buried his face in my coat and began to sob quietly.

'I'm sorry, I've upset you.' Martha Judd had experienced her own sorrow and the thought of someone else's distress, someone younger and brighter, was clearly agonising. 'I wouldn't have reminded you for the world. And the little lad too. Forgive me.' She patted Joseph's head.

He peeped at the woman with one eye. From her roomy coat she drew out a scarlet handkerchief and gently wiped away the tears from his cheek. 'He'll be a great comfort to you, like my Albert.'

I held her arm. 'Albert is a good man. Hannah is very fortunate.'

She nodded thoughtfully. 'Shame they have no little ones, Albert loves children.'

'Indeed. He's been a friend to Joseph, I'm very grateful.'

As I finished speaking she gave me a strange look, her eyes slightly closed, as though she were unsure about a thought that had entered her head. 'Is everything all right?' she asked. 'I know it's none of my business but your mother was very kind to me. If I could help in any way, I'd feel it was a favour to her memory.'

I looked away, knowing that my doubts about Owen were clear from the lines on my face and my reluctance to smile at everyone I met. 'Liza's death shook him badly. He's taking a long time to recover.'

'It seems very cruel, the death of a child. I do understand.'

I tried to relax to her concern. I knew her offer was well meant and didn't wish to distress her by ignoring it. 'I'm sure Owen is no different from anyone else, it's just that everything takes longer.'

'I know what he went through, though I never said at the time.' Her voice grew soft. 'I think he was very brave. It was a pity more young men didn't follow his lead.'

These were unexpected sentiments. 'Thank you, Mrs Judd. That is a generous thing to say.'

'And you tell him what I said, it might help him.'

'I will. Thank you.'

'You take care now and look after that fine lad.' She flicked Joseph's hair with the tips of her fingers.

'Goodbye, Mrs Judd.'

As I watched the woman weave her way through the muddle of stalls, pausing now and again to study prices and shake her head, I felt pleasantly satisfied that I had decided to come to town this afternoon. Perhaps my visit to the church had been in some way instrumental in my meeting with Albert's mother. These improbable notions filled my head more and more these days; I was becoming a superstitious dreamer once more.

'Who was that lady?' asked Joseph.

'That was Albert's mother.'

'She was kind.'

'Yes, she was.' His openness was nearly painful; my one

284

hope was that he had enough good sense to match it, to prevent him from being drawn along by the ruthless and unfortunate.

'Is she going to help father?' he said, making his strides longer as we reached the edge of the stalls.

'Perhaps.'

But he suddenly lost interest as his attention was drawn to the Salvation Army band, which was preparing to play. He watched fascinated as they arranged their shining instruments and set their miniature sheets of music. When they began to play 'See Amid the Winter's Snow' I could no longer contain my sadness.

All those years ago, Becca and I had stood here in the snow, letting the notes drift over us, our minds despairing over Edwin's death. She would hate to be reminded of her sentimentality, so grown up and professional at her teaching in Manchester, and she spared little of her valuable time for her family.

'Don't cry, mummy.' Joseph felt for my hand. 'Liza will be listening, she loved the band.'

1934

21

Tears

Outside the window Joseph was chopping wood and stacking it along the fence for the winter. In this familiar place where his father, during his dark moods, had found brightness and consolation in the plants and trees that he had planted and nurtured and loved with his children, I watched him. He had Owen's awkward way of straightening up between each strike of the axe. I shrank into the shadow behind the curtain; he was at that self-conscious age when he wanted to keep his actions private and unobserved.

But I was pleased with him. We had just returned from Yorkshire, where we had been comforting Edmund. Violet had died unexpectedly at the end of September and the poor man was devastated. Joseph had been a valued ally during the week when the two had walked and talked every day, leaving me free to go through Violet's things and put the house in order. Joseph had felt lonely and vulnerable since his father's withdrawal and he was gratified by the old man's attentions. Sadly, it had been like watching Owen and him together as they disappeared up the lane, Edmund's two steps to Joseph's one.

But my heart was heavy for him. He had the double pain of his father's coolness along with Owen's increasingly strained relationship with me. He had been used to seeing us work on research together but now that Owen was totally absorbed in his own writing he spent longer periods alone or up at the Hall. The poor boy sensed my sorrow and suspected that the cause was not simply the memory of a dead child but something deeper and more fearful which threatened to destroy his family.

In August Alice had suggested that Owen and I go on holiday together, so we had visited the Lakes and Joseph had stayed with her and the boys. The change was good for all of us but I knew that nothing had been resolved and that I was still marking time until the next crisis, which would be the one I dreaded more than any other – Owen's leaving.

It was not simply the idea of his leaving that hurt, that was almost inevitable, it was the thought of the explanations that Joseph deserved and which remained unsaid. Owen was going to escape once more and I would be left to deal with the sad results.

Alice had tried to talk to him while I was with Edmund. She was becoming annoyed with her brother, irritated by his hasty and selfish manner towards everything except his writing.

'I was insulted by his rudeness, I don't know what's come over him,' she had said.

As we sat in the parlour, she became more flustered as she thought back to that dismal afternoon and I more tearful as I imagined my last hopes of reconciliation being snatched away. I thought about Owen in this room with its neat rows of books and carefully placed ornaments and polished furniture. He was out of place. When he sat in the chair he was ungainly as if he didn't know what to do with his long legs when they had to be kept still. And now he hated it because it had been Liza's; the collection of tiny animals in procession along the window sill had been hers. My attempts to create a home for him had become nothing. All the hours I had devoted to his comfort, both emotional and physical, were lost in some wordless response which grew heavier as the days towards winter grew heavier.

'And this house,' Alice had continued, 'what has happened to it? It used to be so happy, now even when it's full of visitors, there's a bitter silence, as if everyone is afraid to show any joy for fear of disturbing its sacred dusty atmosphere.'

'Alice, that's a bit of an exaggeration.'

'No one can live such a joyless existence and I told him so.'

I could imagine his stunned reaction. His face would go visibly pale and he would begin to twist his hands and probably pace about the room. And it would serve no purpose.

'I told him Liza's death happened a long time ago and he shouldn't be thinking of it still.'

I closed my eyes. This was what I should have had the courage to say long ago. 'And?'

'He said he could still see her and hear her as if it were yesterday. I don't know him any more, Ruth. He's a stranger.'

'Alice, I'm sorry, you shouldn't have been drawn into this.'

'Do you know when I was closest to him? When he was away in that infernal war. He wasn't afraid to tell me things. He began to discover himself, didn't he?'

'We've had exactly that conversation, but telling him those things won't help him now. He seems incapable of looking back and sorting something of worth from that shattering experience.'

'But he accepts it, surely that is positive? If he recognises the rewards that have eluded him, it can't be long before he asks himself why and finds the answer.'

'Isn't this all mixed up with his frustrations over

291

medicine? He couldn't separate himself from his father, he needed to prove his own individuality.'

'I accept that – father accepts it – but he had a chance for that in France and he grabbed it. He did exactly what he wanted and the price was his family's distress and his own frustration.'

'You're being unfair to him, Alice. The price was his guilt and his being accused of selfishness and self-obsession. And he's had over ten years to think on his actions.'

'Exactly, ten years. Really Ruth, isn't that long enough? He's avoided facing the difficult questions, the questions which might have made his family life smoother, and now it's all falling away from him – and you and Jo are suffering too.'

'And you said all this?' I could understand now why his responses to me since my return had been so colourless and preoccupied. His guilt and unhappiness were turning into fear.

'He thinks you're so close to Jo that you don't care about his indifference.'

'That's not true.'

'I told him. He was comparing himself to Stanley and Billie; he sees them as the ideal, interested and relaxed because they have nothing to hide from their children – they have nothing to prove.'

'Oh, this is all so wrong. If he'd come to me I would have told him what he has to offer his son – his sensitivity, his thoughtfulness, his love of countryside and poetry, his gift with words. Why does he reduce those qualities to nothing?'

'They're under the shadow of his past, that past that he can't share with his son.'

'But I can't build that relationship with his son for him, only he can repair the damage.'

I felt my head heavy and throbbing as I remembered Alice's words. Joseph was still outside and I stood up where he could see me at the window and waved. He paused and waved back then put down the axe and moved towards the house.

I had to prepare myself for the inevitable. I owed my son the truth. Alice's words had been cruel but Owen had to realise that time was slipping away. Certain moves had to be expressed between people; their love required nourishment just as Owen's plants needed nourishment. Without that attention the relationship would starve and wither. We had to come together before what we had became irreparable. The war had been over for almost fifteen years and its shadow should not darken our lives any more. It had been a mistake for Owen to work with Major Burgon; it prolonged his contact with the past and allowed him to retreat into some murky private obsession, a feud between what his wife and family expected of him and what his stubborn but pragmatic principles demanded.

Joseph stood in the doorway. The far end of the room was almost in darkness as the autumn evening was turning to dusk and his figure in the shadow could have been that of Owen; Owen as a young man just beginning to react to the feelings of others, sensitive to moods and quick to relate to misfortune. He spoke to me several times before I answered then he walked slowly across the room, knelt by the chair and took my hand. Before speaking he glanced round, probably thinking, as I had, what a sad comfortless place it had become.

'Are you feeling well, mother? You look tired.'

'Yes.' I squeezed his hand and looked at the fingers, already marked with broken skin by his heavy work outside. 'I think too much. I should know by now, shouldn't I, that it wears me out.'

'What were you thinking about?' He sat in the chair

opposite the window and leaned forward, his elbows on his knees and his hands folded together. He was going to be better-looking than his father; he possessed a nonchalance that was attractive without being insulting and he didn't wear that intermittent frown that I'd had to accept as a sign of Owen's emotional queasiness. But his blue eyes, which seemed to vary in intensity, could express the same mournful quality that so easily roused sympathy, especially in women.

'I was thinking about your father.'

His hands twisted stiffly and he straightened his back. 'He's upset you, hasn't he?'

I didn't answer.

'You haven't been happy since you came back, and it's more than Aunt Violet's death.'

'Yes, it is.'

'I don't like to see you like this, it's like when Liza…' He stopped and swallowed and leaned forward to touch the animals along the window sill.

'You're a good boy, Joseph. I'm glad I have you to talk to. I used to be able to talk to your father but lately…'

He picked up a tiny monkey made of toffee-coloured wood and rolled it in his fingers. 'Is it about the war, something that happened then? I asked Uncle Edmund but he pretended he couldn't remember. That wasn't true, he didn't want to tell me.'

'Don't ask me now, Joseph. You'll be told when the time is right – and it will be soon, I promise.'

The garden was almost in darkness; the dusk seemed to be swallowed up by it during these late October days. Next month would be the real start of winter – the damp, the fog and the uncertainty that came with shorter days, days burdened with cloudy skies and dripping trees.

I reached for his hand. 'We must go for a long walk before the weather changes. Through the woods to catch the last of the autumn trees and along the river to see the herons. What do you think?'

'Yes, mother, that would be good.' His voice was encouraging but when he looked at me, his eyes were heavy with that grim uncertainty so reminiscent of his father.

22

Shadows

The prospect of Christmas, with still nothing resolved between us and the memory of Edmund in his little cottage bravely preparing for his days alone, made me sad. I had to be more determined about our future together if it was to be a reality.

On impulse, I decided to walk through the woods and call on Albert and Hannah. As I entered the cottage I was glad that I had come. I looked round with fondness. I had almost forgotten the decrepit state of this cottage when Owen and I had first seen it. Hannah and Albert had made it specially cosy with their personalities and their love for each other.

'I thought you had forgotten us.' Hannah smiled uncertainly as she handed me a cup of tea.

'You know how it is, one thing and another. And the days are so short now.'

Hannah nodded and studied me. She knew that there was something wrong. 'You took Edmund home?' she said.

'Yes, it's a shame he wouldn't stay for Christmas.'

'I expect he prefers his own home,' she replied, 'he's quite an independent little man.'

'Did Jo go with you?' Albert was leaning against the range.

I shook my head. 'He's being very mysterious out in the shed, something to do with presents, I expect.'

'Almost a man,' laughed Hannah. 'It doesn't seem five minutes since he was racing around jabbering rubbish.'

'No.'

Albert peered into the mirror over the fireplace to fasten his collar stud. 'Be a love, do me this.' He spoke in a gentle voice to Hannah and while she stood close to him, he watched her features with the tender keenness of a youthful lover.

I had never seen Albert angry or out of sorts over the years I had known him though I remembered how volatile Hannah could be when riled. They had realised a healthy balance of experience, marrying late, and perhaps it was no bad thing that their only contacts with children were other people's.

Albert turned to me with a worried expression. 'Owen was here while you were away.'

'He wasn't too bright,' said Hannah, watching Albert pour himself a cup of tea. 'And he wanted to talk about the past. I left them to it. I can't understand the great mystery and attraction of that past if it was so terrible for them both.'

'Not all bad times, dear.' Albert sat next to her and ran his fingers over his face. The scars had faded and he no longer felt embarrassed or apologetic for them. Only his lack of sight was a bother; one eye was a positive nuisance when you were doing anything practical and many men were driving motor cars now.

'Not for you, perhaps,' said Hannah.

'Women don't understand comradeship, do they, Ruth? That draws the mind back, we can't help it.'

I smiled, recalling Owen's early reminiscences, generously detailed and enthusiastic but requiring my appreciation, which I could never offer unconditionally.

'Women have friends,' Hannah protested, looking at me for support.

'It's not the same, love. You talk about recipes and babies and frocks.'

'Albert Judd, how dare you?' She grabbed his good arm and tried to twist it behind his back. 'You don't know the first thing about women's talk.'

'See what tantrums I have to put up with, Ruth. I should give her a jolly good spanking.'

'You just try.' Hannah snuggled closer and buried her face in his chest.

They reminded me of how Owen and I had been once, and Edwin and Lily before that unspeakable war had destroyed all normal life. I couldn't watch them, it upset me so, especially when I recalled how depressed I had been following my talk with Alice.

Albert could see I was becoming tearful so he suggested that Hannah make a fresh pot of tea. I knew that he wanted to talk about Owen.

'As you say, Albert Judd, but don't go upsetting Ruth with your miserable talk.'

'Don't mind Hannah, she's a bit down on me at the moment. Says there's too much talk of politics and all the goings on in Europe make her uneasy.'

'That's natural. We all want to forget that war.' I glanced at the window sill where Charlotte had put a collection of leaves and berries in a jug for Hannah and thought how brave Billie and she had been since Lily's death. It compounded my annoyance with Owen to see him so resigned to whatever might happen to our marriage. He should take example from Albert and Billie and be more caring. We had loved each other once, desperately, and we might still if it wasn't for his apathy, which seemed to be growing and threatening to drag us further down into some dark place that would destroy us both.

And there was Hannah preparing her vegetables, so comfortable in her simple life with Albert, not making

298

herself miserable seeking what she could not have.

'So what did Owen have to say? I hope you didn't spend all your time discussing the war.'

He hesitated and shifted his feet uncomfortably then sat in the other chair looking down at his cup of tea. 'No, he was worried about Jo.'

I looked up, not surprised by his words. 'And were you able to reassure him?' My voice was painfully sardonic and I looked away.

'He doesn't understand how Jo feels about him. When the lad comes here he's always talking about his father.'

'Is he?'

'It's been hard for him, trying to take the place of his sister.'

'Owen didn't expect that.'

'No, but Jo had to try. He's very unhappy and muddled.'

'I know. I have spoken to him but he needs his father.'

'Owen needs Jo's trust but he is afraid.'

'He'll have to earn that trust,' I snapped. 'Sorry, Albert – go on.'

'I told him he should be talking to you about it.'

'Those words must be etched into his brain by now!'

'I know, I know. Then he should tell Jo the whole story.'

Albert was not so wise; why was it that everyone around Owen knew what he had to do but he could not see it himself?

'If only he would,' I sighed. 'Jo is expecting some demonstration that he still exists.'

'Now would be a good time,' continued Albert, draining his tea and setting his cup on the mantel shelf next to the clock, that clock Owen and I had given them as a wedding present. 'Attitudes have changed. Sympathies have shifted since the start of the Peace Movement.'

I was beginning to tire of this endless debate which was simply carrying us round in circles and not drawing Owen any closer to a reconciliation with his role as husband and father. Since we had lost Liza there seemed no going back to the useful days of discussion which had made us all so content. That small child had taken with her an essential part of our love. Without it we were worthless to each other; we were stranded in some unknown shadow, struggling to find some light in which we could reach out for each other.

'You are so much closer to Jo,' began Albert, and I knew what Owen had suggested before the words were spoken.

'And I'm too close to Owen,' I protested.

'If there's another war – which seems likely, the state Europe is in – it will all have to come out.'

I looked across at Hannah cutting chunks of bread from a new loaf and I wanted to cry. The thought of all that again – it was unthinkable. 'Albert?'

'This Hitler chap, he's more than just an animated revolutionary. He's dangerous, we don't know how dangerous.'

'Oh God.'

'And Owen knows all this. And he knows that Jo's head will be full of all this, just as his and Edwin's were in 1914.'

I was becoming more confused by this conversation. I had come here to talk about Owen and now we were thinking of Jo going off to some new war. I couldn't stand it. 'I can't help him any more, Albert.'

Hannah was laying the table for supper and listening to us.

'He said a strange thing,' Albert continued, 'that he had used pacifism as an excuse for his own loss of identity and bewilderment. He thought that you wanted to tell him to pull himself together and he thought it might have been...'

'Albert!' Hannah raised her voice and frowned in her husband's direction. 'That's enough.' She held onto his arm then stepped forward.

'I felt that way; I wanted to shake him but gradually I admired him because he was prepared to suffer for his views. Oh, I was impatient with his insufferable indecision – I could see you were suffering.' She looked at me with love in her eyes. 'But it's taken years for me to admit it and I didn't want to, not after all that my Albert went through, but I believe he was right. And if there's another war, I hope Jo and Billie and all the other lads say they're not going. Let the politicians sort out the mess, I say.'

Albert smiled at her with admiration. She had a spirit we could all be proud of.

'Thank you, Hannah. I don't know what to say.'

'That's what your husband said.' She held me in her arms. 'And I told him to go home and tell you what he'd told us. He wasn't to make you choose between him and Jo – it was unthinkable and unnecessary. He could hold onto both of you if he regained some of that courage he had in 1916.'

1936

23

Silence

Christmas was almost upon us but the changes outside the window did not excite me as they usually did. There had been a crisp frost over the last few days and the trees were sharp with crystals against a raw sky. Only a few birds were brave enough to leave the shelter of the hedge: a pert robin who strutted along the edge of the path waiting for the crumbs which I always put out in the morning and an impudent blackbird who patrolled the shrubbery, shooing away any competitor for the pieces of apple that he loved.

It seemed that elaborate preparations served no purpose in the house and they were wasted on Owen. For the past few years he had refused to enjoy the celebrations, even for Joseph's sake. And now Joseph was growing too old for party games.

Suddenly I felt angry with my aimless thoughts. The festival had meant so much to us at one time but, like everything else, it had changed over the years, taking on a shabby and purposeless air that merely exaggerated our low expectations. Mother and Violet had gone, father was not very lively and Owen's parents were not enthusiastic for long visits. And with no Lily, Billie and Charlotte would be spending Christmas with Albert and Hannah. Though Joseph claimed not to miss the festive atmosphere, I felt sorry for him. He should not have to suffer the indolence of his parents or the self-inflicted isolation of his father, and I would make an effort to revive a measure of the old fun.

'What would you like to eat on Christmas Day? Hannah can get us a duck or a goose.'

'I don't mind.'

I struggled against my irritation. I hated the way he refused to commit himself to a simple decision, not through any deliberate intention to annoy but simply because he didn't want to think about it. It reminded me of Owen when we had first married and I had attempted to start a discussion on some everyday domestic matter. My questions had been met with glum silences, not intentionally provocative but as a smooth way to accept my choice and make me feel valued.

'You decide, Joseph, please,' I said in desperation.

He peered over the top of his book and there was an odd distracted quality about his eyes that was disturbing. 'Duck then.'

'You're very pale, are you all right?'

He looked at his book and flicked the page. It was unusual for him to show such absorption when I suspected he could not wait to escape my company.

'How was granddad?'

'He's got pains in his legs.'

'He's not a young man, that's to be expected. I'm sure he enjoyed your visit.'

He snapped the book shut and slumped to the back of the deep chair. He took a visible deep breath. 'He talked about father.'

'Doesn't everybody?' I found it hard to keep the bite from my voice. I was finding Owen's insolicitous manner unbearable; I knew that everyone had been urging him to talk to Joseph but there had been nothing, and his pretence that all would be well if he let it be was making our life together impossible.

'Why didn't you tell me about him?'

'Tell you what?' I finished folding the tablecloth, laid it on the end of the dresser and leaned over his chair. He looked up and there was almost panic in his blue eyes. Suddenly, the horror of his words hit me like some terrible sickness that I had been dreading.

'Granddad thought I knew. He seemed to think that I should know. I bet everyone in town knows.' His voice was shaking with coiled-up emotion.

'Joseph, I'm sorry. There is no excuse. We simply didn't tell you.' I closed my eyes to avoid his despairing look.

'I suppose it wasn't important that my father was a conchie!'

'Don't use that word.' I straightened up and slid away from his chair. I began folding the linen into neat shapes, emphasising each crease with my fist on the edge of the table.

'That's right, isn't it, a conscientious objector?' He seemed to be shrinking into the chair as though by doing so he could escape the truth and avoid the pain.

I moved the linen to the end of the dresser and looked round desperately for something else to do. I wanted to show him that I was calm and unmoved but the sight of his white face and twisting hands filled me with such a muddle of feelings – panic, relief, disbelief and hopelessness – that I had to close my eyes and gather myself together before I could trust myself to answer.

I had contemplated this day for years. From the moment Owen had placed Joseph in my arms and I had seen his turned-up nose, his startling blue eyes and long fine lashes, and recognised the helpless trust that was placed on me as a mother, I had lived with this fear, the fear that the truth would one day have to be told.

My mind swung from hope to panic as I considered how

307

to recount and explain it. I was forced to measure just reasons for excuse or how I would persuade him to make allowances so long after the sin. For in my mind now, it had become a sin. The blur of years could not reduce the disgrace of transgression but his confession might have redeemed him in his son's eyes and might have saved his family.

But worst of all was not knowing my son as I should; I could not imagine how he would respond. This came as a surprise for I had always thought we were close enough to share anything without embarrassment or shame. Several months ago Edmund had commended him for his good sense and generosity and I had wanted to blurt it all out and take advantage of those virtues; but Owen had refused to support me, without any acceptable reasons. Now it was too late. Hearing it from someone else – a loved member of his family, a person of traditional values and respected throughout his life for his dedication to the community – was the most disastrous outcome I could have envisaged.

Joseph was peering at me with a curious frown – his father's frown. I tried to identify what might be running through his mind but he was as good as a stranger. Since Violet's death and his hours spent with Edmund, I sensed that he didn't have time for me, or was it my oversensitive imagination? Perhaps this distance between us was a natural step in his move towards manhood. He could not be under my feet for ever.

I began to fuss with the tiny candles on the Christmas tree, needlessly testing their holders and retying bows of ribbon around the top branches. I could feel his eyes on the back of my head, willing me to turn round and give him an explanation for the battered state of his emotions.

'What do you think it means?' I asked calmly, folding my hands behind my back.

'He's a coward.' The tone of his reply was flat. It was the easiest judgement for him to make.

'That's not true. It took courage to live by his principles when everyone else was following orders simply for an easy life.' I rubbed my hands across my apron and sat down.

'They leave their friends instead of helping them, they won't fight; that's being a coward.'

I caught my breath and swallowed the sickening lump in my throat. All these angry words spilling out for which there were no responsible answers; words that I had put together in nightmares, and as nightmares they were not a part of reality, but here, in this cold light with the frost outside and the Christmas tree as some sad symbol of family unity, these words had taken on an aching meaning.

'I'm sorry this has happened, Jo. Your father should have told you in his own way, he might have explained it better.'

'He didn't care. He was only worried what I would think of him.'

'He was waiting for the right moment.' My words were feeble, as I had always known they would be.

'When would that have been, mother? I'm not a child any more.'

'I know, darling.' I rose and caught sight of some greedy sparrows on the lawn, scratching for crumbs. I had forgotten to put out the bread. I smiled as I recalled Jo and Liza sprinkling bread around the garden. 'If it hadn't been for Liza...' I hesitated.

He struck his fists against the arms of the chair. 'Why should that have made any difference?'

'It was too painful. He thought I blamed him and he hid away. He's a very unhappy man, Joseph, he needs our help.'

'We were all sad about Liza, it didn't spoil our lives for good.'

'You're young. Things seem uncomplicated to you. It's not so clear when so much of your life is behind you – the important part.'

'If he'd come to me I might have talked to him. I wanted him to talk about Liza when she had gone, I was lonely.'

'I know, darling.'

'I might have helped him and he wouldn't have had to carry it around with him all these years.'

'Couldn't you try now?'

He shook his head. 'He doesn't want me.'

'For my sake, Joseph, for my love. If you were to go to him you might be surprised.'

'You don't know that. And why should I when...' He broke down and angry tears spilled down his cheeks. 'How could he do that, mother, when all those people were being killed – his friends? How could he leave them to get on with the war alone? None of them had any choice, why should he have been any different?'

'He didn't run away. He was transferred to work in a hospital. He was still doing his part but in his own way.'

'I don't understand how he could change his mind like that.'

'You don't know much about war, and that war was different.'

He thought for a moment. Perhaps he did know about the war. I didn't know what he read up in his room for hours at a time.

'Does Albert know? I bet if he did he would never speak to him again.'

'Of course Albert knows. He's a good man.' I moved round to the front of his chair and knelt down. I tried to hold his hands but he hid them under his knees. 'He understands why your father was driven to do such a thing.'

'Even after what happened to him, those terrible injuries? I don't believe you.'

'Even after that. In a way that made it easier for him to accept. He didn't want anyone else to suffer what he had suffered.'

He pulled out his hands and turned them over, bending and stretching the fingers as though wondering how much of this man would be part of him. Then he stared at me, his brilliant blue eyes cold. 'If only you had told me – I won't forget that.' His face, slightly flushed from the tears, was set in a stubborn mask. He was convinced that he could never feel different again.

I sat heavily in my chair. 'Joseph, you mustn't imagine this to be worse than it is. It happened a long time ago.'

'He's the same man though, isn't he? If there's another war he'll do the same thing.'

That was an eventuality that I had tried not to consider. With Owen's preoccupation with the Peace Movement and his reading about the League of Nations, the thought of another conflict had been neatly parcelled away. It was a subject we didn't discuss. Perhaps we were being deliberately short-sighted to protect ourselves but that was no rare attitude, and certainly no shame with the memory of that earlier war still hovering in the shadows of our life. If it came I knew that he could never carry arms and I doubted if he would be willing to take part in any war-related activity.

'That is a question for your father. You must ask him.'

'I will.' He stood up and tucked the book under his arm. As he turned to leave the kitchen I put my hand on his shoulder.

'Did granddad say what he thought?'

'Granddad was sad.' His tone implied that it was my

fault my father was distressed. 'He said I had missed a lot having Owen for a father.'

'Oh dear.' I thought back to my parents' reaction when they heard of our plans to marry in spite of what had happened. Mother had been determined that I would follow her wishes and more or less damned me to unhappiness if I pursued the unthinkable. But father, ever the diplomat seeking the smoothest path, had given us a guarded blessing and made it clear that if it didn't work out I was not to feel that I had failed.

'But I'll pretend it doesn't matter, won't I?' He was defiant. 'I've still got you and Alice and Hannah and Albert. I'll have to manage without a father.'

'Owen would be hurt if he heard that.'

'Then he should do something about it before it's too late.' He sped from the room.

In a moment I heard him banging his feet upstairs and I knew he would soon be lying on his bed, staring at the ceiling, perhaps waiting for his father's step on the path. I prayed that he would come soon and be in an amiable mood. There was no going back or cherishing the safety of silence any more.

24

Forgiveness

December 18th 1936

My dear Ruth,

This is a strange letter to write. I shouldn't be writing it at all. It is cowardice which makes me express myself in this way instead of facing you but I have held back so often, guarded by some inner vigilance stronger than my own spirit, and this has made me weak. In delaying for a better moment I have lost all those moments.

It puzzles me why you have never tried to persuade me more severely to be honest with Joseph. His happiness has been paramount, hasn't it, so why didn't you make me see that my silence was all part of a moral deceit that was intolerable and, as Joseph grew older, unacceptable? Maybe your years with me have made you into something of a coward too.

My darling, who seemed so resilient in times of heartache, you were afraid for your own inner safety. You wanted nothing less than a quiet existence; no distractions from a bruised memory in which you no longer had faith; no pain to interrupt the progress of your relations with your remaining child. You deserved more compassion from me.

You know your own son so well, you should have seen the time was right for him to accept the truth and badgered me until I accepted the punishment of seeing his contempt and confusion. I've now been denied that punishment and have to stay with this malignant tangle of anger and dissolution, isolated from you all. After my talk with Albert I had made my decision, but of course you won't believe that. It's too easy now that everything is in tatters. What have I to lose?

I cannot forget that day, indeed I should not, for it is part of my punishment. I am haunted by your face; the softness that I love, cruelly smudged by your anger and disappointment and your voice shaking with disbelief at what had happened by an innocent accident.

During the months of our separation all those years ago when words had been our only contact, I had spared you none of the horror, fearing the taint of dishonesty on our closeness, sensing the need for truth and the impossibility of secrets between us. We were still lovers then, spiritually united, and our selfishness and indifference had excuse, in the name of our commitment to each other and our independent survival. But when physical unity took over, the old magic faded. With the reality of a life that had to be lived, came the end of our dreams. There seemed no place for that spiritual element in the turmoil of survival, surrounded by cruel gossip. I destroyed your magic, my love; I didn't allow you to grow into the woman you needed to be. The real horror was not the nightmare of what we'd suffered but our error in trying to forget it, for when the truth was finally dragged out, the agonising wound was reopened and needed drastic treatment.

314

Naturally, I forgive George. He is without malice; except towards those cruel creatures who transfer their disaffection for life to their children. In a way I represent one of those unfortunates, so George could not hold back in his condemnation. I won't think of his part in this – neither must you. The deed is done and we will have to live with the consequences. My resolution to leave for a while has not been changed, I will simply be leaving earlier.

As for Joseph, I rely on my battered instincts, which tell me that his suffering over Liza has cultured a more mature understanding of love. He will meet this new ordeal with a moral defiance which will make him strong and distance him from the pain of our shattered relationship.

You should show him this letter; not because I am trying to heap excuse on excuse, but because it will explain to him why my love for him will not allow me to be with him until I have his forgiveness.

Owen

...He had to be different from now on or there would be nothing for us... This last letter was a part of Owen that had evolved during our turbulent loving years together. It was not part of the shadows that I had dreaded – it could mean the lightness that we both needed to survive.

I wondered what Alice would have done with all this and had to accept that she would never have clung onto such painful remnants of the past. Alice was so practical, so smooth-reasoned and efficient and full of good sense; there was no room in her life for the clutter of lost opportunities and drab soulless memories. She had Stanley, and he had no desire to recapture those dark days. They looked to the future, to a life for their children, set apart from all that their parents had lived through.

'I've brought you some tea.' Alice stood beside my chair and as she looked down at the fallen letters, I recognised a hint of the old Alice in that secret expression; a desire to be close, to help, to soothe without a suffocating concern. It was a quality that had given her the compassion to care for the sick and the injured, the warmth and understanding needed to raise children who were neither too boisterous nor too submissive. It was that perfect balance between loving and giving that had been denied to Joseph.

Owen had been too self-conscious to be relaxed and natural with his growing son; he had been too gently obsessed with himself to listen to the simple needs of a developing personality and count them worthy and meaningful ... and I – I had tried too hard, had been too assiduous in my attentions instead of listening to Alice and Lily or catching signs of warning from my mother's lips. I had surrendered to my son and lost my husband in the process.

'What are you up to? Not digging over that awful past?' Alice crouched by the chair with her own tea and shuffled the tumbled letters. I stared at the envelopes, almost as clean and smooth as the day Owen had sent them.

'I'm sorry, one last look, then...'

'You're going to throw them away?' Alice was relieved, as if she had been longing to suggest it but with Owen's sudden departure had thought it too unkind. 'I have yet to see,' she continued, letting the letters fall into my lap, 'the magical attraction of that past for him.'

I appreciated why Alice refused to think about the unpleasant moments but I also sympathised with Owen's desperate need to let go slowly without losing precious breath. That was my failing, after all. I was unable to distance myself from emotions, my own or Owen's or my child's. I still felt marked by Edwin's death and the emptiness following Lily's sudden accident and the hopelessness of Liza's going. My only means of coming to terms with all this agony was to cling onto the nearest and dearest and take some of their burden of sorrow.

'I think he misses those companions in horror,' I began. 'Those bonds were very special.'

'He has new bonds now, his wife and son. Aren't those important?'

'They helped him to see the whole of himself. We only make his weaknesses more obvious.'

'They would not be weaknesses if he had attended to them earlier.' She was growing impatient and I had no wish to see her upset.

'Don't be too hard on him, Alice.'

'Tuh! I've heard that too often. I'm weary of his endless self-pity and despair when he is surrounded by people who love him.' She strode over to the window and stared out. It was a joyless damp day with bare trees dripping onto the miserable garden. She sighed and leaned over the back of my chair. 'How can he ignore his son? He

317

needs him more than at any other time. And you?' She stroked my shoulder. 'You who have sacrificed everything for him. If he were to walk in here this minute, I would know exactly what to say to him.'

'I'm not trying to excuse him, if that's what you think. I've grown past that but I still love him.'

'I know, my darling.' She held my hand and tried to squeeze some hope into the cold stiff fingers. 'But he is my brother and you are my sister. I love you both and I can't bear to see either of you hurt.'

I sank back and slid the letters to the floor. Their haunting contents were useless and cruel. 'If we'd had another baby to replace Liza. Now it's too late.' My head throbbed from the effect of cradling my grief. 'It would have been easier to bear if Owen had died, at least there would have been no doubts about what the future might hold for Joseph and me.'

'What a thing to say.'

'I don't even know where he is. He doesn't want me to know.'

Alice looked away, shuffling her feet.

'You know,' I said without accusation.

'I can reach him, yes, if he's needed.'

'Meaning if someone dies, I suppose. Death seems to be the only tragedy that moves him.'

'If Jo asked to see him, he would come, I'm certain.'

'Joseph doesn't want to see him.'

'At this moment yes, but in the months to come he may change. Keep that thought at the back of your mind.'

'I feel so useless, Alice. What went wrong? It was all so good in the beginning.' My eyes filled with tears. 'When Owen came back our love grew out of his pain.'

She knew that I was almost at the end of my struggle; what little patience I had left was exhausted. I needed some swift panacea and Alice was the only person with empathy enough to offer it.

318

'When I think of you and Stanley and Billie and Charlotte, I feel so guilty and ungrateful.' I rubbed at my eyes with a lace handkerchief. 'I've had everything. We didn't have to struggle but we still managed to make a mess of it.'

'Don't blame yourself, Owen wouldn't want that.'

'You said something once about losing a child, do you remember?'

'You implied that I was talking rot, that the loss of a husband was far more devastating.' Alice's voice was empty of expression; she would not commit herself to the implication of remembered words.

'And what do you feel now?' I was persistent. This was a concern that had been a quiet shadow on my shoulder for years.

'You were right.'

I nodded although there was a growing uncertainty in my mind. 'Nothing can replace a child, it's true, but if your union with a man is palpable, you become as one, emotionally inseparable, you cannot exist apart.'

'Did you ever say this to Owen?'

'He wouldn't listen. No, that's not quite true. He listened but he gave the words no shape. He became more convinced of his own uselessness; in the end I believed him.'

'What will you do?' Alice held me close. She sensed my stiffness and I knew that she would find it hard to forgive Owen for what he had done to me even though he was her brother.

'I must be strong, for Joseph's sake.'

'Even though you feel you've made the wrong choice?'

'It's not down to choice. I should have been more determined, met his uncertainty head on and argued him into accepting the present as it is instead of what he wished it to be – an insipid decorated image of the past.'

Alice smiled. 'That sounds more like the old Ruth.'

'I wish I could understand what happened. Since the children...' I drew in my breath, shutting out the almost painful euphoria of those first moments of joy when there was no one else in the world but my husband and my babies. 'I lost that unique part of myself. It was snatched away in all the clutter of motherhood, the emotional numbness of having to share every part of your body and soul with someone so small and selfish.'

'It happens to us all,' nodded Alice.

'Not you, Alice. You retained most of the old you: your cheerfulness, your order, your relaxed approach. I was baffled by the emotional challenge – loving Owen was challenge enough. Do you think Owen and I might start again? It's not too late?'

She slid her chair close and peered into my face. 'Give him time. You need a breather to adjust to what has happened. You might believe that you had it easy compared to others but you're wrong. What you took was a serious step, committing yourself to a relationship so soon after the war. And you lost a dear child, not a mere baby.' She paused, allowing her words to settle. 'Liza was a tiny person, she had personality, and was a part of you and Owen and Jo. It was agony for you but don't forget that Jo needs your love and support, perhaps more than Owen did. He is still forming his own life. What comes from now on will shape and determine his future.'

I had to believe it. Alice gave advice without implying criticism; she could be sensitive and strong at the same time, so whatever she offered would be taken in good faith or discarded without fear of bad feeling.

'You're right. Why are you always right?'

Alice flapped her hands, dismissing my certainty.

'To think I have resorted to a succession of crutches to help me through the bad times – uncertain dreams and miserable hopes gleaned from too much poetry and even religion. You've survived without any of it.'

'Stanley had strength enough for both of us. He had to stay one step ahead or his disadvantages would show. He's the most zealous character I know; determined and assiduous to a degree.'

It was clear that Alice's loyalty was divided between her disabled husband and her unfortunate brother but she invariably succeeded in tempering her remarks with fairness. These two men who had made such an impact on my youth and been such an intricate part of my life, they were alike as vinegar and honey. When I thought of Stanley's vigorous excitement in living and compared it with Owen's quiet unblinking acceptance of all that happened, I felt a funny bubble inside that I was afraid to burst. I had to keep it full and shining as I had done on so many occasions, occasions when I should have exploded and let my enraged feelings spill out.

'Thank you, Alice.'

'You will be all right, Ruth? You won't do anything desperate?'

'Of course not.' For once I believed in my own strength. 'Joseph needs me and I hope Owen will need me again ... sometime.'

'That's the spirit. Now come and see the boys, they're dying to hear about Jo. I'm sorry he's not here.'

'He likes to be with George.' My voice softened. 'Especially since he found out. I think he wants to make amends. Poor father, he blamed himself for Owen going. What made it worse was Owen's total inaction with father. No anger or bitterness, completely insensitive until it was too late. It would have been easier for father if Owen had shouted and raved instead of sulking.'

'It's not in his nature, is it? He prefers to turn away from bad feelings and differences. He thinks they'll disappear.'

'Except inside himself, he seems to cling onto those,' I said sharply.

'That's Owen, you won't alter that – well, not in a hurry. I didn't warn you about needing the virtues of a saint before you took him on, did I?'

'You did not.'

'Would it have made the slightest difference?'

'None at all,' I answered with conviction.

1938

25

Echoes

This was not like other summers. The rain began in April and it was still falling now in the middle of June. It seemed that every morning when I opened the curtains there was nothing but a smoky sky and dull silvery spots of rain. The lilac that grew close to the house had bloomed and drooped, its scent drowned by the careless rain. That lilac had always been a vital part of my spring, with bunches dropping their musky violet petals onto the kitchen window sill and filling the garden with a headiness which reminded me of my bedroom at home when Edwin had spilled a bottle of perfume on the rug.

It was difficult to focus on sunnier things when all around was so colourless and when the precious notes in my memory were growing faint and the outlines of images were losing their comforting shape. Even my son's brightness was no consolation as he grew in self-confidence and slid away from questions and advice.

Only this morning I had seen him off on a walking weekend with a friend and he had refused my company to the station. I was proud of my courage as I prepared his breakfast, packed his sandwiches into his rucksack and waved him off from the kitchen door. He had turned at the gate with a smile and a wave, a replica of one of his father's farewells; it had almost left my spirit in tatters.

And since then I had been unable to stir from my chair near the window. The clock on the dresser told me an hour had passed and there were still dishes on the table and the floor to be swept but I was drawn back to the garden and Liza's rose bed.

I found some scissors and a basket and was soon outside snipping off the neatest flowers to put on the table. They were well established now and their scent had been lifted by an early shower and swirled around the house. For a moment I held my breath, my eyes closed, and the child's helpless laughter at some conspiracy with her brother drifted across the garden. I usually banished such tricks but this time I would be stubborn and find consolation in the sweetness of a joy preserved.

'Excuse me, I hope I've come to the right place?'

A man's voice, lilting and slightly breathless, was carried through the branches of the lilac behind me. Before I turned I heard his footsteps across the path and caught the scent of orange that preceded him.

'I'm sorry, I should have written, I know, but I came on impulse.' He was rubbing one hand down the side of his tweed jacket and the other was grasping a parcel of orange peel. He took my hand and shook it with an old-fashioned vigour that was faintly amusing. I didn't believe he was a creature of impulse; his enthusiastic greeting disguised a self-effacing quietness that was evident in his averted and unsteady gaze.

I took the orange peel and tossed it onto the compost heap and when I turned back he was bending over one of Liza's roses, his hands cradling the deep pink petals. From behind, he looked older and, suddenly and inexplicably, I knew who he was. There was a familiarity about the gentleness of the gestures with the flower.

'Maurice.' My voice almost failed me.

He looked over his shoulder, a broad smile breaking up

326

the patches of sunburnt skin. 'How do you know me?' He was still clasping the rose.

'I feel I knew all Owen's friends.' My voice was too melancholy and I put on a smile to answer his. 'He wrote such detailed and wonderful letters. You might have been sitting around me as I read.'

He straightened his back and I saw how tall he was. 'Should I feel flattered or ashamed?'

'Oh, there was nothing to be ashamed of...' Then I realised that he was teasing. Perhaps my first impression of a shy and reticent being was misplaced.

'I'm sorry, I couldn't resist it, you looked so serious.' He shrugged his shoulders.

I struggled with the words from so long ago. Was I confused? I could not recall the characteristics of every comrade that Owen had described but I felt that a sense of humour had not been an attribute of Maurice's.

'Have I upset you?' He was beside me, lifting the basket of roses and holding out his arm.

For a moment I could not answer. The years had vanished and the man beside me was my husband on that first afternoon in the little house. We had made such plans for the garden but the roses seemed to dominate now, with the lavender clinging to the edges of the plot.

'Owen isn't here,' I said in a flat voice.

'It's you I've come to see.' He plucked one of the roses from the basket and held it out to me.

I pushed it into my blouse. His skin was parched and there were wrinkles around his eyes and forehead where he had screwed them up against the glare of the sun. 'You've just missed Joseph, he left this morning for Wales.'

'That's a shame, I should like to have met Owen's son.'

The words caused a heaviness in my chest as if some great trial or pain was on the other side of tomorrow. 'Yes, Owen's son,' I whispered without thinking.

'I've heard so much about him. Owen is very proud.'

I was tempted to answer with some hurtful remark but controlled my impulse. We began walking towards the house and he held the door open for me and waited until I asked him to sit down. He appeared uncomfortably tall in the tiny kitchen and had to bend his head to avoid the beams.

Without asking I began to fill the kettle but he beckoned me to sit with him. In that moment I had a sudden and terrible premonition that he had come as a messenger of Owen's death. He seemed not to notice my unease, intrigued as he was with the jumble of nearly nineteen years of our occupation in this home.

'I like your little house. It's cosy to an old bachelor like me.'

'You're not married, then?'

He shook his head. 'Stella found someone else while I was away, someone more acceptable to her parents.'

'I'm sorry.'

'It's a long time ago. I've grown used to a solitary life, I quite enjoy it.'

'It must have happened to a lot of young men.'

He stared out into the garden. A rabbit had crept from under the lilac and was grooming his face and whiskers as he sat under the roses. 'Owen was fortunate.'

'Yes.'

'You were here when he got back.'

I said nothing.

'Don't you want to talk about him?'

'I've talked and talked until I feel my head would explode with all the words.'

'But not with Owen?'

'No, not with Owen, not recently.'

'Don't you think you should?'

'In the beginning that was all we did.' I was starting to

feel uncomfortable, fearing that Maurice had come on a mission to prepare the way for Owen's return. 'But now I've done with all that. There are no more words and the sentiments are dried up completely.'

I leaned forward to tap the window as the rabbit stood up and began to nibble the rose leaves. 'They were all spent in those letters. Did he show you those letters?'

'No, they were between you. He was careful about keeping you separate.'

I had suspected it but never been able to make Owen admit it. 'I wonder sometimes if he took in all I said. We seemed to understand each other, even towards the end when he was in that dreadful prison hospital. I tried to say the right things and I believed in what he was doing.'

'He never doubted it.'

'But when he came back it was as if all that had never been. He didn't mention what had passed between us yet he was obsessed with the other parts of the past.'

'He didn't want to spoil your part, it was special to him.'

'Tell me about him – how he was out there. At times I feel he's had two lives.'

'You may be right. When we first met he was shy and unsure of what he had to do. But we all were at that stage. He quickly realised he would have to adopt a lighter, more urbane attitude. It was impossible to live a life out there that didn't involve others.'

I smiled. 'That lightness doesn't sound like my husband.'

'No, it wasn't easy but he gradually relaxed as the men took to him.'

'You talk as if it were only yesterday.'

'Such things don't fade. You can't forget them.'

'But do you want to? I felt Owen was clinging onto such things for some unhealthy kick he got out of them. When I tackled him about it he became resentful and shrank into awkward silences. He was almost sulking. It was very bad for Joseph when he was growing up.'

'I'm sure.' He rubbed at the edge of his jacket and I suspected he found it difficult to show sympathy for my position without denying the loyalty he held towards his friend.

'When I tried to pull him out of it by referring to the letters and how different he was in them, he was afraid. He felt exposed. He'd given me everything in those letters, his very soul, and he had nothing left of himself, no secrets to hold that made him complete and individual. That was when he began to realise that he had nothing to offer his son.'

'And that made it impossible for Owen to confide in Joseph?'

'You know then?'

Maurice nodded and for a moment his grey eyes held mine in a sad look, a look that reflected all the regret and hopelessness that I had carried over the years and which had become so large a part of my existence since Owen left.

'He went to France to find what he had lost, that unique part of him that had drawn you together and made you love him.'

'But why? I don't want him to be the disturbed hero he was when he came back. His ideals were all very noble at the time but ideals don't support a family, they don't satisfy the questions of a growing son or relieve the grief of a lost child. And this is no time for heroes any more.'

He leaned forward and offered his hand. 'Please don't be upset. I didn't come to stir up sorrow.'

I shook his hand away and blinked back hot tears. 'Then why did you come? Have you a message from Owen?'

'He doesn't know I'm here. I met him, it's true. We talked for days about so many things.'

'Mostly the war, I suppose.' I was defiant against my feelings towards this man, not simply because he had shared moments with Owen but because I sensed that he had come to see me for genuinely unselfish reasons, for my sake as much as his friend's.

'No. We talked about you and Joseph. I don't need to tell you that he didn't want to leave, do I, but when Joseph found out he felt excluded from your lives.'

'That happened long before.'

'All right, but his isolation became complete. His one wish was to save you and Joseph from more pain, you must understand that.'

'He could have said all this.'

'He knew that if he became mixed up in explanations he wouldn't be able to leave. He loves you too much – both of you – and he felt he'd let you down so dramatically that redemption wasn't on offer.'

I stood up, flicked at the cushion on the back of the chair and began to clear the table. 'These words are all very well but they're simply more excuses because he couldn't face up to what he had to do. It was simple, he would have had my support, all my love, but he failed.'

Maurice's face revealed nothing of what he was feeling. I suppose he owed it to both of us to keep his emotions squeezed up tight. He probably shared his friend's creed that emotions are too precious to waste. Owen had tried to live by that creed but sadly it became too fragile to hold together. His caution had cost him an identity during a time when showing an acceptable image to the world was all-important. There was a peculiar inconsistency in his reactions; although I had reassured him that what people thought of us was irrelevant, he was conscious of how his behaviour was deflected on me.

'He never doubted your love and in his terms he did his best. Owen was concerned with values when success

331

and acceptance were measured in material terms. Values could not be gathered up and invested for the future; they were not a quality that could be used in any defence against accusations of weakness. As you said, ideals are expensive.'

I had stopped what I was doing, the tablecloth folded in my arms. I recognised Maurice's words; they represented what I had believed but had been unable to express to my husband when he most needed it. I also knew that Maurice was able to explain it far more expertly than Owen could ever have done.

I laid down the cloth and crossed to the window. It was almost midday and a watery sun was high in the trees; it hovered, a shimmering lozenge, distorted by a haze of moisture-laden air. I spoke without turning round. 'What do you do, Maurice?'

'Me?' He seemed surprised by my query. 'I'm a teacher, nothing grand. English and classics at a minor public school.'

'Ah.' I understood his gift of clarity.

I swung round, smiling, with open arms. 'I don't know why I feel so exquisitely happy all of a sudden. You haven't told me that Owen is coming home, have you?'

He shook his head. 'He'll probably have to come back to England soon, with the situation in Europe.'

'Yes, he will. And I don't think he has anywhere else to go.'

I sat down, more relaxed than I had been for weeks. I had forgotten the value of simple talk and the chance to listen to a fresh voice.

'So it's not too late for him?' Maurice appealed.

'No. But there won't be any more talk about the past. It must all be buried with the dust and the tears. We have to begin again.'

I felt strangely content and optimistic. I made him some

sandwiches and we ate them by the open window, with the scent of roses wafting in. He told me of his holiday in France and his plans for the new term. I felt an immediate affection for him. He should have been close to someone, someone to share his love of literature and the classics; he should have had children. I suspected that he was a lonely man and invited him to stay at Christmas. 'Who knows, Owen may be here, and you can pick up where you left off.'

'Would you mind that?' He seemed concerned about upsetting me.

'Why would I mind? If Owen were here I would put up with anything.'

August 1939

26

Darkness

Revelation of Owen's history might so easily have driven Joseph and his grandfather apart but I recognised a new closeness between them. The younger man was a comfort in the old man's empty hours. I know that at one time my father had feared that Joseph, as an only son, might become solitary and thoughtful like Owen but he had encouraged him to develop a more outgoing and inclusive temperament.

We had been closer since Owen's departure too, but I was uneasy about our being so dependent on each other. It was not easy to explain to an impressionable young man who had no one else to love that he should guard his affections for his mother.

I seemed to spend more time sitting by the kitchen window; the quiet memories of Liza were warm and manageable, the pain blurred by time. But there was a different uncertainty at the back of my mind. Since Germany's invasion of Czechoslovakia the previous October, another war seemed a certainty – the only question was when?

For months the newspapers had been stuffed with Mr Hitler's unashamed devious movements in the Rhineland and Austria; it was horrifying to contemplate but Germany's avaricious hunger for power would not be deflected. Joseph and his grandfather had listened to news of the

Czechoslovakian invasion on Owen's wireless and Joseph was with the old man now, going over the week's news.

I preferred to keep such hideous happenings smothered by more beautiful thoughts. The roses were almost past their best now but their perfume still drifted across the evening air through the open window. There was a step outside and Joseph walked in. I was always pleased to see him, his resemblance to Owen was a slight compensation.

'Good time?' I asked as he leaned over me to offer his cheek.

'Yes.' He looked concerned and I held onto him.

'Are you all right?'

'I wish you wouldn't spend so much time alone, mother. It can't be good for you.'

'I like my own company, I don't feel alone. You forget your father was an habitual wanderer, returning home at godless hours, wet and weary after a day in the country, but there was always a sense of his presence even when he was away.' I recalled the books left open on chairs, scraps of paper with odd verses of scribble poked into shelves or propped up on the dresser; his battered Harris tweed trilby hung on the end of the stairs or drying over the mantel shelf. Joseph would not have noticed such signals of his father's quiet occupation.

'And now, when there is hardly any of him left?'

His words made me sad. 'I think about you.'

'You shouldn't brood.'

'How do you know I'm brooding?'

'Sitting here by the window, almost in darkness, what more can you be doing?'

'They're not all sad memories. Your father and I were happy once.'

He closed the window and sat in his chair. 'I know. I often wonder if he'd had the attention and encouragement that I've had from you and granddad and Alice whether

338

he would have had more confidence. Maybe he wouldn't have felt so overwhelmed by the weight of the unknown.'

'Perhaps.' I was gratified that Joseph was so perceptive. 'It's a shame he can't share your concern.'

Joseph leaned towards the window and ran his fingers along the sill. A sudden wind scattered some rose petals that lay near the path and twirled them under the window.

'Granddad thinks he would have left anyway, even if I hadn't found out.' His voice was controlled; his initial anger had dissipated months ago and he could talk about his father with a maturity tinged with feeling.

'He may be right.' I was not willing to enter into another lengthy discussion on Owen's unfathomable motives.

'I was too young to understand, he was right.'

'Joseph, you don't have to go over all this again...'

'I want to. I want you to see that I tried to understand. I'm not looking for excuses but I can try to see what he did through your eyes, I owe that to you.'

Although they seemed similar, I could see that Joseph possessed a certain amiable brashness that would have been foreign to his father. There was more resolution in his manner, more self-assurance, and he knew exactly where he was going. However, this was not without its worries. It reminded me of the reckless confidence displayed by the young in the months leading up to the last war. Challenges didn't unnerve them; they found it easy to hold a clear vision of what was expected of them and, as they moved through those final breathless months of freedom, the summit of their confidence was the perfect balance between enjoyment and fulfilment and their joyous energy, coupled with a serious sense of duty. Even Owen experienced a measured enthusiasm of sorts.

'Oh Joseph, if you could have known him before the war…'

'It was like now, wasn't it? All this uncertainty is very exciting.'

'Don't be too excited. War is not something to be enjoyed. I hate to think of you heading towards the same disastrous events.'

'This war will be different,' he said, his voice more animated. 'We can't run away from it, it's too late.'

I shivered at the thought of him being sucked into that spiralling fascination with conflict and fighting for right that so easily obsessed the young.

'I don't want to think about it.'

'Mother.' His voice was now softly appealing and I had to look into his dark eyes and respond with attention. If I ignored him it might appear that I was careless of his wishes. I nodded, knowing what he was going to say.

'If it happens, I will go.'

I closed my eyes. My mind was suddenly filled with a farrago of notions; I should speak to Alice, to father – should I tell Owen? Joseph knew that I'd had a postcard from France before Christmas and Maurice had been back to the house in February.

'Will you tell him?'

When I opened my eyes he was standing up with his back to the window and it might have been Edwin there, breathless and exhilarated at the prospect of hurrying off to France. I blanked out the image, afraid to perpetuate the fate that might be reborn by the likeness.

'Joseph, I don't know.' I looked to the garden for distraction. It was growing dim, as if some stealthy spirit were spreading a curtain of fine muslin across the sky to keep everything hushed and untarnished for another day. With the sunshine gone, I didn't want to think about the

340

agony of uncertainty. To go through all that pain again...
My son, suffering as Owen had suffered...

'Did you tell granddad?'

He nodded, bowing his head so his face was barely visible. 'He knows exactly what to say. He seems to have an instinct for kind good sense.'

I hesitated, taking his hands and pressing them to my cheek. It was a miracle to me how that tiny helpless baby could have grown into this full energetic young man.

'Can you forgive him, Joseph?' I let his hands fall.

'It's not about forgiveness.' He paused, fumbling for words that would not distress me. 'I don't feel wronged any more. The anger has gone but the damage to you has already been done. I worry about your recovery.'

He had turned away and was staring out of the window. The garden was grey and silver in the shadows, unrecognisable as the place where I had watched him run and play as a child.

'We must try to pardon him, Joseph.' My voice had the reasonable quality that would be familiar to him but there was a hint more persuasion. I hardly remembered losing my temper with him. 'Maurice was so certain that he was repentant.'

'Why must we do it all?' He was making one last attempt to justify his feelings over the past years.

'We're not. He is trying.'

'One tiny postcard and you think he's sorry. I suppose if he sent you one of those wordy letters you were so fond of, you would forgive him anything.'

'Jo, that's not fair. You must understand that his life has revolved around pacifism. He doesn't want to prolong this disharmony; it's against all he believes in. It's up to us, Joseph.' I tried to turn him round but he would not look at me.

'I can't promise.'

'That's all right, at least you're not saying no.'

341

27

Starlight

We had taken to watching the stars together. It was soothing and undemanding and allowed us a closeness that did
not require deep conversations. Joseph's previous lack of
interest in the heavens surprised me for he had always
cherished a fascination for the natural – perhaps the vast-
ness, the impenetrable distances defied his imagination.

My father had helped him to buy the telescope and
by chance my attention had been caught. I enjoyed the
intimacy of our shared place in the back bedroom of the
little house. The darkness made me feel secure and my
son's nearness and muted commitment to what he was
doing reminded me of Owen when I had first known him.
I didn't think he would enjoy being reminded of that
resemblance but at the close of a particularly unpalatable
day, when we were both feeling frayed and restless, I told
him.

'I know you won't want to hear it but it gives me a peculiar comfort.'

He didn't turn away, as I had expected. Over the years
since Owen's leaving he had matured quietly, adopting his
role as man of the house with modest confidence, taking
over decisions that had previously fallen to his father,
without a murmur. This combined easily with his job up
at the Hall, where he tended the gardens.

In the darkness I couldn't see his face but I knew by

the tilt of his head that he was measuring my words. That was part of my comfort, that blindness between us, leaving only soft space for our feelings. Years of seeking the sun had made me weary and I felt relief in the stillness of shadows. After all that I had suffered I should have distrusted such abstractions, but there was no easy escape from my natural inclinations.

Joseph put his eye up to the telescope and swung it in a gentle arc so his profile was visible against the grey light from the open window. After several minutes of silence he spoke without changing his position. 'I do understand and I don't mind being reminded that Owen was my father.'

'Thank you for saying that.' I touched the back of his shirt, aware of the warmth of his body under the cotton twill. 'I am afraid to talk of him.'

'You shouldn't be. It has become easier with time. Sad, but sometimes I think I've forgotten what he looks like.'

'That happened to me during the war. He was alive only in his letters. I'm sorry now that I let them go, it would be something...'

'No, that was right. They gave him the excuse for sustaining his preoccupation with the past. You needed a neat break, everything gone, a new start.'

'It didn't happen, did it?' I gave a sigh.

'If you'd asked him to come back, he would... It was for me that you kept quiet?'

I nodded, running my fingers down his arm then folding my hands in my lap. I had grown used to being patient and even now, when I lost sight of why I was waiting, it seemed a peaceful occupation. 'It's now when I might be losing you that I can contemplate him coming back. It's very selfish of me.'

'Not at all. You're too severe on yourself.'

'I wish you weren't going.'

'I must.'

'Why?'

'I thought we'd talked about it, decided I have no choice.'

I sat up stiffly, rearranging my hands on the arms of the chair, feeling the cracked leather under my rigid fingers. 'Why did this happen? God doesn't like me very much. First, my husband, then my baby and now my son. I can't bear to think about it.' I sobbed, and it didn't seem so bad in the darkness.

'Mother, please don't make it worse. I will be safe. This is a different war, there won't be such casualties, it's organised and efficient.'

'That's propaganda put about to make you happy. They're doing exactly as they did before – stirring up patriotism and feelings of duty when in the end those fine feelings will be nothing – you're going to kill and be killed.'

'Mother, please.'

I would not let him speak. 'This war will be just as ghastly. They have bigger guns and bigger bombs. They have no intention of telling you the worst, it would be crazy.'

'This doesn't help. Try to think of everyone else, young people who must risk their lives for freedom.'

I lowered my head, ashamed. 'Of course, you're right. As usual I think only of myself. It seems to be my unfortunate habit, doesn't it? When Owen was away I could only think of my happiness and getting him back; when Liza was lost I was concerned only with my distress, I refused to see you or Owen in your pain. I ignored his depression as irritating self-pity – he was so expert at portraying that. And now if you go – I will be alone. Edwin was right. He gave me a warning once. If it all collapsed and went wrong, it would be my fault, I would have to face life with nothing.'

344

'That's a particularly hurtful and callow remark.'

'I don't think you understand. He was referring to my stubborn disposition.'

'It's not selfish and stubborn to love your family.'

'It can become an obsession. It can destroy those fine nourishing feelings that you may need to survive alone.'

'It hasn't been easy for me, this decision to leave. I could have been more resolute, I clung too much.'

'But that's what mothers are for.'

'You've given so much of your life for me, you deserve some time to yourself. Now is your chance.'

'I don't want freedom at that price, I don't need it.'

He was dismantling the telescope to put it away in the case. This was the last time we would sit in this room, so close, yet so far apart. We didn't know each other's thoughts as we had in the past. We had shared secrets, anticipated questions, been prepared for each other's needs, however trivial or fantastic.

'Take this for granddad, he should have it.' He snapped the case shut.

'You'll be back, won't you leave it here?'

'He may as well use it while I'm away.'

'As you wish.' I tried to muffle the desperate sadness I felt.

'Those maps downstairs, he can have them too.'

'You might have taken them to him, explained how to use them, he would have appreciated that.'

He pushed the case away and walked to the window for the last time. 'I'm sorry, it's too painful. He's an old man, I don't know if I'll see him again.'

'Of course you will, you'll have leave.'

'I dare say.' He turned with a frown. 'I suppose father will have to come back ... the war?'

I nodded. I tried to imagine them together again, the only man I had loved and this young man for whom he had found it so difficult to feel affection after his daughter's untimely death.

'What are you thinking?' He was beside me, helping me from the chair.

'It seems a long time since you were together, father and son – truly together – sharing and enjoying each other's company. You did once, didn't you?'

'We did,' he smiled. 'I have those days to look back on at least.'

'Will that be enough for you, some tired cold memory from your childhood?'

'What else can I hope for?'

I looked away.

'Will you see Charlotte before you go?'

'She'll be at the station.'

'Good.' The dark blue sky was suddenly brimming with stars. In a few days Joseph would be looking up at that same sky as Owen had done before he described it to me. I grasped his arm as we left the darkened room and the brightness of the stairs made me screw up my eyes. 'How do you feel, tell me the truth?'

'A little nervous. Relieved that the months of waiting are almost over. These last few years have been a peculiar muddle, one moment we were set for war, the next there was uncertainty. I wouldn't want to live through that again.'

'Well, remember poor Charlotte left behind.'

'As I'll remember you every day.' The ghosts of Owen's words were there as a comfort but also a wicked reminder of my loneliness.

'It's come too soon.' I left his arm and peered into the tiny parlour. Everything was still and dark, as if the house had been abandoned to the spirits. I glanced at the hearth, with the fire laid ready and tiles freshly polished and an odd thought disturbed me. In my memory there were several hearths, together with the men I had known. They had been the family's spiritual centre; Edwin, my father, John Webb, all standing in front of them reflecting on some domestic problem or planning some new venture. Even Joseph had knelt before this one, studying his books and maps, talking over his shoulder as I sat sewing in the old chair from Lilac Avenue. But Owen was never part of that image, almost deliberately he kept back, as if in defiance he refused to be part of that intimacy and cosy conformity.

I could hear Joseph in the kitchen, filling the kettle and clattering cups and saucers. It came naturally to him, that simple domesticity. I would miss his unobtrusive vigilance for little problems and my happiness. I might console myself that Owen's absence had perhaps made my son a more adaptable and considerate person. That would have pleased his father as much as he needed to feel pleased with the habits of existence. I took a last look round the parlour and closed the door. I would spend my time in the kitchen in the months to come, close to my most heartfelt memories.

'Sit down, mother.' He watched me standing uneasily by the door, as if I were a stranger in my own house, afraid to disrupt the comfortable familiarity or blanch the hopeful days that must surely come. I was suddenly strangely disorientated, as though my limbs no longer belonged to my body and my head was floating somewhere above, looking down on the kitchen. I could reach out and touch my son, busy with his tea-making, but I was too far away, my fumbling would not reach him.

'Mother, are you well?'

'I'll be better when tomorrow is over.'

'You should have let Alice come tonight, she would have distracted you.'

'No, tonight was for us, you and me.'

'Don't say it as though it's the end of everything.'

'It may be, for all we know.' I stared at him across the table. That table where I had watched Owen clean his boots so lovingly, where I had argued with Alice, always good-naturedly, over the children, and Liza had upset her pudding.

'Perhaps you shouldn't come to the station?'

'I want to. I always regretted not seeing your father off. I was haunted by a ridiculous fear that I had conjured ill-luck by not being there. Maybe his existence out there was doomed by some strange colourless spell because he left without the blessing of my farewell.'

'Mother, please don't.' He tried to catch my fingers but I snatched them away, clutching at the collar of my dress like an elderly distracted woman.

'I'll have my tea, then I'll be ready for bed.' I smiled, at once calm and in control. 'Don't worry about tomorrow, I won't let you down.'

'You could never do that.' He kissed my forehead and flicked at the grey hairs curling round my face.

It was a painfully special day and I had time to take care with my preparations. I wore a maroon check suit that Joseph had always cared for and pushed my hair under a soft grey hat around which I fastened a black silk scarf. Alice had been with us since the early hours, making endless cups of tea and distractedly polishing windows. Her two sons had already gone and she was searching for tasks to take her mind from them.

'Are you sure you have everything?' I asked for the third time.

Joseph was leaning against the dresser, totally uncomfortable in his stiff khaki. 'It's too late now if I haven't,' he smiled, tapping his bulging kit bag. 'All fastened up.'

'Oh my Lord, why am I so terrified?' I flopped at the table and Alice pushed the teapot towards me. 'No more, I'll be ill. Did you feel like this, Alice?'

'You'll be fine once we get moving.' She glanced at the clock on the dresser and took her coat from the back of the door.

'You look very smart.' Joseph put his hands on my shoulders and held me at arm's length. 'I'm very proud of you.'

'What nonsense.' I flicked at the collar of his uniform as if removing a piece of fluff that wasn't there. 'I'm the one who should be proud.'

'I think we should be going,' said Alice. 'I'll go on ahead in case the bus is early.'

Joseph gave the kitchen a final fond look before he closed the door and hesitated on the doorstep. There was a delicious scent of lavender; it was glistening from an earlier shower and its perfume drifted all around the little house. He bent down and plucked a few flowers and pushed them into my buttonhole.

There were too many people at the station. I felt oppressed and angry, as if they had come deliberately to spoil my final moments with my son. Hannah and Albert were there but their presence was polite and unobtrusive; they hung back quietly until they thought I wouldn't mind. Albert spoke earnestly to Joseph for some minutes and concluded with a laugh and a hug. Hannah was trying not to cry but when Joseph leaned forward to hold her she collapsed onto his shoulder. Alice came to the rescue and led her to a seat from where they could watch the sad nervousness of everyone else's farewells.

Then Charlotte arrived, tiptoeing up to him, the ghostly double of her dear mother, with her wispy golden hair and slender figure. She was wearing a coat of delphinium blue and for a moment Joseph simply stared at her with a helpless expression. When he offered his arm they strolled to the end of the platform, talking softly, her head gradually falling onto his shoulder.

I was dazed with a mixture of distress and impatience. I wanted it not to end, so my son would remain with me, but I felt weighed down by the unendurable heaviness of my heart and the trial of controlling myself before all these strangers. As a distraction I set myself a task: I would try to put names to all those painful faces and imagine how they would address each other in the first of those thousands of letters that would fly back and forth across the sea... Darling Emily, Dearest John, My Own Louise, Beloved Eric ... I closed my eyes for a moment and felt the silk scarf at my throat brush against my cheek from the sudden breeze as a train slid by on the next platform. I could keep my eyes so until it was all over, it would be so much easier to bear. Let me remember my son hugging Hannah and Alice and holding onto Charlotte's delicate hand with such calm tenderness.

'Dear Ruth.' A voice seemed to drift out of the breeze from the departing train. I felt it was my imagination and didn't care to open my eyes until I sensed some other person close, blocking out the watery sun.

At first I thought it was John Webb, as he had stood all those years before at Edwin's death, hunched and grey-faced at the grief he had stumbled on by chance. Then I blinked and the features softened into a younger, more taciturn expression – John's son.

'I hope you didn't mind my coming?' Owen sat beside me.

I didn't know what to say. I couldn't say his name even though it was never out of my mind, especially over these past months since Joseph had enlisted.

He stared down at his boots, the leather worn and dusty

from all his walking. 'I should have let you know, I'm sorry.'

'How did you know?'

'Alice. Don't be cross with her.'

I sighed. 'I'm not cross.'

'What then?'

'I don't know.' I couldn't bring myself to look at him; it was enough to feel his breath on my face as he spoke, to feel the comforting movements of his body beside mine as he folded his arms and crossed one leg over the other. 'Owen?'

'Don't say anything, not now. This is Jo's day.'

'Yes.' I was wishing that I had been more prepared, my thoughts and feelings carefully sifted and arranged, but knew it would have made no difference. I would have felt the same warm confusion preceded by hours of panic, building up to this moment. Everyone else seemed to have disappeared; there were only the two of us on the platform.

'Have you seen Joseph yet?' I slid my hand down his jacket and felt for his hand. It was cold and trembling.

'I thought we would see him together, you and I.'

'Of course.' At last he relaxed and allowed his fingers to curl inside mine. It didn't matter that there were no words between us. All those years of sharing, however troubled, had made some mystical connection that made talk unnecessary. 'You'll see a change in him.'

Owen nodded gently then kept his head on one side as he saw his son strolling back along the platform with Charlotte on his arm. He frowned, unsure of the picture, no doubt thinking, as I had, that it could have been Edwin and Lily.

They stopped and Joseph let Charlotte go. He came forward, hesitating, staring down at us still with our hands laced together on the seat.

'Hello Jo.'

'Father.'

I feared a scene, here in front of all these strangers, but his voice was firm and resolute. He beckoned to Charlotte.

'You won't remember Charlotte.'

Owen nodded and held out his hand. 'As pretty as your mother, my dear.'

She blushed and gave a tiny bow as though she were meeting someone important, then she excused herself politely.

'Well.' Joseph sat down heavily on the end of the seat and stretched out his long legs. 'This is a surprise.'

'You don't mind?'

'Why should I mind?'

'It's an odd situation, seeing you off like this – where you're going, I mean.' Owen's voice was shaking as if he had not dared to contemplate how this meeting might develop.

'Thousands of young men are doing it, it's nothing extraordinary.'

'Not many will have a father like yours.'

'No.' He glanced at Owen and impulsively put out his hand. 'I'm glad you came, for mother's sake.'

He kept hold of his father's hand and looked at him with a directness that Owen found disarming. 'I don't think we should talk about the past, it's not the time and it will only upset mother.'

'Thank you Jo, that means a great deal to me.'

'We've all changed. I hope that I've grown up.'

'I can see that's true.'

'I must concentrate on getting through this. I don't want to think about mother and Charlotte worrying about me. Will you take care of them?'

'You know I will, if your mother still needs me.' He leaned forward to see my face between them.

Joseph rose unsteadily. A train was chugging into the

station but there was little sense of urgency about the way it hissed to a halt alongside the platform. The guard was flinging open doors and shouting down the platform as everybody stirred from their last precious moments.

For a while, I didn't move from the spot where I had made my goodbye. Owen watched from a distance, not wishing to intrude on our final private moments. I moved towards him with open arms.

'Tell me what you feel,' he whispered.

'Feel? Senseless and empty. I can't even feel angry with those ridiculous men in the War Office any more.'

'Would it help if I stayed for a while?'

I stopped, considering the changes in his face. He looked tired. His hair was thinner and his eyes, though the same rare dark blue, were dulled by heavy lids. His startled expression had vanished as if there was nothing left to astonish or disturb him. I didn't feel the need to reply. Pressing my body close to his, I led him towards the bridge that led out of the station.

Out of the shadows and sadness of the station buildings the sun was high and shimmering in the cool sky. I turned my face upwards and tore off my hat and tossed back my head so my hair tumbled free round the shoulders of my jacket. With some temerity Owen put out his hand to feel the curls and closed his eyes as if he wished to obliterate all those jaded and unforgivable years.

'What do you think,' he said, suddenly smiling, '*Gerontius* is on in Manchester next month. Would you come with me?'

I nodded, recalling all those delighted tears when I had first heard it. 'There is nothing I would like more.'